A RULE of LIFE

To Elaine,
Very best!
PB

PATRICIA BRANDON

To contact the author for media engagements or for signed copies, email to pgaddisbrandon@gmail.com

ISBN 978-0-578-88355-7

Interior design and cover design:
Deborah Perdue: www.illuminationgraphics.com
Editor: Therese Elliott: Therese.elliott79@gmail.com

Dedication

To NANCY BONDY KINDY

*You are loved and missed in this world more
than you could ever imagine. I will never
forget you, my dear friend.*

Proverbs 3:5-6

Geaux, Tigers!

Rat's Ass.

Acknowledgements

Cyndi Tucker and Tavia Copenhaver McCuean: Thankful for the Merrie Woode days, the friendships we made that have lasted through all the years!

Natalee, Charlotte, Gaylen, Christa – My Du Kum Inn girls: How I have thought of you (and all the Merrie Woode girls) over the years! No doubt you are as special now as you were then!

Lyndsay Garner Hostetler, Merrie Woode Media Coordinator and Performing Arts Director: Thank you for the time and care you gave me in the archives room and corresponding with me about Merrie Woode history from the beginning.

Dr. Fredric Mau, National Certified Counselor, TeleMental Health Provider, Hypnotherapist, and Certified Instructor of Hypnosis (and those are only a small part of all the international credentials!): Your training and meticulous historical perspective on the subject of hypnosis was invaluable for this story.

Elaine Zachary McElyea: Thank you so much for sharing with me about the Zachary House, Zachary's General Store, and some Cashiers history! And for being my friend since high school!

Hebrews 5:1-4

For every high priest chosen from among men is appointed to act on behalf of men in relation to God, to offer gifts and sacrifices for sin. He can deal gently with the ignorant and wayward, since he himself is beset with weakness. Because of this, he is obligated to offer sacrifice for his own sins just as he does for those of the people. And no one takes this honor for himself, but only when called by God, just as Aaron was.

CHAPTER ONE

Camp Arden Woode for Girls – Laurel Valley, North Carolina, 1919

Otha Moses, the camp cook, wiped her hands on a stained apron, handed the young counselor a plate of fresh oatmeal cookies, then crossed sturdy ebony arms. The alfresco kitchen in the mountain woods and the rush of a proximate waterfall insulated yet another conversation with the preoccupied young counselor. *Soul searching, this one seems to be, always curious.*

"Now, I ain't one to talk," Otha began, "but I don't believe Harvey Bryson carried that child to Doc Halsted like he said. He and that no-count white trash, Chester Graves, ain't never done nothin' good."

"So, it's true?" Tricia Grimball frowned, fluffing long dark hair from underneath her gray uniform camp shirt. "A girl was attacked in town last night and that man, Chester, was killed?"

"That's what Harvey Bryson said. Now Chester's dead and that poor girl don't remember nothin' but a sack pulled over her head and somebody trying to drag her off. Harvey said a strange

– 1 –

man grabbed her and they come up on him. Said he's the one what killed Chester. You know what I think?" Otha's eyes narrowed to razor slits. She wagged a finger at the pretty college girl. "Harvey Bryson is a damn liar. Them two hoodlums attacked that child. But I think I know who saved her and killed Chester."

"You do?" Tricia felt her body shiver. "Have you told anyone? The sheriff?"

"No!" Otha was adamant, dark eyes blazing. "Ain't nobody gonna believe me, even if I did. But I feel it in my bones. I believe it. The Sin Eater, he's the one that done saved that girl."

"Sin Eater," Tricia repeated. "What on earth are you talking about, Otha?" The beloved cook spread her hands wide, pale palms gleaming in the deepening twilight.

"When a person dies, they go to heaven. Well, if they first asked for forgiveness and love Jesus. Only sometimes they die sudden before they can ask forgiveness. The Sin Eater, he agrees to eat they sins to take them on his own self, so the dead can go on to Heaven."

"That's crazy!" Tricia blurted out, then wished she had not. "I mean, are you sure? I've never heard of such a thing."

"Folks here been into the mysteries a long time. Nobody knows who the Sin Eater is. He hides in black clothes and a hood to cover his face. The family of the dead give a signal, and he come the evening before the funeralizing, prays to take on the sin, and eats the food and wine they leave on the body." Otha hesitated. "I don't trust everybody, but you a good girl, Miss Tricia. You got an honest heart."

In a visceral place where risk and fear meet, Tricia felt the beckoning call of the unknown with each word Otha uttered about this bizarre phenomenon. It was a far cry from the prescribed, predictable life she'd fled for the summer. It was why she came to this place; to breathe in the lifeblood of an unknown world. To understand that the knowing would likely consume her, grow her up, perhaps in ways she had yet to imagine. Every fiber of curiosity sparked from deep within her.

"You said he says a prayer. What kind of prayer?"

Otha scrunched up her face, palms up once more, and whispered.

"He prays for the sin to come into him. He say that he pawns his soul for the sins of the dead person. Then he eats and drinks the food. Sometimes, it's a meal and sometimes it's just corpse cakes. After that, he leaves quick. Every now and again, folks throw potatoes after him, to chase off all that sin."

Tricia stood in silence, staring at the simple but wise cook. This was creepier than the New Orleans witchcraft and voodoo her best camp friend, Nancy Baudette, had told her about.

"Corpse cakes? What in the world are corpse cakes? And what about the local priest, what does he think of all this?"

"A priest only does the funeralizing. He don't have nothin' to do with no Sin Eater. He know it goes on, but he don't pay it no mind. He know some people need to have they kinfolk sins all gone before they can be buried, is all. Folks don't think anyone, even a preacher man, can guarantee salvation, unless they sin is all gone. Now corpse cakes, they just biscuits for the dead. Sometimes the dead person's initials are carved into 'em."

Tricia could no longer contain the faint smile that spread across her face.

"Otha, these are modern times. We even have Model-T cars and a spur line train that can bring people from Hendersonville to Lake Toxaway. How could such a thing as sin eating still exist?"

She thought about the likes of the Dukes, the Firestones, and the Vanderbilts, who had their own private train cars in which to travel, until the horse-drawn carriages that go the rest of the way from Toxaway to Laurel Valley took them for the remainder of their journey. It wouldn't be long before even those were nonexistent. Best of all, women would soon be able to vote. And this beautiful brand-new magical camp, just for girls was a testament to modern change.

"Are you sure there is still such a thing as this Sin Eater man?" The expression on Otha's face convinced Tricia that the older woman would remain undeterred. "I've just never heard of such, is all," she added.

"Miss Tricia, you mark my word." Otha was adamant. "The Sin Eater, he around. And he ain't no bad man. Never hurt nobody that I know of. He just a poor soul trying to do right and probably feed his own family."

"One more question. What made you think that the Sin Eater was involved to begin with?"

"Well, it all happened going on the road toward Highlands, not far from where the Parker family lives. There was a funeral up the road apiece the next day for old Luther, a farmer. Likely they wanted the Sin Eater that night. The young girl, she out playing with her brothers, and they run off and left her, you know, like they was teasing her, like boys do. That's what they done said. Only she didn't come home. She showed up laying on the porch at Doc Halsted's. And Chester Graves showed up dead. So, Harvey had to say something. I think 'ole Harvey hoping that Priscilla ain't gonna remember nothing and that nobody will ever know what happened. Like them others."

"Others? What is it, Otha? What are you not telling me?"

The cook looked down at her hands and back up again.

"Back in the winter. Back around New Year's Eve. A young girl done disappeared from around Franklin, in the next county. This girl about sixteen, maybe. They say she likely just run off with some slick talking city man that promised to treat her good. She was friendly with the men folk. But I think somebody grabbed her. And it happened in Dillsboro, too. Early October. That time, a young colored girl was supposed to be arriving on the train with her brother."

Now Tricia stared at the camp cook.

"What are you saying, Otha? These girls disappeared and no one knows where they are? What did the brother of the Dillsboro girl say?"

"That's just it," Otha stared at Tricia, shaking her head. "He gone, too. Disappeared, him and his sister. He just a boy, younger than my Samuel. Ain't nobody heard nothing from neither of 'em. They never arrived at they granddaddy's house."

"My God." Tricia put a hand over her mouth. "Otha, are you saying the girls and the boy all just vanished? No one knows what happened to them?"

"Somebody knows," Otha snapped. "Somebody with blood cold as that ice box. Somebody evil and rotten."

The camp bell sounded to signal evening program time. Tricia was glad for the small reprieve to process all she had just heard.

"I have to go now. Thank you for telling me about the Sin Eater. Thanks, too, for these scrumptious cookies you fixed for us counselors." She smiled at the cook, who once again whispered.

"You didn't hear none of that stuff about Harvey Bryson and Chester Graves from 'ole Otha Moses. They white men and I'm jes' an ole' colored cook. But if you want to know more about the Sin Eater, that no count Chester Graves' funeralizing will be Thursday. And if anybody needs the Sin Eater, Chester's wife sho' 'nuf know he will need forgiving, with all of his no-good ways. The Sin Eater will be paying 'ole Chester's sorry carcass a visit tomorrow evening, you mark my words."

Tricia ran the whole way, past the long line of poplar-sided Adirondack makeshift cabins that dotted the lakefront, past the small outdoor chapel assembly area, through the game field and scrambled up the long wooden steps to the great gathering room known as the Castle. She slid through a mass of giggling campers into a space on the floor beside her four cabin charges. They were the youngest girls in camp, each about eight or nine years of age, all from affluent families, and she had grown to love each one.

"Tricia, do you have line duty tonight?" Natalie, the shy, sensitive pixie-haired blonde whispered as her eyes cast a worried plea. "Would you stay in the cabin until we go to sleep?"

"What's wrong, sweet girl?" Tricia smiled as the youngster laid her head against her shoulder. "I don't have duty tonight, but I was planning on staying in the cabin awhile with you girls before visiting with some of the other counselors down in the Ark. I always stay until you are asleep when I don't have line duty, don't I?"

"I'm scared. Some of the older girls are saying that the Wampus Cat might have attacked a girl in Laurel Valley and that he could come to Arden Woode next."

Tricia gave Natalie's arm a reassuring squeeze. The Wampus Cat was the legendary creature in camp lore that appeared when a camper went on the first overnight camping trip to Toxaway Mountain. In the wee hours of the night, the creature would kiss a camper on the nose while she was sleeping, leaving an orange spot that strangely resembled a mercurochrome stain, and took a few days to diminish. To be kissed by the elusive Wampus Cat had become a fast status symbol at Arden Woode.

"Whoever told you that is pulling your leg," Tricia offered, "like maybe some of the older girls trying to tease you. You know the Wampus Cat is all about good activities, not scary ones. Remember when the Wampus Cat came around when we went on our first overnight on top of Toxaway Mountain?"

"I remember," offered Christa, her brown head of hair bobbing up and down as she giggled. "He slobbered all over Chuck's nose and she looked like a clown for a whole week." More laughter from all but Natalie.

"He liked me the best, so that's why he kissed my nose like that," Charlotte, the impish tomboy affectionately known as "Chuck," rubbed her nose with her hand and shook her head full of short dark blonde curls.

"That's not true!" Gaylen, the last of Tricia's four campers shot back, grinning and wrinkling up her freckled face. "The Wampus Cat likes me the best. He told me so." Bursts of merriment erupted from the girls.

"Okay, ladies, let's enjoy our evening program and we will talk about all of this when we get back to the cabin." Tricia pointed to the stage and drew their attention to the large sheet hanging from above for a puppet show production of Alice in Wonderland, done by a cabin of campers. Leaning toward Natalie, she whispered, "I don't want any of you to worry, or let others cause you to worry. We will talk and figure it all out."

Natalie gave a soft smile of relief and held Tricia's hand throughout the announcements and short program. She continued to hold tight to Tricia's arm all the way back to the security of their cabin, the last one on the line next to the dining hall and swimming docks. When nightgowns were donned and metal cots pushed together, all huddled around their counselor, sock feet crossed and waiting for another bedside discussion.

"Let's have it, "Tricia started. "What exactly have you been hearing today?"

"A girl got killed by a monster," Gaylen said, her freckles dancing across the smiling face. Shock value was a premium for her. Not to be outdone, Chuck chimed in.

"Yeah, and the monster is out there waiting to chomp on another one."

"Come on, you guys, I don't think that's all true, is it Tricia?" Christa held a death squeeze on her stuffed bear, named Baltimore for her hometown, and glared at the others. She exuded common sense, even for one so young. Tricia crossed her legs, rested elbows on her knees, and cradled her chin in both hands.

"Let's sort this out, why don't we? Here is what I know to be true because the adults here have shared as much. A girl from Laurel Valley, about twelve or so, was grabbed by someone while she was walking home last evening. She is not dead. Another man rescued her. It is believed to have nothing at all to do with this camp in any way. It is likely that it had to do with some of the town folk. Most people are very good and love to help others. Yes, there are a few out there in the world that are not nice people, but they are not in this camp. We go out of our way to protect each other and practice safety, right?" Tricia decided to leave out the part about a dead man unless the girls brought it up. "So, let's be clear. The Wampus Cat did not do this. We are all safe here. Besides," Tricia grinned, "if anyone came around here, I'd kick him, then I'd grab his head and box his ears in! Then I'd tickle him like this!"

Reaching for Natalie's arms, she tickled underneath them until the young camper began to laugh, then reached for each of the other girls, who grabbed their pillows and started the epic mock battle. Tricia let the four wear each other out until the quiet bell sounded. Then, she tucked each in for the night, said evening prayers, and waited patiently on her own cot until she heard the rhythmic breathing of exhausted sleep.

Slipping on a thick cardigan over the gray middie and long green tie that was part of the standard camp uniform, she fluffed hair from underneath the collar and grabbed the small Delta lantern from beside her cot, along with Otha's oatmeal cookies. Easing the screen door shut and making her way down the few steps to the lakeside path, she stopped first to let the line duty counselor for the first three cabins know that she was going to the Ark, and then stopped two doors down at Nancy's cabin. Tricia whispered through the screen.

"Nan? Hey, Baudette, you in there?"

"Yeah, I'm coming, Grimball, hang on." Nancy appeared, shaking her head of short black hair and wrapping her arms around shivering shoulders. "Lawd, it's cold in these hills this evening. My girls were all wound up about the girl that was attacked in town. It's all they could talk about. I thought my Dottie was going to cry a river."

"Natalie was the same way. She is the sweetest little thing, so sensitive. We had a pretty serious discussion about it. Hey, speaking of, I need to tell you about my crazy conversation with Otha before we get to the Ark. You are not going to believe this foolishness. But it needs to stay between our group for now. Otha would feel pretty betrayed if the word got out, and it could actually be dangerous for her." Tricia proceeded to relay most of what the cook had shared. "And," she added at the end, "Otha says that she thinks that this Sin Eater person will be going to the home of the man that was killed to eat his sins, or whatever."

Nancy stared at her with unbridled disbelief.

"Holy hell. This sounds like black magic voodoo back home." She whispered with a hint of distinctive French Cajun. Nancy was a rising senior at Louisiana State University, from small town New

Roads, Louisiana, and had been Tricia's best friend from the first day of camp orientation. She was in charge of the Nature Nook area where the campers learned about the mountain land, the flora and fauna that were its inhabitants. Everyone liked Nancy, with her ready smile and home-grown wit. She was a good Catholic girl, raised on a farm on the False River in a large and loving family that embraced their faith and rowdy fun. Tricia envied her and the warm way in which she spoke of home.

"Yeah, it's all bizarre for sure. But don't you want to see it? I mean, aren't you curious even a little bit?"

"Curious, yes. But there's all kinds of that weird stuff back home in Louisiana. I don't need to go looking for it. I've seen plenty of it."

"But have you ever heard of anything like this? Him, I mean, the Sin Eater. You know, to see if he really does what Otha says? Aren't you the least bit curious about this wild and bizarre ritual?"

"Aw, Grimball, damn, I don't know! Besides, how are we gonna do that, anyway?"

"Well, the way Otha told it, Chester Graves's funeral will be Thursday, so the Sin Eater will visit on Wednesday night. Curiosity is killing me. I've never seen anything like this."

"But what if the Sin Eater really did kill that guy, Chester? What if he attacked that girl and, if he sees you sneaking up on him, what then? I don't know, Grimball, this is the craziest thing I've ever heard."

"And what if the Sin Eater is really the one that saved that girl? What if the guilty guy is still out there? Then what?"

"Then whoever did the killing sure enough isn't going to take too kindly to us snooping around. Besides, the person who is doing the sin eating – I can't believe I'm even giving credibility to this guy – doesn't want us sneaking around anyway. And he's got to be a little crazy, too, don't you think?"

"Yeah, maybe. I need to think it all out. But if I can find out, I want to know. I've got to know."

"Why do you have to know? Why, Grimball? This could be bad stuff, right here."

"It could. But when could we ever see life like this, straight out of mountain lore? I don't know, I just feel drawn, I have to know, is all. I'd never get to do this kind of thing back home. Proper young ladies just don't go off on adventures like this, of course." Her voice exaggerated the ooze of southern unwritten law.

"Neither do sane people!" Nancy shot back.

"Okay, point taken," Tricia grinned. "For now, we have to protect Otha and what she said about the Sin Eater and the other men. Remember, she could be in serious danger if anyone thought she was blaming any white man for anything, no matter how bad they might be."

"I'll think about it. Maybe. Considering we probably would have a lot to do to actually pull it off quickly, it's going to be hard to make it happen. It may not be possible with our schedules, you know."

"Maybe not. But don't you want to know? I mean this is like forbidden ancient secrets! I really think I might be able to work it out, since I'm on trip craft staff and have regular access to a vehicle. But, Nan, only the four of us that share the same day off, only our group, can know anything about this. No one else."

"Why would we tell anyone outside the group?" Nancy laughed. "They'd think we'd lost our ever-loving minds. Which we likely have."

"I swear, Baudette, I thought you'd be right at home about this, with all of that swamp magic and curses ya'll got down there in bayou country. So, you in?"

"Aw, geez. You're not gonna let up about this, are you? Yeah, okay. I guess I'm in. I can blame you when we go down together!" Nancy laughed. "Why not?'

Tricia felt the coolness of the night and the light breeze coming off a moonlit Emerald Lake as they approached the Ark. A chill traveled the length of her body. Camp Arden Woode had already introduced her to people from places she had never been or even heard about. Now she was alive, exhilarated at the prospect of facing potential danger and discovering a strange new world. But somewhere in the deep recesses of intuition, she could feel something more. The choice to stray into the dark unknown, to be an interloper, would most certainly bring risk and test her mettle as never before.

While she had no way of knowing what lay in waiting, she knew beyond question that her life would be inextricably and forever linked to these mountains, these people. It was a risk she felt compelled to take, though she had no idea why or how it would end. One thing was certain. Her parents would forbid her involvement, which only served to enhance the desire to pursue the strange story.

As they made their way through the dark stillness, Tricia breathed in the lush greenery surrounding Emerald Lake, the stark face of Bald Rock Mountain, and the cool summer scent of pristine woods. These mountains of western North Carolina, especially here, were the embodiment of paradise. From the moment she had seen the job advertisement posted in the student union building at the University of South Carolina, she knew summer work at this new camp just for girls would be the excuse she needed to make her own escape. Away from the stale, humdrum life she led, and away from an overbearing boyfriend she had initially idolized, but now found demanding and dull.

Escape was finally possible from parents who declared war on each other often, and who dutifully, in the name of proper guidance, stifled any exploration of what or whoever she aspired to be. Her younger sister Maddie wanted to be the perfect society wife that their mother expected them both to be, and her two brothers seemed poised to pursue legitimate careers as well, but Tricia felt the looming thrill of nonconformity. Her parents had all but forbidden any pursuit of her dream to write, calling it "an untenable profession for a woman," but the desire haunted her still. They likely would not be pleased that she had already published articles in their Columbia newspaper and at the university, under the nom de plume of Belle Boudica, a name derived in part from an ancient Celtic warrior. Much as she did not want to disappoint them, the prospect of life with Daniel Middleton had become constricting, more like a life sentence than a life.

As the oldest child, Tricia understood and even embraced her place as a respectable young Southern woman. There had been a time when marrying anyone might have been salvation, a reason to leave home. But there had to be more- much more – life to live than adherence to the boring timeline already mapped out for her. As a young child, she had been terrified of spending even one night away from her parents in case they had a fight bad enough to dissolve the family. That had not happened, as her parents would likely never defy societal expectations, though the possibility had seemed ever present when her father would storm out of the house when angry. Through the tender growing up years she discovered that, regardless of the path her parents chose for her, she would never know her own self-worth and place, until she found the wherewithal to venture forth, to break free, even if only for a summer. This might be her chance.

Aside from the recent opportunity to commute to college during the day, choosing to leave the watchful and restrictive eyes of home had been the best decision of her life, at almost twenty years old and ready to graduate in the coming year. She was pre-destined to become a teacher, only if Daniel, for whatever reason, became unable to provide for her.

The real expectation from her family and Daniel's, would be that they would marry after he finished law school next year, and begin the perfect couple journey. At first, she had been flattered that he picked her. He was handsome, smart, and ambitious. Early in the courtship, she had loved hearing about his goals and dreams. But her dreams and needs were never a priority for him. What was it her mother had said? *Lay your own needs aside. We women sacrifice like that.* Now Daniel seemed stuffed and rigid, poised to work in his father's practice, and ready to claim his place among the town elites. She, too, had always wanted to one day marry, have children, take her place in an adult world. But the way he looked past her, didn't hear her if another man was in the room, brought about a sense of sadness, a feeling that they would share children and not much more. Tricia felt a pang of guilt at the doubt she hid from everyone.

But it was 1919, after all, and a time of great upheaval was just over the horizon. Prohibition of alcohol had been approved in January, though it would not be enacted until later in the year. The country was in the midst of "Red Summer," the bloody race riots in the larger cities that continued since winter and largely the result of white supremacist attacks. Congress had just passed the nineteenth amendment giving women the right to vote, which would happen once ratified. Child labor was no more, and the great World War had been brought to an end with the recent signing of the Armistice. The world was finally safe for all.

Change was coming, especially for women. Many universities and colleges had begun opening their doors to females, even if just as day students. It was a good time to strike out on an adventure before settling down. Maybe this summer was the diversion she sought. Perhaps it would ready her for being a good wife and mother. Tricia could feel the promise of challenge and discovery like the stirring of the air just before a storm. She wondered if the obsession with this local mystery and strangeness, the seeking of truth and the fantasy of saving another, might be her own way of finding resolution for her personal struggles. Somehow, she had to find out. What she longed for was the courage to act with conviction, with the decisiveness of a lightning strike, to be a force that would leave its own indelible mark in this world. If only she knew what to do and had the courage to see it through. Maybe she could save herself, too.

CHAPTER TWO

The Ark, a small wood shack crafted in the Adirondack style like the rest of Arden Woode, was built right at the water's edge of Emerald Lake. It was exceptionally quiet on this night, with only the four young women who had become fast friends at camp sitting inside. Sparsely furnished with worn chairs, an old brown cloth sofa, and a spartan wood table for eating or games, it was the beloved location for counselors to sequester from their young charges for a few moments of solace and camaraderie.

"Otha told you all of this? You believe her?" Cyndi Turner swung her long legs over the arm of the chair she had been sitting in and nibbled a bite of one of Otha's oatmeal cookies. Tall, fit, and statuesque, with thick dark hair, she was in her final year at what was now The Industrial Institute and College for the Education of White Girls but would soon be changed to The Mississippi State College for Women. She was a canoe and sailing instructor at the camp.

"I do," Tricia responded with no hesitation. "Otha is not formally educated, no, but she is of impeccable character. I believe that what she is telling me is what she knows and is what has gone on in these hills for years."

"So, let me be sure I'm understanding all of this lunacy," Tavia – short for Octavia – Copelinger shook her light brown bob that fell to her chin and smiled wide enough to show most of the perfect white teeth against a flawless complexion. She came from a prominent Florida family, was attending Auburn University, and served as the archery and badminton instructor. "You're saying Otha believes that this Sin Eater man may, or may not, have killed somebody, or was the hero who rescued the girl, and that he will be at this Chester Graves person's house right before his funeral? And that he will eat food off of him, drink some alcohol, and take on all of his sins?"

"That's what I'm saying, as odd as it sounds." Tricia hesitated. "At least Otha believes he was the one that probably saved the young girl. And Otha said his burial was going to be Thursday, and therefore the visit of the Sin Eater would be on Wednesday, the night before. Who's in, besides Nancy and me? We need at least a driver and a lookout, if I can get the camp vehicle."

"Nancy, you agree to do this?" Cyndi glanced at Nancy, who was stretched across the sofa, tugging on her green bloomers to get comfortable.

"Grimball talked me into it. I guess Louisiana voodoo isn't the only weirdness around. It would be something wild to do, and definitely an adventure, huh?"

"How do we know we can all go, first of all, then to be able to get the auto, and not get caught? I mean, this could be really dangerous if this bizarre Sin Eater individual sees you or us?" Cyndi was critical and logical, which would no doubt be helpful in any endeavor.

"I don't have all the answers just yet," Tricia offered, "but would you consider it, if I can work it out?"

"If I do it at all – and I need to think about this – then I'm driving," Cyndi added. "I've driven my father's Model T and also the camp vehicle once when we pulled the canoes to a river. Besides, if we need to make a fast escape, I see pretty well at night here."

"Wait. Wait a minute," Tavia stared at Cyndi, her eyes wide in disbelief, as she reached for a second cookie. "You really are considering this? Lord have mercy, we are all gonna die! This sounds creepy to me. You know, like the devil or something."

"No, actually not the devil at all," Tricia intervened. "Just some misguided, but well-meaning folks, really. Otha says that the Sin Eater is a poor member of the town who gets paid for his service by the family of the dead. In doing this, he feeds himself, collects money for his family, and truly believes he is absorbing the sins of the dead person. Yes, it's crazy backward and a bit morbid, but this sad soul apparently really needs the money and the food bad enough to submit to such."

Tavia frowned as Tricia continued.

"She says that the preacher around here doesn't like it, but pretty much ignores it because it is a part of the lore in these parts. I suppose they think it will eventually die out, with all of the progress in the area. But you have to admit, it is fascinating, isn't it?"

"Weird as hell, if you ask me!" Tavia suddenly jumped to her feet as if stung by a bee and moved to the sofa. "Get me away from these danged cookies! I could eat them all," she squawked, laughing. Not wanting to lose momentum for her plan, Tricia reached for a cookie and thought about the next step, smiling as Tavia shoved Nancy's legs off the sofa so she could sit beside her.

"Hey, easy on the goods, girl, my legs are tired today." Nancy playfully pushed Tavia's shoulder. Tricia grinned, loving the sisterly camaraderie with these young women that she had not known a month ago. The relationships were part and parcel of what made this camp so special.

"Okay, Baudette, which of these secret spy roles would you like, if we can pull this off?"

"Well, I'll tell you right now what I'm not doing! I'm not going to be the runner, no, no, no. So, if Cyndi is driving, I'll be the lookout. I'll be excellent at saying when we need to get the hell out of Dodge! Tavia, I don't see anything wrong with two lookouts, what do you say?"

"I think this is insanity, is what I say. I don't know – just too crazy."

"You know," Tricia offered, sensing victory with three willing participants thus far, "how about this, T? If you really are skeptical – and I can understand that – we may need someone to stay with our girls. You know one of us is likely to have line duty tomorrow anyway, right?"

"Oh, so now I have to stay here, while ya'll go off and chase some backwoods yahoo that claims to eat sins?" Tavia grabbed a sofa pillow and tossed it at Tricia, who batted it down and smiled, sensing that consensus was near.

"So, everyone is in agreement that we can at least try to check this out, if everything works out otherwise?" Tricia asked.

"Whoa, wait!" Cyndi held up a hand, shaking her head. "We don't know for sure about this Sin Eater person, if he is a good guy or not, or perhaps one of the other men who tried to hurt that girl or any of the others that are missing. How do we protect ourselves in case someone approaches the car? What about you, Tricia, if you're the one that is actually going to try to see all this nutty stuff?"

"Well, we won't be out late, really, just after dinner and back before Taps, probably. I don't think anything will happen."

"We could take one of the megaphones," Nancy offered, "or maybe one of the .22 rifles from the range?"

"A rifle is not a bad idea, but it might be hard to smuggle it out of camp and back. We could take a megaphone though. At least we could make lots of noise with it. Besides, at least three of us will be there." Tricia said. "I really think we will be alright.

"Let's keep the proverbial horse in front of the cart," Cyndi said. "How about we find out all the details and then we can work out the rest? I mean, this may not even be possible."

As usual, Cyndi was the voice of reason, an anchor amid the excitement of a potentially dangerous mission. Tricia was happy just to have agreement among them and an adventure in the making.

"Hey," Tavia waved her hands in the air. "Changing the subject abruptly, but has Lorene Hogue talked to anyone beside me about going to a real high-class juice joint around here on Friday night after dinner, where we can meet some hoofers to spin us around on the dance floor a bit? Who has line duty that night?"

Tricia bristled, thinking of the loud, brash counselor who was in charge of coordinating the evening programs for the camp and often acted as if she were the only one on staff with any sense.

"Lorene Hogue?" Nancy's head snapped to attention, as she smiled at Tricia, then Tavia. "Why's she reaching out to us about going anywhere? She seems to have a real burr up her butt for Grimball, here. Always making kind of sarcastic comments about anything she does or says. Everybody here is great, except her."

"Yeah, she's from somewhere in the mountains and knows this area pretty well. Said she and Rachel want to take us out awhile to bury the hatchet since we got off on the wrong foot with her. Especially Tricia."

"She said something to me, yeah," Tricia offered, "But I really didn't pay her too much attention. I think she's full of hot air. I don't trust her."

"Well, maybe we should give her a chance?" Tavia insisted. "After all, it might be fun to go out for a little bit and meet some men with real class. What do you say?"

"I'm out," Cyndi said, "I've got line duty on Friday and need to be sure my girls are rested and ready for their canoe trip on Saturday."

"I'm in," Nancy grinned. "Tricia, that's not your night for duty, is it?"

"No, it's not. Actually, both my girls and Tavia's are spending Friday evening with their parents vacationing at the Laurel Valley Inn for some family night event there."

"Come to think of it, so are mine," Nancy mused. "I think a large majority of our campers have parents at the Inn. You know they are having a big Fourth of July celebration there next Friday night that the whole camp has been invited to attend. So, Tricia, c'mon, this will be a free night off and could be fun. We might meet some real gentlemen there, who knows?"

"Okay, okay, I'll do it. Only because you and T will be there. I still don't trust Queen Lorene. But it can't be late at all, because I have to get Cyndi's girls packed for their river trip along with another cabin and help transport them, too."

The female banter continued for another thirty minutes before Tricia reminded all of the promise of secrecy regarding what that Otha had shared. They left the Ark walking in silence back to their respective cabins, as night conversation traveled with ease around the lake and through the long front row of tiny dwellings. Tricia crept into her cabin, latched the door, slid into her gown, and snuggled beneath the heavy woolen blanket against the mountain chill. For a few moments, she listened to the soft hum of night fowl, thought about the events of the day. Visions of her family, of Daniel Middleton and the life she had escaped for the summer loomed before her. Closing her eyes, she marveled at the sound of a distant saw whet owl, its guttural cry soothing in the darkness, and smiled at the prospect of the days to come, the adventures that lay ahead, as sleep finally overtook her.

CHAPTER THREE

Reveille sounded crisper than usual, as the morning sun creeped into a cloudless blue sky and over the edge of Bald Rock Mountain, sending an almost blinding sheet of sparkling light across Emerald Lake. Perfect mornings such as this reminded Tricia of her fortuitous decision to spend the summer here.

"Okay, ladies, rise and shine," she said. "Time for another fun day in paradise!"

Mock moans emerged from the girls, who slid out of bed to don the standard camp uniform of a gray flannel middie sport shirt with a green tie and dark green serge bloomers. Brown high sneakers laced up just over the ankle and, on this day, each of the girls chose to tie their hair back in a scarf that sat across their foreheads.

"Well, I see that the Du Kum Inn cabin girls have all decided to be quadruplets today. Should I wear one of those, too?" Tricia asked.

"Yes, wear it, please!" Natalie grinned as the others echoed the sentiment. Tricia tied her own dark green scarf around tossled hair, pulled it slightly forward to match the look her girls had created, and slid the green flannel band emblazoned with a white "C" over her left bicep.

"If you weren't wearing your counselor armband, you could be a camper!" Natalie breathed, smiling at Tricia.

"Goofball, she is one of us!" Chuck hissed.

"Okay, let's get these cots made and get this place spic and span for inspection. We're going to show everyone that the girls of Du Kum Inn can earn those inspection points just as much as Bum's Rest and Doxology, right?" Tricia referenced the cabins of the older girls who had become quite competent in achieving inspection excellence since the start of camp.

"Yes, Lorene said to tell you not to worry, because there's no way that we can do as well as Doxology in getting our points because we're the youngest." Gaylen offered.

"She did, did she? Tricia frowned. Lorene, again. "Well, we will just see about that, won't we, my sweets?" Tricia waved a hand in a circle, as if hovering over a crystal ball, and lowered her voice to a growl. "I see something amazing! I see the youngest showing the oldest. I see the girls of Du Kum Inn demonstrating so much progress that they will absolutely show our friends in Doxology what we can do! We will climb to the mountain top! Victory will be ours!"

"Yeah, let's go get them! Get 'em!" Chuck shouted, as her cabin mates began jumping up and down."

"Hey, hey, hey," Tricia intervened, "if we are going to get this done, we had better put our money where our mouths are and get busy in here." The girls erupted in laughter as Christa stuffed a rolled-up dollar bill into her mouth.

"Like this?" she mumbled incoherently, smiling.

"That's so silly," Natalie smiled. "She didn't mean that!"

"Girls, I hate to stop the fun, but seriously, if we're going to smack the bloomers off of those amateurs in Doxology, we better get busy, now." The girls roared their approval and snapped to attention. "We need to be ready by the time the breakfast bell rings."

Tricia began hustling about the cabin, assisting in the task at hand. She recognized the fierce unspoken competition to meet this challenge perhaps more so than her campers. Not for the earned points for a specially cooked dinner, but for the sheer pleasure of shutting down Lorene Hogue. The noise in the cabin dulled to a hum as the girls were singularly focused on their mission. They became worker bees, buzzing about until the nearby dining hall bell sounded. As they shuffled down the steps to breakfast, Tricia laid the broom beside the door after one last sweep.

"Oh, I almost forgot!" She gave a sly smile to her crew at the bottom of the steps. "Hugh Carson taught me how to make a pine sachet with ground up needles while we were on that tubing trip down the French Broad. They smell great and even deter a few critters! I've been saving them for a special occasion for you all, but I think we should get them out now." With a quick dive into her bedside chest, Tricia retrieved five delicately scented sachets tied with green vine and placed them on each pillow. "There, that should do it! A winner, for sure!" She double-checked the height of the roll-up canvas shades, pulled the door shut behind her and made her way to the dining hall with the excited residents of Du Kum Inn.

As they filed inside, Tricia waved to Otha and her friend Nancy, who, along with her young charges from the Linger Longer cabin, were on breakfast duty, placing steaming hot bowls of oatmeal and apples on the family dining style wood tables, along with pitchers of cold milk from the icebox. They chose a table close to the great windows overlooking Emerald Lake and awaited the meal blessing from Hugh, one of the assistant directors, and head of the hiking and trips program. Tricia felt a light tap on her shoulder, as she unfolded a napkin and reminded Chuck to remove her elbows from the table.

"'Morning, Tricia," Lorene Hogue had stopped momentarily on her way across the dining hall. "Good luck with inspection today – as always. Hey, looking forward to Friday, too."

"Grrrrrrr," Tricia muttered under her breath, smiling and waving to Lorene, as her Du Kum Inn girls all turned to see what her response would be.

"Down, girl," Nancy Baudette leaned in to whisper as she serviced Tricia's table. "Don't let her get to you, she's trying to goad you into a response."

"Just once. I just want to beat her one time," Tricia whispered back between gritted teeth. "Why is she so damn competitive with me?" Aloud, she said, "Girls, if we don't get a perfect inspection today, we're going to keep at it, right? I'll ask around and find out what we need to work on. But if we are successful today, then we will have started something great, for sure, and we can do it some more."

"If we get it today, we whoop and holler!" Gaylen grinned, as the other girls chimed in their agreement.

"We can," Tricia stated emphatically, "but we also play it slick. We give them our sugar-sweet smiles and enjoy the recognition with grace and dignity and class." She stopped and gave an evil grin to her girls. "Let's let our work speak for us! Go on and finish your breakfast and be sure to sit together in the Castle this morning for the announcements."

The chatter turned to the activity offerings for the day, which included horseback riding, archery, crafts, and swimming or sailing. Tricia smiled, listening to the banter, as she reflected on the growth of each of the girls. Christa had become more of a quiet leader, while Natalie was overcoming her shyness and was skilled beyond her years in kindness. Gaylen was the sharp-witted extrovert, while little Chuck was the fearless tomboy. Her eyes drifted to Lorene and her girls laughing long and loud together, no doubt at some inane joke, as they shoveled the last bites of oatmeal and began to take their table accoutrements to the counter for Otha, her assistant, and Nancy's cabin to finish cleaning.

When the bell rang for dismissal, the remaining campers in the dining hall scurried to begin making their way to the Castle for the daily announcements and inspection points earned. Tricia and her girls walked with the campers from Mushroom, the cabin next door, and climbed the big stairs to the indoor assembly area. The wooden stairs seemed to magnify the stomping sounds of their shoes as they entered in excitement.

"Let's sit more toward the back, today," Tricia said, "so that if we are successful today, everyone will have to turn around and look for us, what do you say?" Her girls clapped their hands and nodded approval as they found their place together on the floor. "Now remember – good sports, right? No pouting allowed."

"I'm going to scream if we get perfect points, Tricia, I can't help it," Gaylen breathed, her eyes wide in anticipation. Tricia smiled back.

"Okay, I'll scream too. But we do need to be good sports and not brag about it, right?"

"Right!" They sat cross-legged on the floor and waited for the director of the camp, Dammie, and the head counselor, Mary, who had both been instrumental in the development of Arden Woode, to begin the devotional, with the assistance of one of the cabins. Tricia loved the contemplative start that always brought balance to the hectic and fun days. They bowed their heads and listened as the morning prayers were offered. When done, Dammie beamed at the gathering of girls and staff.

"Well," she began, "here we are getting close to the end of June and we've had such a grand time, haven't we?" All roared their approval. "But there's much more to come, you know. Today, we will finish our activities as usual, and for tonight's evening program, Lorene has planned some fractured fairy tales, with the girls of cabins Bob White, Wynkin, and Nod doing what I'm sure will be some amazing acting for us." Loud cheers responded, as Tricia and Nancy exchanged glances. "Since most of our Arden Woode families spend vacation time at the Laurel Valley Inn, and are there for the holiday, we have all been invited to be their guests at their Fourth of July celebration next Friday night!" More cheers. "They will be preparing quite a feast with barbeque, corn on the cob, watermelon, and fresh peach ice cream that we will help churn!" Eruptions and squeals filled the Castle as Dammie and Mary motioned for quiet.

"Now, the big announcements for today's cabin inspections!" Dammie turned to Mary, who waved her clipboard in the air. Tricia stole a glance at her girls, who were all holding hands and looked beyond cute as they waited with patience. "We are happy to announce that we have a cabin today that has earned their first perfect inspection." Tricia placed a hand on Natalie, next to her. "Please give it up for ... our youngest girls in Du Kum Inn! Congratulations, ladies!" The clapping and cheers for Tricia's girls were thunderous, particularly from the cabins belonging to Cyndi, Tavia, and Nancy. When the cheering subsided, Tricia heard Lorene's raised voice just above normal speaking, for all that were close by to hear.

"Well, congratulations, you all finally got lucky." Tricia turned to look at her and made a regal bow.

"Skill. Pure skill and perfection from my girls," she said, not waiting for a response from Lorene, but winking at Nancy's group, who were also sitting nearby. When the excitement settled, Dammie spoke up.

"We need a quick meeting with counselors before today's activities begin. Campers, when you leave you, Mary and Hugh will walk with you to your cabins and the washroom and you will remain in your cabins until your counselor returns. You are dismissed. Have a joyful day!"

In a flurry of activity, Tricia's girls hugged her excitedly, embracing their green camp ribbons, and disappearing amid the youth as they

exited the building. When the room was once again quiet and she
held the attention of all, Dammie examined the group for a moment,
as if to emphasize the importance of her announcement.

"As you all have heard already, there was an attempted kidnapping of a young girl, almost aged thirteen, just at twilight or so, right
outside of town last night. The girl was rescued and carried to Doc
Halsted's house, where she was left on the porch by one of the men
involved. She sustained a blow to her head of some sort and does
not remember anything that happened. Her family is devastated, of
course. They are goodhearted mountain folk, I'm told. The sheriff has
asked that we take her in with us for the remainder of the summer
so that she might experience all that is Arden Woode, and hopefully
some normalcy. In doing so, it is also hoped that she might eventually
recover from the trauma of the attack and remember what happened.
We are placing her with The Sign of the Hemlock cabin of girls, since
they only have three campers there. Hugh and Mary arranged for
her supplies and uniforms. She will arrive tomorrow for breakfast. In
the meanwhile, no one is to talk with her about her experience at all.
No comments or questions about the traumatic event. The campers
will not be told that she was the one attacked, and she is aware of
that. Should she begin sharing information voluntarily, you need to
bring that to our attention immediately, but don't discourage her from
talking with you. Mostly, be a good listener for her. Above all, we want
her to be safe and happy. Treat her as any other camper, otherwise,
and bring any concerns to me, Mary, or Hugh. Understood?"

"Oh," Dammie added, "her name is Priscilla Parker. A very sweet
girl, I hear. If anyone should ask, she is arriving late because she

has been assisting a family member who was left very weak from the Spanish flu. If there are no further questions, you may go attend to your campers and have a wonderful day!"

Tricia, Nancy, Tavia, and Cyndi found each other as they made the slow walk back to their cabins.

"I wonder what she does remember," Cyndi mused. "I guess not much right now."

"And we can't ask her," Tavia added.

"But we can keep an eye on her, befriend her," Tricia offered. "Who knows what she might remember eventually?"

"Hey, any ideas for a plan for that Sin Eater craziness?" Nancy asked.

"Not yet," Tricia admitted, "but I will have an idea, once I can talk with Hugh today. I'll let you know as soon as I know for sure."

Cyndi and Tavia branched off to their respective cabins, while Nancy walked on with Tricia.

"This is wild that we're going to have this Priscilla Parker right here with us. Think she knows anything at all?" Nancy said.

"I don't know," Tricia said, "but I have a really strong feeling that we're going to find out."

CHAPTER FOUR

Hugh Carson, the director of the trip craft program at Arden Woode, had already opened the supplies hut and was sipping on a second cup of coffee when Tricia arrived. An accomplished member of the paddling and whitewater racing community, there was nothing about a canoe or running a river that he did not know. As a college professor at The University of the South in Sewanee, Tennessee, who had extensive knowledge of physics and mathematics, he was adamant about every camper learning to execute their strokes correctly and learning at their own comfortable pace. Proficient in hiking, climbing, and the layout of western North Carolina, Hugh was the consummate mountaineer, who loved the land with everything he possessed, and was passionate about sharing that love with others. Of average height and build, with a full head of brown hair, Hugh was a nice-looking man who Tricia assumed to be approximately the age of her own father, perhaps between forty and fifty years of age. He seemed much younger in spirit and agility. His felt hat, pungent pipe, and ebullient personality had become mainstays around the camp, and he was easily one of the most loved of the administrative staff. He went on every trip outside of the general camp area, taking great pride in transporting campers in the back of the camp truck and was a wealth of information about the surrounding territory, rivers, and the local lore. He remembered every camper's birthday with a special note thus far, and Tricia had no doubt that he would continue doing so throughout the year.

"Well, there she is, my astute helper from South Carolina, an achiever of a perfect inspection." Hugh smiled, as he reached down to pet his dog, Hala, that he had found wandering the previous year while on a Nantahala River trip. The dog was of medium size, with a soft brown and white fur coat, a mix of some sort, and went with Hugh everywhere, especially on boating trips. Hala was as beloved as Hugh to all the girls and staff, and as obedient to him as she was loyal. Tricia bent to rub her neck and pet the soft coat of fur.

"Good Wednesday morning, Hugh! Looks like we start packing for the Dam Swim trip for Sign of the Hemlock and Pow Wow for tomorrow? Are they still going to camp out across the lake, too?"

"Been thinking about that. Now that we have our new camper joining us tomorrow, and she will be placed in Sign of the Hemlock, Dammie, Mary, and I have agreed that an overnight trip on her first night here would not be in her best interest. We think she needs a few nights in her cabin to feel safe here and bond with her cabin mates and counselor."

"That makes good sense."

"I think what we are going to do is let those cabins have just a day trip for now. Let them do the one-mile Dam Swim from camp as planned, eat the mid-day meal over there and play some, then paddle back in the canoes that we can deliver there in the truck. I understand that Priscilla knows how to swim, just not sure how well. We can let her swim some, ride in the canoe otherwise, and get some personal and extended swim and canoe lessons. Plus, she would get some more bonding time with a small group of girls and stay pretty busy for the day and will have adult eyes on her at all times. We can fit those cabins in on an overnight later. That way, she can start her regular routine with us on Friday, and she will have solidified some friendships a little better. What do you think?"

"I think that sounds perfect," Tricia said, her mind racing ahead, as she focused on a way to make the secret agenda work.

"Well, that part is taken care of, at least." Hugh smiled. "Now I need a favor. Lorene asked me to participate in one of her fairy tale skits tonight – I'm the wolf in Little Red Riding Hood – so I was wondering if you might consider taking my place so I could deliver the canoes this evening after we finish using them today?"

"I may have a better idea, if I might offer it," Tricia mentally held her breath and watched for clues from Hugh. "How about this? The girls would much rather see you as the wolf than me, and you already know your lines, I'm sure. What if I took the canoes, paddles and cork vests over, along with some firewood, and perhaps have Nancy and maybe Cyndi help me? They are not in the skits and don't have line duty. I know Tavia would watch our girls and we would be back before taps, of course, since it's not that far."

"Hmmm." Hugh pondered the idea, taking a sip of coffee, and firing up his pipe, the puffs of aroma filling the air. "You really wouldn't mind doing all that?"

"No, not at all, and it makes more sense, so you could do the evening program. We could have everything ready for tomorrow and that way, the truck would not be necessary to use for the trip at all, since the canoes would already be there when you all arrived."

"You know, I think that will work," Hugh winked, "and I don't have to give up my cameo appearance. So, how about if I get started packing the supplies for them and you go check with Otha for the meal items for us, and then check with Nancy and Cyndi, too, to be sure they are available to help. I'm sure someone can, but don't want to leave that to last minute."

Tricia nodded in affirmation, as she gave Hala a pat on the head and bounded out the door. That was much easier than she thought it would be. Now to finalize the mission. Otha was inside shuffling items around in the icebox and pulling out utensils for the mid-day meal when Tricia found her.

"Good morning, Otha, I came to see about the meal for the campers doing the Dam Swim tomorrow."

"Well, hello, there!" Otha seemed in good spirits today. "Yes, that is on the schedule. You need snacks and dinner, right?"

"No, ma'am, they are not spending the night. You know the new girl is coming, Priscilla Parker? They will only need lunch and perhaps an apple for later." Otha frowned and closed the drawer of utensils.

"Priscilla?" she stared hard at Tricia.

"Yes, the girl from the other night that someone attempted to kidnap."

"Why she coming here?"

"I think they want to help her relax and feel more normal, you know, to help her recover. They say she doesn't remember anything about that night. Her family agreed to it and the sheriff in town asked if we would take her." Otha stood still and quiet and appeared lost in thought for a moment.

"Well, I guess that might be good for her then."

"Otha, you remember what you told me last night?" Tricia lowered her voice. "You know, the Sin Eater? You said Chester Graves' funeral would be on Thursday, so the Sin Eater would come tonight? You said if I wanted to know, you would tell me. Where does Chester Graves live?" Otha spun around to face Tricia, her eyebrows knit tightly together.

"Girl, what nonsense you done got up your sleeve, now? You ain't fixin' to get yo'self and me in some big trouble, is you?"

"No, ma'am, not you. Just me. I'm taking some of the canoes after dinner to the Emerald Lake Dam area for that trip tomorrow. They are going to swim there after the morning program tomorrow."

"And you think you gonna jes' walk up and visit with the Sin Eater, is that right?" Otha shook her head. "That ain't gonna happen. The Sin Eater, he don't talk to no one." Tricia hesitated, wanting to be sure her next words were taken seriously.

"No, not exactly. I'm not planning to talk to anyone, or for them to even know I'm there. I just want to see him perform his ritual, is all. I'm fascinated by what you have told me. You said you could tell me about the funeral, remember?"

"Yeah, I remember, but I 'sho 'nuf didn't think you'd actually want to go see it. You got more nerve than I thought, Miss Tricia, you sho' do. Damn foolish nerve."

"I'm stubborn, too." Tricia grinned. "At least that's what my parents say."

"They ain't wrong," Otha said, pulling out a basket from underneath a metal cart. "But if you really want to know, I'll tell you. Don't be sayin' nothing to Miss Dammie or Miss Mary, or Mr. Hugh that I done told you. I need this work, and I like it here."

"Otha, you know I love you more than grits and butter. As much as I love my own mama. I'm not going to do anything to get you in trouble, I promise. Does Chester Graves live far from here?"

Otha crossed her arms and tilted her head in the direction of the woods behind them.

"When you go on the main road out of the camp, you go to the left, toward the dam. But before you get to the dam, maybe a mile down the road, you gonna turn left again. You will see a sign tacked to a tree with a picture of an apple and a peach on it. Sometimes folks sell produce there during the mornings in the summer. Turn left right there. Chester Graves' widow, she live down that road a piece. Past an old empty house on the right, then down the road a little more, also on the right, is her place. An old white farmhouse, with a porch and a few rocking chairs. If you gonna try to see inside, you best take something to stand on. How you gonna get there, anyway?"

"The Model T truck. Nancy and Cyndi are going to help me. It's all figured out. If we can leave here shortly after supper, will that give us enough time to get to the area before the Sin Eater does whatever he does?"

"If you first in line and eat and leave immediately, then likely so," Otha nodded her head. "The Sin Eater, he knows how to sneak around kinda quiet like. If he do see you in the road, he gonna maybe go around you through the woods, anyway, or just avoid looking at you at all. He knows how to get around these parts. He may even keep a horse around. Ain't too many folks live back there, no how. Them folks that lived in that old shack you first come to, they done gone off somewhere, ain't nobody there now, so you can set the truck right there. Walk down from there."

"Otha, I promise, all I want to do is see what he does. I'm going alone to Chester Graves' house. Nancy and Cyndi will wait for me in the truck."

"Lawd, I shoulda never done told you nothin' about this, child. Don't you let nothin' happen, you understand? I will never forgive myself if something happens to you."

"If he's not dangerous, then it will be fine, and I'll come tell you about it later."

Otha shook her head once more, muttered something under her breath, and motioned to the cupboards, as she began picking through the fresh red apples in a basket on the floor.

"Some pork beans in there, pickles, some chocolate bars, cinnamon crackers and a tin of them little marshmallows, too."

Tricia found the necessary items and Otha helped her assemble the biscuit sandwiches and fill the trip canteens with water and bug juice and set them all in the large icebox. She packed for eleven people, including Hugh. When all was prepared, Tricia gave the cook a heartfelt hug and hustled off to find her friends.

Nancy was instructing a group in edible and poisonous plant life in the area when Tricia eased in the door of the Nature Nook. All of the campers greeted her and laughed together as they began to sort their leaves, berries, and flowers into labeled cups on the big table.

"Hey, Baudette, Hugh wanted me to ask you a favor, got a minute?"

"Hang on, be right there." She pointed a finger at the girls. "Remember, we do not eat anything, right? Nothing ever, unless a qualified staffer gives you the go-ahead. Just sort them out. You can help each other, too. Okay, Grimball, what's going on?"

Tricia motioned her over so that they could speak without the campers hearing the conversation.

"It's a go for tonight," she whispered. Hugh is in one of the skits and gave me permission to take the truck to carry the canoes and paddles for the girls over to the dam area. He said you, Cyndi, and I could line our girls up first for dinner, and as soon as we are done, we can get the boats and leave. Tavia will sit with our kids for the evening program and get them back to the cabins, if needed. But we should be back by then. Otha says Chester Graves' place is pretty close."

"Oh, lawd, damn, Grimball!" Nancy laughed softly. "We really are gonna do this. We're gonna do it?"

"Yes. Yes, we are. If by some chance, we get to the dam and plans change, we can adjust if we have to. Can you get hold of a megaphone? And that big bucket there, can you bring it?"

"Yeah, I can do that. What's the bucket for?"

"Otha said I might need something to stand on to reach a window, just in case."

"Aw, geez. We are so gonna get in trouble if we get caught."

"No. No we won't. I got it figured out. We made a wrong turn, and just got lost and I went to the house for help is how we can swing it. It's gonna be okay. Otha says the next closest place is vacant and Cyndi can park there, keep it running, and wait on me. If we time it right, it won't take long, I promise. Y'all just be ready to take off when I get back. Maybe we should back the truck into the driveway. We'll figure out the rest when we get there. I need to go let Hugh know we're set to go. Will you let Cyndi know?"

"Yeah, I'll see her soon, maybe. But we can tell her at lunch, too."

"Perfect. I will check with Hugh about how much gasoline he thinks we have and make sure everything is set. Probably need our jackets, too. Stockings maybe, at least for me, since I'll be in the woods some and it will be chilly."

"Hey, what about a lantern?"

"Too risky. Will just have to let my eyes adjust to the dark. Besides, Otha says he usually comes around twilight or so and I figure it may not be too dark when it's time for me to get back to the truck."

"So, we're doing this, Grimball," Nancy said again, staring at Tricia.

"No stopping now. The adventure begins," Tricia whispered, her eyes wide.

"That's what I was afraid you'd say. I'm saying a prayer for safety. For all of us. I think we're going to need it."

"Aw, c'mon, Baudette, you know this is going to be great. I mean, when could we ever get to do something like this again?" Nancy cocked her head to the side and whispered.

"Never. Never would be good, Grimball. I can't believe I let your behind talk me into this."

CHAPTER FIVE

Judging from the amount of early evening light, Tricia surmised that they were departing Camp Arden Woode close enough to the right time to carry out the clandestine mission. Darkness came with relentless precision in the mountains of western North Carolina and tonight, timing was everything. Cyndi smiled as she climbed into the driver's side of the 1918 Model T truck.

"This is newer than my father's, but it drives the same. Acceleration up here on the column, right pedal is the brake, the middle one that sticks out some is the reverse, and this left one here is the clutch."

"Just so you can drive it, and keep us out of harm's way, that's all I need to know." Nancy glanced up at Tricia, who was standing in front of the vehicle, as Cyndi initiated the start up. "Got enough gas, right, Grimball?"

"Yeah, plenty. Hugh got a whole can of gasoline from Zachary's General Store. Let's get these canoes dumped at the dam so we can do what we planned." Tricia walked around the back once more and tugged on the ropes that held three canoes sandwiched with care in the cargo area. Motioning for Nancy to slide toward Cyndi, she climbed into the truck and pulled the door shut. Cyndi worked the pedals with only minimal difficulty, and they eased forward onto the small dirt road, winding their way around Emerald Lake.

"You really think you're going to get to see this Sin Eater person Otha upset you about?" Nancy looked at Tricia, who kept her eyes on the road as they made their way out of camp and turned left onto the main road. "Not too late to back out of this insanity, you know."

That thought had crossed Tricia's mind, but she knew stopping now was an impossibility. Whatever it was that was driving her to witness the morbid ritual the camp cook had described was too strong to ignore. She breathed in the sensual chill of the pre-dark air and felt her body shiver underneath her Duxbak jacket. Every nerve was on fire, ignited by the forbidden. Even the summer scent of the mountains, thick with the loamy smell of damp dirt, rhododendron, and mountain laurel, made her giddy with anticipation.

"I've never been more excited. Or more scared."

"Now she's scared," Nancy poked a finger at Tricia's shoulder.

"I brought a small lantern, just in case," Cyndi added, motioning underneath the wide seat, "and Nan and I decided a whistle made much more sense than the big megaphone we'd talked about earlier."

"Great idea," Tricia smiled, as Nancy pulled the whistle from around her own neck and handed it to her.

"That way, if you blow it, we know to run away, too." Nancy quipped.

"Funny, Baudette. You're a real weak sister, you know?" Tricia returned the friendly jab, then folded her green camp handkerchief into a triangle, placed the widest part over her forehead and tied the corners at the back of her neck to keep her long hair away from her face.

"I may be a pushover, but at least I'll be alive!" Nancy grinned, as Cyndi eyed the landmarks.

"There's the sign with the apple and peach on it," she exclaimed, pointing. "So, we turn in there as soon as we're done with these canoes, right?"

"That's the plan," Tricia added, "and we should not have much more to go at all."

A little further down the road, the dam entrance came into view, and Cyndi navigated with ease, despite the bumps and dips in the road, into a clearing where the boats would be left. A wood railing for tying up horses, and a three-sided shed stood to the left of the entrance.

"Perfect, no one is here. Let's get this done before it gets much darker. Otha said the Sin Eater comes around sundown, and I want to be in place when he does."

They moved with purpose, loosening the ropes and leaving the canoes turned upside down, with the paddles stuffed underneath.

"Where are the vests?" Nancy turned to Tricia, as they finished the delivery.

"Decided to leave them at camp. The girls will have them while swimming to the dam, as needed. Okay, we're done. Let's blow this joint!"

Cyndi guided the truck back onto the main dirt road. The few Model T's that graced the nearby Laurel Valley Inn and the local horse-drawn wagons had worn it almost smooth. When the sign bearing the apple and peach appeared once again, the girls noted their surroundings, and Cyndi maneuvered the truck into the off road.

"Okay," Tricia felt her breathing become more rapid and her pulse quicken. "Look for the old run-down white shed Otha said would be on the right, and we will back it up in there and get as far from the road as possible."

"Think that's it, coming up there?" Cyndi pointed to the weathered and dilapidated shack. It appeared more gray than white. Tricia surmised the difference in description to be the result of abandonment and natural weathering.

"Yeah, that's got to be it. Otha said the next house a little further down was the Graves place."

"Shouldn't we drive past the house to see how far it is from here?" Cyndi asked. Tricia glanced at the deepening crimson streaks across a partially clouded sky and the long shadows announcing impending twilight, then darkness.

"I don't think we should chance it. I want to be sure I have a good idea of the lay of the land, so to speak, and that I can stake out a good place to hide, so I can see him arrive. I can sit here another minute or two and work on my nerves, but don't want to take too much time." Tricia double-checked the whistle around her neck. "If I use this, y'all come to the road and wait for me there, ready to take off. If I don't show up, well…" Tricia's voice trailed off.

"Well, what? We can't leave you here!" Nancy stared, wide-eyed.

"We yell for you, that's what!" Cyndi said, "Then we go get help if you don't answer or show up. That's the plan. But Otha has already said that she thinks the Sin Eater is the hero here and that Chester Graves and this Harvey Bryson guy are the ones that probably tried to kidnap Priscilla Parker. So at least Otha thinks he's not dangerous or evil, if that means anything."

"It means something to me, for sure. Otha is a simple, kind-hearted woman. I know she's not educated, but she's got more sense than many. So far, I believe her. Alright, it usually gets dark around eight or so," Tricia mused. "I figure we should be heading back to camp by then. I mean, if he comes at twilight, like Otha says."

"Cyndi's right. It'll be fine. Just be careful." Nancy gave a gracious effort at reassurance. "You better beat it now, Grimball, if you're really serious about doing this."

Tricia took a deep breath and opened the door, stepping down onto the hard-packed dirt.

"We're doing this," she murmured, trying to find her courage once more. "I'm going to do this. Okay, keep it running." She gave a light rap to the door panel. "See you soon."

Lifting the large metal bucket out of the back of the truck, then removing her jacket and securing it around her waist, she glanced skyward. Once night arrived, it would be unforgiving in its opaqueness. She began a steady jog down the road, taking care to stay as close to the edge of the trees on the right-hand side as she dared. Woods stretched as far as she could see. As she rounded a slight bend, she saw what appeared to be a clearing and a pathway. Getting closer, a wood house became visible, situated at the back of the lot, exactly as Otha had described it. A worn porch sprawled across the front and a white piece of cloth was hanging on the front door. On a small stand beside the door, Tricia thought she could make out the soft glow of a candle. This was the place.

She figured she had gone down the road a half a mile or so, visualizing the landmarks with every step for the way back when it would be much darker. She made her way along the edge of the trees, taking care to remain where she could see the house in its entirety, as well as anyone approaching the front door. The only visible light inside the home was coming from a room on the right side of the house.

Stopping beside a large white oak, she stood in silence, taking in her surroundings and picking a few leaves and pieces of debris off of her thick, dark stockings. Only woods across the dirt road, with no other building in sight. Otha was right, she would likely need the bucket to stand on to reach the windows. Squatting down beside the tree, Tricia wondered, for a fleeting moment, what Daniel Middleton back home would say, if he could see her now? For that matter, what would her parents think? No doubt, she already knew the answer to both questions. Pushing the intrusive thoughts aside, she scanned the surrounding area again as daylight began to melt into evening darkness.

A veil of ethereal light, soon to give way to the night, was still present when she saw him. He came from across the road, an apparition emerging from the thick verdant woods. Tricia felt her entire body shiver. Black garb covered him in totality, the long hood hanging over his face and the layers of cloth floated about like a druid high priest, as he moved in silence toward the house. The image evoked a gallimaufry of fear, excitement, and curiosity. She watched, mesmerized, as the Sin Eater removed the white cloth from the door as it was opened for him by a woman, most likely the deceased Chester Graves's wife, and then closed behind him.

Tricia studied the house carefully. Still only one light that she could see inside. Carrying the bucket beside her, she crouched low, making her way as fast as she could across the side yard to the big window that emanated the dim light. It had been raised four, maybe five, inches. Was it open for the fresh mountain air, or to allow the smell of death to escape? She gulped a few times, as her throat tightened with apprehension. No sound came from the room. Placing the bucket upside down, she stepped up with one foot and grasped for the ledge to steady her balance. Surely, they could hear her heart thumping in time with the pounding in her head. The curtains were pulled, but a small gap remained. Tricia inched her way to the tiny open space and finally dared to peek inside.

The scene before her was even more macabre and disturbing than she had envisioned. The body of Chester Graves was dressed in a white shirt with dark pants and a jacket, his arms crossed about his chest. He had been laid on an old iron bed, his dark hair slicked back against an eerie paste of alabaster skin. On his stomach was a wooden tray that held a container of food and a sturdy metal cup. Something that she could not discern was folded next to the cup. The woman, still stoic and silent, raised an arm and pointed to the tray.

The Sin Eater positioned himself with his back to the window and placed a sizeable black cloth pouch on the bed. With great care, he removed a small wooden plate with similar utensils and a cup and placed them on the bed also. To Tricia's surprise, he laid a black Bible next to the body and placed the unknown item inside the cloth bag; perhaps payment for services rendered. The woman approached the bed from the other side, picking up the plate of food while never looking at the face of the Sin Eater, and scraped the meal onto his plate, then poured what looked like red wine into his cup. For a moment no one moved. The Sin Eater opened his hands, palms up over Chester Graves, then placed one hand on the Bible, and spoke the eerie words in a low, deep voice:

"I give easement and rest now to thee, dear man. Come not down the lanes or in our meadows. And for thy peace I pawn my own soul. Amen."

Tricia shivered, feeling an unexpected rush of compassion and sadness for this mysterious man who had just willingly sacrificed his salvation, his eternity, for another. Did he truly believe in what he was doing or was he so desperate for sustenance and money that he would participate in this spiritual con game, regardless? The woman turned her back to the Sin Eater and placed a hand on the doorframe, standing motionless and silent. The Sin Eater picked up his plate, eating until nothing was left, and draining the cup in one tilt. His methodical execution of the morbid process was done with a silent, but unmistakable, reverence. Tricia found him more intriguing and sympathetic than she had imagined. He returned each item to the black bag with deliberate and gentle motions. Without warning, the woman turned back toward him, looking down at her feet, and clasping both hands together. With unflinching calm, she whispered aloud.

"Did you kill my husband?" Tricia froze, quite sure this was not part of the strange and bizarre process. The woman waited on a response that did not come, then started out of the room, before turning back once more, her voice quivering. "I thank you."

The Sin Eater stood for a moment longer as she disappeared from view. Picking up the bag, he retrieved the money given to him and laid it back on the tray, before securing it once more at his side. Leaning down toward Chester Graves, he placed a hand on the dead man's arm.

"I'm sorry," he said softly, the mournful emotion almost tangible.

Tricia's sharp intake of breath caused a loss of balance on her precarious perch. She grabbed for the ledge, but to no avail, tumbling to the ground as the bucket landed sideways and rolled a few feet away from her grasp.

"Oh, God!" she breathed. "Damn it!"

Her ankle had rolled under her full weight and she felt a slight twist. Hobbling to her feet, she tried to take the steps to the metal bucket with care, gripping the container and stealing a glance at the window. He was not there, but he had to have heard her fall. Breathing harder, she turned to make her escape.

From the darkness, the Sin Eater appeared, towering before her, motionless and foreboding. The long black hood covered his face, except for the mouth and jawline, which was set and tense. Tricia gasped in surprise. His nearness was frightening. With a slow and steady motion, she raised her hand to her throat, a scream threatening to erupt. Feeling for the whistle, she took a step back. The man did not speak, nor move. A light breeze brushed hair across her face and caused the clothing of the Sin Eater to billow in the air like a ghostly apparition. Tricia thought his head tilted a miniscule degree to one side, as if he were trying to read the "C" on her counselor arm band. Still, he made no move toward her and remained silent. Sensing that there was no intention of hurting her, she felt a tiny wave of relief gathered from deep in her chest. As if on cue, the mysterious man spun away and began moving with rapid strides toward the woods from where he had come, the black robes floating about him in the cool chill of night air.

"I – I don't believe you killed Chester Graves. I think you saved that girl!"

The words tumbled out of her mouth before she had given thought to them. The Sin Eater ceased moving and turned toward her for the briefest of moments, still saying nothing. Fear rose in her throat once more. But just as quickly as he had stopped, he bolted for the woods, disappearing into the darkness and leaving her shaken and alone.

Tricia felt her lower lip quiver and realized just how close a brush with potential danger she had come. Yet, somehow, she was not convinced that this man, for whatever he might be, was a kidnapper or intentional killer. Rubbing her forehead, she took another deep breath and began a brisk walk toward her friends, as swiftly as her tender ankle would allow. The wind and the crisp evening air were a soothing balm of relief against her skin, now flushed and warm. When the sound of a rumbling engine began to get louder, and the lights from the car brighter, she knew security was close at hand, and tried to run, her heart threatening to burst inside. Nancy jumped out of the truck and grabbed her by the shoulders.

"Are you alright? What happened out there?"

Tricia leaned into her friend, the tears trickling down her cheeks, and soft sounds trying to emerge. The intensity of the macabre scene and relief that she had not been hurt gave way to an avalanche of emotion.

"Tricia, what happened?" Cyndi demanded. "Get in, now!"

Tricia released her hold on Nancy and leaned against the truck, brushing the dark hair away from her face and trying to hold herself together. She pulled the handkerchief from around her hair and wiped her eyes.

"Yeah, I'm okay," she finally managed, as Nancy scurried into the truck beside her and slammed the door. "You aren't going to believe this. I'm not sure I believe it myself."

As they pulled off toward the camp, she relayed all that had happened. The girls gasped in disbelief when Tricia told them about coming face to face with the Sin Eater and all that had occurred. Finally pulling through the gate to Arden Woode, Cyndi slammed the brakes hard, staring at Tricia and Nancy, as the quiet safety of the camp surrounded them once more. She tapped her fingers on the steering wheel and turned toward the others.

"Ladies, what in the holy hell have we gotten ourselves into?"

"And what are we going to do now?" Nancy added.

"I can't think, I don't know, I need some more time to pull myself together and think." Tricia said, leaning against the back of the seat and rubbing her face, as if to wipe away what had just happened.

"How about we sleep on it tonight? We can decide tomorrow when we have some time to talk again. Maybe we just forget about it now."

"Forget about it?" Nancy was incredulous. "Grimball, all this adventure you wanted, and boy, oh boy, have we stepped in it! Hip deep, we are! No way, we can't forget about it now! You heard that woman thank him for killing her damn husband, and him saying he was sorry he did it! You're so far in it right now, you're almost on the other side of it! We can't just do nothing!"

"Look, I know what I heard," Tricia offered, "But he didn't exactly say that he did it, and ya'll didn't hear the sorrow, the pain in this man's voice. I don't think he was the one that hurt anyone. And if he did kill Chester Graves, I think it had to have been more to protect Priscilla than anything. Keep in mind, he didn't even try to hurt me, and he could have easily done so, and ya'll would have never seen my sorry self again!"

"Okay, okay," Cyndi, ever the voice of reason, hesitated. "There are a lot of things we don't know. Did he mean, 'I'm sorry you're dead', or did he mean, 'I'm sorry I killed you? And did he give Chester Graves's widow back the money because he felt bad for her, or because he felt guilty? Let's say you're right. If he's not the killer, or the kidnapper, then there's likely only one other person that leaves."

"Harvey Bryson," Nancy said. "Otha seems to think Harvey and Chester were friends. Which means, if the two of them were in cahoots, 'ole Harvey is going to definitely blame the Sin Eater for all of it and save himself."

"Oh my god, it's worse than that," Tricia realized, aloud.

"What do mean, Grimball?" Nancy looked puzzled.

"If the Sin Eater is really innocent, and Harvey Bryson is guilty, then Priscilla Parker could be in real danger, if Harvey thinks she might remember anything at all."

"No matter which one is guilty, that girl is still in danger – and so is anyone near her," Cyndi added. "And what about you, Tricia?"

"What about me?"

"The Sin Eater knows that you heard every word and that you know about all of this. You could be in danger, too. He had to have gotten a pretty good look at you. You had your handkerchief on your head, keeping your face very visible."

"I just don't think he is evil or dangerous. I just feel it, is all. Something about him. I think Otha is right, it's not him, at least not intentionally. But one thing seems certain – he was there for all of it. He knows exactly what happened."

"This is so unbelievable, "Cyndi shook her head. "I think that, yes, we should all sleep on this and approach it with clear heads tomorrow. We figure out what to do and go from there. But whether we want to be or not, we're in too deep to back out now. The Sin Eater saw your camp uniform, Tricia. And he definitely saw your face. He knows where to find you, if he has a mind to."

CHAPTER SIX

Tricia rolled over and opened her eyes as the early morning sunlight weaved its way into the Du Kum Inn cabin. It had been a night filled with tossing and turning and interrupted sleep, if any at all. All four campers were hovered over her cot, as Natalie gave her arm a gentle shake.

"Are you okay? You're usually the first one up, making sure that we are ready for breakfast and inspection."

The girls were dressed in their uniforms and the cabin was spotless except for her own space. Tricia jumped out of bed, tossed her nightgown aside, and began donning the gray middie shirt and dark green bloomers, along with her flannel counselor arm band.

"Please tell me the breakfast bell hasn't rung yet!" Delighted giggles erupted from the campers, as they volunteered to make her cot and put away her gown.

"No, silly," Gaylen squealed in delight, "we just let you sleep until it was almost time."

"You must have been very tired, Tricia. We tried not to wake you," Christa added.

"You all are angels. The best ever in the world. How did I luck out with the absolute most wonderful girls at Arden Woode?" More giggles. "Okay, let me get my shoes laced up and we can head to the dining hall. The new camper is supposed to be here for breakfast, and I want to be sure we all say 'hello' and give her a warm welcome."

"I'm going to give her a pine sachet like Tricia made for us," Natalie said, holding up the small bag of cut needles.

"Well, I'm going to give her this necklace I made in crafts yesterday!" Chuck exclaimed, placing the beaded trinket around her neck with pride.

"I can give her one of my swim caps," Gaylen piped up, not to be outdone.

"Hey, whoa, ladies," Tricia laughed. "This is not a competition for the best gift, and you don't have to give her anything at all but your friendship. Just think about how you might feel if you were coming late to camp and did not know a soul here."

"How about if we give her the pine sachet and say that it's from our whole cabin?" Natalie asked.

Tricia smiled. Natalie was such a tender and kind-hearted child. Tricia made a mental note to include her generosity in the next personal letter that was sent to each parent. She had already begun to feel how hard it would be to tell her girls goodbye at the end of the summer.

"Nat, I think that would be lovely and a nice little token from us as a cabin. What do you say, my sweet ones?"

All nodded in agreement, as they bounded out the door and made their way to the dining hall. Nancy and her girls caught up to them, as the breakfast bell rang, and the campers all migrated up the stone steps to the front porch and into the eating area.

"Grimball, you get much sleep?" Nancy whispered.

"Hardly any at all for most of the night," Tricia admitted. "My poor girls were so sweet, they got dressed and cleaned up around me, can you believe it? I was beat. They woke me when they were done. I can't stop thinking about it all."

"Yeah, me neither. Maybe we can talk some later." Nancy frowned and pointed a finger in front of them. "Hey, look there, outside by the path that goes around back to the outside cooking area. You ever seen that buckboard and horse here before?"

Tricia looked where her friend had directed. Otha was motioning the rider to move the wagon further around behind the dining hall.

"No, never. Visitors are usually limited to Sundays after our morning service."

"Well, the fellow sure seems to be getting some ganders from us counselors."

"Maybe. Hard to tell," Tricia mused, taking in the lone muscular man in the seat holding the reins. He appeared to be taller than average, with dark hair that brushed under his chin, but not touching his shoulders. A dark grey small-brimmed work cap sat atop his head. His white collarless shirt had sleeves that were rolled to elbow-length, with suspenders and dark duck cloth trousers. His work boots were sturdy, like those of the farmers back home, maybe made from the strongest kangaroo leather. "He looks okay so far. I can't see his face, so I'll reserve judgment. It looks like he's maybe making a delivery for Otha."

Before Nancy could respond, the sound of a knife pinging loudly against a glass got the attention of all in the dining hall. Dammie was standing beside a demure, pretty young girl, with straight blonde hair secured at the nape of her neck. Long, wispy bangs hung over timid eyes. The Arden Woode uniform seemed to swallow her lean frame, and her shoes had been worn almost past their usefulness. Tricia winced at the obvious diminished circumstances of the new camper and the out of sorts way that she must have felt.

"May I have everyone's attention, please, before we have our blessing and eat breakfast?" Dammie smiled and placed a hand on the girl's shoulder. It is my distinct pleasure to introduce our newest camper to the Arden Woode family. Please introduce yourselves later to our new friend who will be with the Sign of the Hemlock gals. Now, help me welcome Miss Priscilla Parker to Arden Woode! We're so glad you are here, Priscilla."

The embarrassed girl peeked around the dining hall, blushing and smiling, and raised a hand in greeting. The entire assembly of girls rose to their feet, clapping and cheering for the newest member, and shouting words of welcome. *Another reason this place is so special,* Tricia thought.

When the meal was done, the girls of Du Kum Inn left to find Priscilla to give her the pine sachet. Tricia waved them off, with instructions to save her a seat in the Castle for morning devotional and announcements. She found Otha outside cleaning and boiling water over a hot fire. The young man was still there, wiping his brow after having unloaded what looked to be a good amount of fresh cabbage, tomatoes, cucumbers, watermelon, sweet potatoes, and a metal container of fresh milk.

"Hi, Otha. Hello," she offered to the man.

"Tricia, this here is Mr. Ewan, from up the road at the Laurel Valley Inn. He gonna start bringing us some goods every now and again, so Mr. Hugh don't have to be going for 'em so much."

"Hello, Mr. Ewan," she tried once more.

"Just Ewan," he said, with no emotion. "Ewan Munslow." She surmised him to be close to her age, but he seemed more serious and reserved, and she thought she detected perhaps an Irish or Scottish accent. He was rather handsome, with an intense ruggedness to his personality and deep coal grey eyes.

"It's a pleasure to meet you, Ewan."

"Mr. Ewan, this here is my favorite counselor of all," Otha beamed. "She and her girls help me out so good when it's their turn out here. And they the youngest ones here." Ewan softened some-what in demeanor but spoke only to Otha.

"Otha, if I'm going to call you by your first name, you have to drop the 'Mister' from mine. Agree?" The man finally gave a hint of a smile as he addressed the camp cook.

"I told her the same thing," Tricia grinned. "Took me forever to get her to stop calling me 'Miss' either. How about it, Otha? Agree, for me and Ewan, here?"

"Lawd have mercy, you both gonna get me fired. Alright. If 'n I slip up, now, and do otherwise, don't be fussing at me."

"The truth is, Otha, where I come from in South Carolina, it's considered proper manners to refer to those older with the appropriate title before their names. But at Arden Woode, we're all family, remember? Besides, I've already told you I could adopt you for my mama." The cook shook her head, smiling, as Tricia continued. "I came by to talk with you about last night, but now I have to get to the Castle shortly, so I will speak with you later. Ewan, it was nice to make your acquaintance."

As she turned to leave, she saw a book sitting on top of the outside preparation table.

"*The Man Who Lost Himself*," she read aloud, picking it up. "An Irish author, is he not? Didn't he write '*The Blue Lagoon*'? This is yours?" She looked at Ewan, who was now staring at her with something close to cordiality, and added, "I should like to lose myself sometime. Is it worth a read?"

"Yes, to your first three questions, and I don't know, to the last. Hugh Carson just gave it to me, so I've not read it."

"I would love to know if you like it." Tricia returned the book to the table. "Well, good day again to you both," she said, turning to walk back through the kitchen area and up the small hill to the Castle, where her girls were waiting with space between Christa and Chuck.

"Tricia, have you met Priscilla Parker yet?" Natalie asked.

"No, not yet. I thought I would wait for a better time. I will see her shortly when they leave for their dam swim and picnic. It might be easier for her with everyone she must be meeting now."

"I like her, she's very nice," Natalie said. "She seems kind of shy like me."

"Does she, now?" Tricia smiled and rubbed the top of Natalie's head. "Then I'm sure she's a doll. But you know, Natalie, I think you're really coming out of your shell, young lady." Natalie beamed.

"Coming out of her shell. You mean like a turtle?" Gaylen, ever the jokester, bent an arm in front of her face and laid the other on top of it. Lifting the arm on top upward, she peeked through the open space. "Look, I'm a turtle coming out of my shell!" The girls laughed at the silly fun and began copying Gaylen's turtle imitation.

"What am I going to do with you four?" Tricia grinned. "You all are the bee's knees, you know?"

"Now, we're camp bees!" Chuck began to make a buzzing noise and flap her hands in the air, which the others were quick to replicate.

"Thank goodness," Tricia whispered, smiling, as Dammie and Mary proceeded with the devotional, inspection awards, and daily announcements. Tricia's girls were excited about the activities for the day, which included archery, dancing, and tennis and swim time after lunch. "Alright, ladies, please have fun and be careful today! I'll see you at lunch and rest time!"

"Bye, Tricia," they yelled in unison. "See you later!"

Tricia caught up with her friends for a quick meeting before they all had to attend to respective duties.

"Tricia, I thought about you all night," Tavia looked at her, shaking her head. "I can't believe all that Cyndi told me about this weird Sin Eater person. And, good heavens, everything that you found out! I know we can't all talk so much now, but this is huge. Huge! Anybody have any ideas?"

"Maybe telling Hugh," Cyndi offered.

"Or the law around here," Nancy added.

"I don't know," Tricia said. I didn't sleep until early morning. I could not get it all out of my head. My girls actually had to wake me up, and I'm usually dragging them out of their cots. I'll say this, though. I asked for adventure, and now we've got more than we bargained for."

"We?" Nancy grinned. "No kidding! We have gotten into some deep stuff. It's way bigger than any of us thought."

"I think I'd like to talk to Otha some and feel her out a little. I also want to meet the new girl, and maybe when Hugh comes back, see what he knows about it all, or perhaps Dammie and Mary, but I know they have their hands full right now."

"Well, maybe for now, we just let it be and think about it some. We don't want to take any wooden nickels, you know," Cyndi added. "Maybe tomorrow night, when ya'll go to the joint, or after, you can find some time to talk. I can catch up with you later. It's not like we have to hurry to do anything."

"True," Nancy said. "I just wish we could be sure no one was in danger."

"I was going to try to get in a brief word with Otha, but the guy from the Inn was still there. Apparently, he is going to be delivering some produce and milk from the farm there. His name is Ewan Munslow and he seems nice enough. I think he may be Irish. Kinda on the serious side, though." Tricia smiled. "But he seems nice enough."

"You talked with him?" Nancy grinned.

"Oh, not much at all. About a book that Hugh gave him, mostly. I guess we'll be seeing him around more."

"Why are you blushing and smiling?" Nancy asked, winking.

"Oh, c'mon, don't start!"

"Poor old Daniel," Cyndi smiled. Tricia smiled back.

"The more I'm up here, the more I don't want to marry Daniel."

"Well, girl, you best be thinking on how that conversation is going to go," Tavia said. "I wouldn't want to be in your pantaloons when that happens. Doesn't sound like your folks are going to be happy about it, either."

"I can't think about all that now," Tricia put her hands up in the air. "Okay, we can continue this later. We've all got to get to work."

As they dispersed to their various duties, she made her way first toward the trip craft hut to help Hugh with carrying the last-minute items to the docks.

"Well, Tricia, good morning! I have to thank you and Cyndi and Mother Nature for carrying those canoes to the site early. That was a splendid idea and it all worked out quite well." Hugh smiled, grabbing his hat and pipe and whistling for Hala to follow.

"It was nothing at all," Tricia grimaced inside at the self-preserving lie she had just told, especially to Hugh. "Glad to have been able to help. Hope the skits were great fun, and the girls all enjoyed you as the wolf."

"Yes, good Arden Woode fun, of course. Let's head on down for the cork vests at the boat house, grab those, and the emergency kit. We will put a few extra in the canoe with the two counselors and a few in mine. The food should go in their canoe, as Hala will be with me. Once all that is done, you can retrieve the food items." Hugh gave his dog a gentle hug, then locked the trip craft hut before they made their way down the path to the bracing waters of Emerald Lake. Tricia eased into the conversation about Priscilla with caution.

"Hey, I haven't met the new girl yet, but my campers welcomed her with a pine sachet." Hugh beamed, knowing he had first taught Tricia that skill. "They said she loved it. By the way, I couldn't help but notice, her shoes are in terrible condition and I was thinking maybe we could take up a collection for some new ones for her."

"Yeah, I noticed that too," he said. "The shoes slipped by me. She's going to need some nice stockings as well. It would take quite awhile for new items to arrive here, and she could use them sooner rather than later. I'm thinking about asking one of our gals about the same size to give her an extra pair and then we can contact our more well-off camper's family for perhaps a new pair."

"That would work, I think. She seems quite lovely, maybe a bit nervous. I suppose that is only natural, being the only new one. Do you know for sure if she can swim?" Hugh hesitated, watching Hala chase a squirrel in the pathway.

"I don't think she swims much or has ever been taught how. Played in creeks, that sort of thing, but has not been in a large lake. The swim instructor will put her in the crib to assess her ability level." Tricia smiled at the reference to the training and assessment area in the lake that the campers had affectionately christened "the crib". "If she can't maintain twenty minutes by herself, she won't participate in the swim without a cork vest. Otherwise, we're going to let her choose where she wants to ride. I'm hoping that perhaps she will sit with me and Hala, here, and I can begin giving her some canoe instruction and let her paddle some."

"I would think she might like that a lot," Tricia noted, then pointed toward the lake. "It looks like the counselors have got the cork vests already and are sizing them up."

"Excellent," Hugh replied, "our Arden Woode gals are on top of the situation, as usual." Reaching the docks, Hugh adjusted his hat and gave short, precise directions for the eight young girls and the two counselors to follow. "We always have a buddy system in the water, so everyone should be paired with another to watch out for while we are swimming. Remember, this is not a competition or a race. It's only the opportunity to see how much you've learned about being in the water, knowing when to use different strokes, and how to stay in touch with what your body is telling you to do. Of course, we will stop and float for a few minutes with the cork vests. If anyone needs to be in a canoe, we can do that also. Once we get to the dam area, we will rest, play some, have a noonday picnic, rest some more, then head back in the canoes. It's going to be a wonderful day." Hugh tipped his felt hat to the new girl. "Miss Priscilla, I understand, is going to accompany Hala and me in the back canoe, while our two counselors are in the other one. I bet, by the time we reach the dam area, she will be really getting the hang of paddling."

Priscilla grinned, a wide, happy smile that did wonders to enhance her appearance.

"Hugh, I'm going to go get our food items and canteens from the dining hall. Might I borrow one or two girls to help me carry them?" Tricia asked. Hands shot up in the air, and volunteers clamored to help. Tricia pointed to one and then glanced at Priscilla, who also had raised a hand, but remained quiet. "Priscilla, I would love to have you help us."

The two campers chatted in casual girl-speak, as Tricia listened. Priscilla was not overly conversational, but did try to participate, to fit in, as they walked to the dining hall. Otha Moses was busy preparing for the other meals of the day and organizing the small inside kitchen area.

"Good morning once more, Otha," Tricia greeted the cook warmly. "We are here for the trip food for the swim to the dam today."

"Well, hello there, girls. Help yourself to the icebox and those sacks on the counter there." She glanced at Priscilla. "You must be our newest young lady. We glad to have you here."

"Yes, ma'am. I really like this place. Breakfast was delicious, too."

"Lawd, child, if you liked that, you gonna love what Otha has coming up. Macaroni and cheese, peas and corn, and some sliced ham. Fresh peach cobbler for dessert."

"Oh, that sounds wonderful. That sounds like Christmas to me!" Priscilla clasped both hands together and smiled. "I can hardly wait!" Otha, pleased with the excitement about her cooking, looked up at Tricia.

"You know what I think we should do? We ought to have us a Christmas in July feast, that's what. We got lots to be thankful for at this here place, we sho' 'nuf do!"

"Why, Otha I think that is a fabulous idea! We could draw names and exchange presents that we make each other here at camp. And sing Christmas carols around the campfire and maybe decorate a tree, too! Do you mind if these girls and I share your idea with Hugh and he can share it with Dammie and Mary? After all, Priscilla, here, helped provide the inspiration for it. We're so glad she's here with us."

The young girl looked pleased that she had helped to create an idea for camp. She gave Tricia a grateful smile. Otha wiped weathered hands on her apron and placed them on her hips.

"Yes, indeed, tell Mr. Hugh. You girls best be getting along now, and take care that you is safe on that water, you hear?"

"Oh, Otha, the man that was here this morning, Ewan? What does he do, exactly?"

"He the one up at the Laurel Valley Inn that runs the farm there. Sees that all the produce is ready for serving. He help out there all kinds of way. Ewan, he's a good boy. He's good to me, too. Mr. Hugh so happy that he gonna be bringing us fresh vegetables and fruit, eggs and milk, and maybe even a chicken or two." Otha smiled. "He a nice-looking fellow, too, don't you think so?"

"I wasn't really paying attention."

Otha chuckled, shaking her head. "I think he was, maybe."

Tricia blushed, glancing at the two campers who were also smiling at her, and picked up the canteens. She grabbed the sacks of food and started for the docks. "I'll come back in just a few minutes, Otha. I did get to see that thing you were telling me about, by the way. Let me get this group on their way. See you shortly!"

Otha turned to look at the young counselor, dark eyes wide.

"Lawd have mercy. You be careful. You be mighty careful."

"Don't worry, it was all fine. Well, mostly fine, I promise."

When the dam swim participants were settled in the water and the rest in the two canoes, Tricia waved them onward. "Hugh, take care of your passenger there, she's already becoming an Arden Woode girl with her idea for a camp activity. I expect she will be paddling away when you all return. Priscilla, we are so lucky to have you here!"

"Bye, Tricia! See you when we get back," Priscilla yelled, waving both hands in the air.

Tricia stood for a moment, watching the swimmers as they navigated the chilly waters of Emerald Lake, and offered a silent prayer. *Lord, let that sweet girl find her way and recover her memory so that the responsible ones are brought to justice, and she is safe. May we all be safe from harm.*

CHAPTER SEVEN

In the outside cooking area, Otha was roasting a large ham while she shelled peas and husked corn. A sturdy, striking young colored boy was slicing peaches. He resembled Otha, around the eyes especially. Tricia figured him to be around fifteen, possibly older or younger.

"Tricia, this here's my son, Samuel. He helping me out some this morning before he have to go do his chores. Samuel, this is Tricia."

The young man raised hesitant eyes to meet hers but did not stop working.

"Hello, Samuel. Otha told me she had a son. Pleasure to meet you, and good to have you here."

Samuel nodded and smiled, his eyes drifting back to the task at hand, but said nothing.

"Could I see you for a quick minute, Otha? I just wanted to ask you about last evening."

Otha lifted a basket of peas and motioned for Tricia to follow her into the kitchen area inside. She pulled a large wooden bowl from a shelf and began the shelling process, tossing the peas in the bowl and the pods in an empty basket. Tricia reached to help her.

"I miss doing this with my grandparents," she smiled. "If I help you, we can get more done and talk, too."

"I reckon that damn fool Chester Graves is having his funeral today." Otha shoved more shells into the basket.

"I suppose he is," Tricia said.

She relayed the events of the prior evening, up to the point where she spoke to the Sin Eater. Otha stopped her shelling and stared, raising her hands in the air.

"My sweet Jesus!" she breathed. "Did he talk to you?"

"No, not a word, just like you said. He stopped walking and turned to look at me. But then, he took off and ran to the woods in the direction of where I saw him come from."

"And he done left that money for the widow Graves, you say?"

"Yes, ma'am. Left it right there on the bed beside the body. Otha, do you think it's possible that the Sin Eater meant to kill Chester Graves?" Tricia lowered her voice even more. "Do you think he could possibly be the one that tried to kidnap Priscilla?"

"No!" Otha was emphatic in her defense of the mysterious man. "No, I don't think he would hurt no one if he could help it."

She reached for another handful of peas.

"I think that the Sin Eater, he come up on Chester and Harvey trying to grab that girl to do harm to her. He come up on 'em, and he try to help her. I think that he killed Chester while trying to save her, and that no good Harvey Bryson ran off to save his own hide. I think the Sin Eater carried her on down to Doc Halsted's place.

Left her there so no one would know who he is, is what I think. But Harvey done told everybody that it was him what carried that girl to the doc's place. He says he left her there to go get help for Chester. I don't believe a word that come out of his sorry mouth."

"Okay." Tricia thought for a moment. "Then if the Sin Eater did not try to take Priscilla, this Harvey Bryson person knows that the Sin Eater was there and that he also knows all that happened. What do you know about Harvey?"

"I know he come from lots of money."

Otha's mouth twisted into a disapproving sneer.

"He done been spoiled rotten by his mama and daddy. His daddy a judge up there in Highlands, and they say he alright, but old Harvey's just lazy as they come. Always looking for an easy way out, never lifted a finger for nobody but his own self."

"From the looks of the Graves place, they weren't that well off. How did Harvey and Chester become friends?"

Otha chuckled, dropping a handful of peas in the bowl.

"Harvey got into the mysteries around here with Chester when he met him in a juke joint drinking that hooch. Harvey had money and Chester didn't, but they just alike inside. Bad seeds. Everybody 'round here know it. The way I hear it, Judge Bryson give Harvey some land for lumbering and farming. I don't think he does much with it. 'Ole Chester did whatever Harvey wanted him to, at least that's how I hear tell of it. Poor Mrs. Graves never had herself much of a husband, if you ask me. Good riddance."

"Has Harvey told his father or the law in these parts about what happened?"

"I suppose he did. But he probably didn't talk much about the Sin Eater, because Harvey knows the Sin Eater don't want no problems. He don't want no one to know who he is, neither. Harvey knows that's why that girl was left on Doc Halsted's porch. As long as the Sin Eater don't say nothing, old Harvey ain't gonna say nothing much about him. I reckon that's why Harvey ain't given too much of a describing of the Sin Eater and just been telling a made -up tale about a strange man that tried to grab that girl and killed Chester. Harvey done made himself and old dead Chester out to be heroes. He say that he the one that done hauled Miss Priscilla yonder over to Doc Halsted, left her there and went back to get Chester's body, but he nothing but a damn liar, and everybody knows he's trash, but ain't nobody gonna say it out loud."

"Otha, this is important," Tricia leaned in to whisper, "do you think Harvey knows that Priscilla Parker is here? Do you think he would hurt her?"

Otha frowned, shifting with discomfort while running a hand through the peas to be shelled.

"I sho' do. Yes, ma'am, I sho' 'nuf think he would hurt her if he thought she might could remember things and talk. No one ought to leave that girl alone, not ever. He probably know she's here, too. I s'pose most of the little towns will know it soon enough, since gossip travels faster than anything else 'round these parts."

"What do you think I should do?"

"Nothin', you don't need to do nothin' at all!" Otha was adamant. "The Sin Eater ain't gonna bother you, and neither will Harvey Bryson, as long as he don't know none of this that we know. You don't want him finding out what you know. Otherwise, all Harvey wants to do is chase women folk and drink and live off his daddy. Leave his sorry behind be."

"What age is Harvey?"

"He probably a little older than you, maybe. Likes to dress like he something. But he's up to no good." Otha crossed her arms and looked at Tricia. "That girl, Priscilla, she the only one might be in danger if Harvey catches wind that she remembers anything."

"Do you think Judge Bryson would defend his son even if he is guilty? You said that the judge was not like Harvey."

Otha snapped a pea pod open and tilted her head to one side.

"I don't rightly know for sure. I hear he's an honest sort, but 'ole Harvey is his son. Main thing is, we don't need Harvey Bryson or his kind anywhere around this place. He's a bad seed, no matter who his kin is. And I think he would stop at nothing to save his own sorry hide. Chester Graves done got what's coming to him, if you ask me." Otha shook a pea pod in her direction before snapping it. "You stay away from the likes of Harvey Bryson. He ain't never gonna amount to nothing good. And nothing good will ever happen to anyone that takes up with him. Nothing!"

Tricia headed back toward the trip craft hut, recalling all that Otha had shared, and all that she needed to accomplish before the noonday meal. There was wood to be chopped and other trips to be put on the calendar and organized. The day would pass quickly, as would the time before the arranged outing with Lorene Hogue. Something about the upcoming evening still felt suspicious. Lorene had made off beat comments, given her backhanded compliments, and played silly pranks since camp had started. Everyone else had laughed, not fully understanding that Tricia was far from amused by her antics and didn't understand whatever it was that she had done to be the target of such treatment. Maybe the girl was really reaching out and deserving of the chance to make things better. With a bit of luck, they might even find more information about the terrible events surrounding the attempted kidnapping of Priscilla Parker and something more about the missing, or the mysterious Sin Eater.

CHAPTER EIGHT

"Looks like there's a few folks already here."

Lorene Hogue gestured toward the handful of jalopies parked close to the run-down clapboard building, and a couple of horses and wagons tethered to a railing on the far-right side of Buford's Place. A weathered porch sprawled across the front, with a few steps up to the single door entrance. To the right side of the porch sat two local men in overalls, plucking and strumming away on an old banjo and fiddle. In the afternoon light, the place seemed benign enough.

"There's an interesting touch," Tavia nodded toward the musicians and smiled.

"Don't let the casual outside fool you, it's a much nicer joint inside. Rachel and I will let you three out here at the door and we'll park. Wait for us here."

"I smell a rat," Tricia whispered as Tavia and Nancy climbed out of the camp passenger vehicle in front of her, their summer skirts brushing her face.

"They've been pretty nice so far, let's give them a chance." Nancy whispered back, then added, "Tricia, your hair really looks pretty tonight. Did wearing it in a braid all day give it those soft waves?"

Tricia smoothed her white and light-grey pinstriped cotton dress and smiled with approval. "Yes, I washed it and let it mostly dry after our swim this afternoon, and then braided it during quiet time. My girls got to see the waves all fluffed out before they left with Hugh for the festivities and night with their folks. Gosh, it feels weird to have these brown kid top heels on after all this time in our camp shoes. I'd almost forgotten how to fasten them up."

"You were saying, about that rat," Tavia grabbed Tricia's arm in a frantic motion, and pointed to the camp vehicle that rolled onto the main dirt road back toward the tiny town of Cashiers. "I think we've been literally taken for a ride."

"Hey!" Lorene yelled to them. "We thought we'd introduce you ladies to the finer things in life. No hard feelings, right? We'll be back in a couple hours or so. And don't forget who's still queen!"

Ripples of laughter drifted back to the three counselors now standing on the front porch of Buford's Place, as the "oogah" sounds of the camp passenger vehicle horn faded into the distance.

"We're so going to pay her back. If it's the last thing I do this summer!" Tricia swore between gritted teeth. "I knew that girl couldn't be trusted. Why is she after us so?"

"Not us, Grimball. You. She's got it in for you for some reason." Nancy shook her head. "However, we've got to figure out a plan pretty quick here. What're we gonna do?"

"We could just sit out here on the steps and wait for them to come back," Tavia offered. "No telling what's inside." Noting the curiosity from the porch maestros, she added, "Of course, we could take our chances inside too. They did say it'd be a couple hours."

The raucous sound of predominantly male voices and the hum of a harmonica wafted through the old clapboard walls from within. Shades were pulled over the single windows so that only a soft amber light peeked through to the outside.

"Well, we got dressed up – at least as much as we could at camp – so I say we check it out." Tricia gave a gentle push on the front door and faced her friends. "How bad can it be, right?"

They eased their way inside, with Tricia in front. The wood floors of the old building creaked and moaned with each step, and the room was adrift in a smoky haze and the strong smell of alcohol. A handful of men buzzed around the two pool tables, laughing and clapping one another on the back as they made their competing shots. By the back door that no doubt led to the banks of the roaring Chattooga, two men jawed back and forth in loud, indiscernible voices, oblivious to all else around them. Without warning, a whiskey bottle was snatched from the hands of one, who slid weaving to the floor when the other administered a dull thwack of the bottle to the side of his head.

"Oh, God. This is bad," Nancy whispered. "Real bad. Except for that floozy-looking gal in the corner there trading spit with the old guy, we're the only women in this place."

"And we're definitely overdressed." Tavia added, noting the attire of most mimicked that of the men on the front porch. She rubbed her hands together, trying to keep calm, as the rush of activity came to a momentary halt. All eyes rested on them.

"Um, hello, how are you tonight?" Tricia announced, smoothing her damp palms against the soft cotton dress.

"Oh Jesus, help us," Nancy said behind her, as Tricia pressed forward.

"We're from Camp Arden Woode, down the road there in Laurel Valley." She gestured behind her in the direction of the camp. "Some of our fellow counselors decided to play a prank on us and left us here for a while." Tricia paused. "We sure could use some help from gentlemen such as yourselves."

"That's the plan?" Tavia whispered, forcing a desperate smile.

"When in Rome," Tricia whispered back, then turned to the amused crowd once more. "Perhaps maybe you could teach us how to play the billiards before our friends get back here. Which will be shortly, I'm sure."

"If my great grandmamma was here, she could put an old-fashioned gris-gris on 'em," Nancy whispered again. Tricia and Tavia stared at her, eyebrows raised. "You know, put a root on 'em. Cajun voodoo. We could use it."

"We're so dead," Tavia muttered. "They'll never find our bodies. Maybe our bones will wash up somewhere down the Chattooga."

A young blonde-haired man exchanged a laugh with the other men, then sauntered toward them. Tricia guessed him to be close to her age, perhaps a little older. He wore dark pants and a light-colored shirt, rather than the prevalent overalls.

"Why, sure thing, Darlin'. We can teach you fine ladies all you want to know and then some." He turned, smiled once more at the approving men, then cast a lascivious stare at each of them, bowing low in a gesture of exaggerated chivalry. "I'm Harvey Bryson, ladies. Who might you be?"

"Harvey Bryson?" Tricia repeated, turning to face her friends, eyes wide with expression, hoping they made the unspoken connection. Their eyes told her they had. Before she could respond, a shadow of a man made his way toward them from a darkened corner of the room. Tricia felt instantaneous relief when Ewan Munslow came into focus. He was dressed in work clothes, much the same as she had last seen him. His expression was stern, his voice serious.

"Excuse me, Miss Grimball, might I have a word with you?"

"Aw, come on now, Munslow," Harvey chided, "you can't handle her, much less all three of these beauties. Go back to your whiskey. Ladies, shall we?" He gave a nod toward the billiard tables.

"A word, Miss Grimball?" Ewan insisted, his eyes bearing down on her.

"Hello again, Mr. Munslow," Tricia smiled. "Ewan. What an unexpected and pleasant surprise."

"For both of us," he replied, not smiling.

"Tricia," Nancy spoke up, recovering a sense of safety in the presence of Ewan Munslow. "Why don't you join us after you've spoken with your friend? Tavia and I are quite sure that Mr. Bryson here will keep us in the company of gentlemen while teaching us the finer points of billiards, and perhaps regale us with a local tale or two?"

"I can hardly wait," Tavia smiled, the sarcasm evident to the females only. Harvey Bryson linked arms with the reluctant girls as if he were escorting royalty.

"Ladies, you're in good hands, I assure you."

"Laissez les bon temps rouler," Nancy waved a hand in the air. "Let the good times roll."

"You French, Darlin'?" Harvey leered as Nancy now fully embraced the clandestine mission they had chosen, flipping fingers through her short black hair.

"I am tonight," she laughed, "but most of the time I'm from Louisiana."

"There's my cue," Tavia added, rolling her eyes toward Tricia, "no pun intended. Rack 'em up."

The trio laughed with giddy rowdiness, making their way to the billiard tables. Tricia turned to Ewan.

"Are they going to be okay over there? Harvey Bryson seems to be a bit of a rake, if my first impression is correct. And it does not appear that the two of you are friends."

Ewan Munslow stared at the revelry on the opposite side of the dimly lit room.

"Harvey Bryson is a man of questionable means and perhaps even more so of character. But I think your friends will be alright for the short time that we will be here."

"We don't exactly know how long we'll be here," Tricia frowned.

Ewan leaned closer to her, finally smiling. She was disarmed at how handsome it made him look.

"I have the carriage from the Laurel Valley Inn. If your friends don't mind riding in the back with a few supplies from Zachary General, I can take you back to Arden Woode before things get out of hand. We'll keep a watch on them."

Now Tricia grinned, fully appreciative of his presence.

"Yes, that would be wonderful. Thank you. I'm so glad you were here."

Ewan guided her first to the bar area, where he procured whiskey and an extra glass, then to the tiny table tucked in a far corner. He pulled a chair close for Tricia.

"I'm not going to pour you much whiskey. Everything here is made courtesy of the locals and is quite strong, although this is actually pretty smooth. I won't be offended if it's not to your liking."

Tricia breathed in the strong aroma of alcohol and tobacco. In an instant, images of her father, brothers, and male relatives emerged. Such was the scene when they'd gather on the back porch to enjoy a smoke and a drink while they recapped their week. As a child, she would sit on the floor, close to the kitchen door, overhearing conversation not meant for a woman, much less a child, about politics and business. Meanwhile the women would gather in the sitting room, chattering about food, fashion, children, gossip, and on occasion, venture into the realm of politics and the like, usually left to the men folk. For an instant, she saw Daniel Middleton's face, and heard his voice admonishing her for being curious about male conversation. *Don't concern yourself with such,* he would tell her. Ewan Munslow didn't treat her that way. She lifted the glass to her lips and took the smallest of sips, coughing only briefly.

"I'll have to get used to it." She closed her eyes for a brief moment. "But I like the way it sends soothing warmth all the way through my body."

Amused by her response, Ewan smiled, taking a bigger sip from his own glass and relaxing against the back of the wooden chair.

"So, Tricia Grimball, I did like the book. You should read it." Seeing her confusion, he added, "*The Man Who Lost Himself.* By Henry De Vere Stacpoole."

"Oh that, yes, I would very much like to read it."

Ewan crossed his arms, studying her face.

"So why do you want to lose yourself? Remember, you said so the day I met you when we were talking with Otha?" Tricia did remember. She wasn't sure she was ready to share the real reasons with him. She knew she found herself drawn into his directness and it awakened a desire for the honesty and realness she craved in her own life. She took a deep breath and looked into the piercing eyes.

"Do you ever feel like you're not really the person everyone sees? Or maybe that it's partly you, but that there's so much more inside that's dying to get out? You know, like living up to the expectations others have for you, but secretly wanting something more?" Ewan leaned toward her, his forearms resting on the table and his face close to hers. She shivered under the intensity of his gaze.

"What do you want?" The question both surprised and disarmed her. She hesitated, wondering if he would belittle her for the response.

"Freedom," she said softly. "Freedom to choose who I want to be, what I want to do, who I want to love." She gave a wistful smile. "Back home, my folks have one idea about how I should be. They want me to be a teacher. That is, they want me to be educated to teach, if something should ever happen to the soon-to-be-lawyer that they want me to marry. They really don't want me to have a vocation at all, especially the one I want. Then, I should have two or three children at least, and throw elegant and successful garden parties."

She smiled at Ewan and took a sip of whiskey.

"You still haven't completely answered my question, Miss Grimball. What do you want to do?"

"I want to write," she whispered, as if her own words were illegal. "I want to write intriguing stories about fascinating people and places, about what is happening in our vast world. I want to seek out a story, whether it's good or bad, and explore it. All sides of a story. I want to make people think. I do want children one day, and even to be married, but I want it to be with someone that I can look up to. And someone who sees me the same way. Someone I can't imagine living without."

Ewan drained the whiskey glass and stared at her, tilting his head and leaning forward on his elbows, his chin resting on locked fingers. She felt as if his gaze had penetrated her soul.

"You came here to escape those expectations? Or perhaps more accurately, to find your own way?"

"Yes! Yes, that's it, exactly, to find my own way. But at the obvious risk of disappointing others that I love and care about."

"If you disappoint others, it's only for a season. If you are not true to yourself, the disappointment will last a lifetime."

His words set off a firestorm inside and she found herself fighting back tears. He had boiled it all down to the essence of what really mattered; what she knew deep inside. Once acknowledged out loud, she would have to act.

"You sound like you have been there before. What's your story, Ewan Munslow?"

"I saw what you did there, the deflection." He smiled. "There's no big story."

He shook his head and eased back into his seat once more.

"My father was from England, married an Irish girl, and they decided to settle in Westport, County Mayo, Ireland to raise a family. That's where I spent my early years, hence the Irish accent. It is a truly magnificent place, full of history. My mother became quite ill and died when I was young. I had an older brother who joined the British military and was later killed early on in the war, after my father and I had already come to the States. My father was a farmer and had also become quite the chef over the years and cooked for well-to-do folks who had a hand in helping him procure a job at the Laurel Valley Inn. We came here in search of the American dream, I suppose. That, and my father wanted a fresh start. I was thirteen at the time. I worked right along beside him, learning to farm the land, fish for mountain trout, and provide local fare for the inn. I even cooked a bit with him, all up until I went to Rutherford College, in Brevard."

Ewan smiled at her, shifting his weight in the chair and running a hand through his dark hair.

"When I was almost twenty, my father had gone with some local men on a mining expedition. North Carolina is known to be teeming with valuable gemstones and gold. In fact, the lake there by the camp and the inn sits on an old mining site. At any rate, there was a rockslide and all eight men were lost."

"Ewan, I'm so sorry. You lost your whole family."

Tricia felt a rush of sympathy for him. No wonder he came across as serious and aloof.

"Yeah, it was hard for a while. But I had learned much from my old man, and thankfully, could step into his shoes as the head farmer and local foods procurement person for the Laurel Valley Inn, so I quit my schooling, fully intending to go back. By then, the inn had grown in reputation and the decision was made to hire a formally trained chef. So, I live in the farmhouse behind the inn and now provide much of the produce for the camp, also. It's a good living, for now."

"For now?" Tricia crossed her arms on the table, leaning toward Ewan. "Do you want to do something else besides farming?"

"I love this place, the land. The people here are as good-hearted and hard-working as they come. I could be happy here all my days. The Laurel Valley Inn provides a link to culture and gentility, I suppose, and fascinating people come here. My secret dream, if one could call it that, is to become a physician. I was a good student while I was in school, and some said I showed promise, whatever that means." He smiled at her again. "I still read every medical book I can get my hands on and have observed a doctor or two when they come to the inn. I've even learned from some of the remaining Cherokee who live in these parts. They believe in a strong connection between the body, the mind, and the spirit. I learned much from them as we all battled the Spanish flu."

"Ewan, why don't you go back to school somewhere to become a physician, if that is what you truly want?"

"I've thought about it a lot. I have saved up money in my twenty-six years and my father left me what he had worked so hard for, too. But one also has to have the backing of a qualified doctor and school credentials to proceed. I have not been but to two years of higher-level formal learning, nor do I know a prominent physician well enough to vouch for me. There is one very well-known and excellent doctor that lives here with his wife during the summer now. Their place is called High Hampton and his name is Dr. William Halsted. He is one of the founding professors at Johns Hopkins Hospital in Baltimore. He started the first formal surgical residency training program in the country. I have not had the pleasure of a conversation with him. His word is all I would need. But I would have to convince him I would be worth it. No small task, I'm afraid, as I'm sure there are others who have much more formal education than I."

Before Tricia could respond, Ewan tapped her arm, motioning to the billiard tables. Nancy and Tavia were once again wrapped around Harvey Bryson and had begun to sing camp songs, much to the amusement of the onlookers. Even the couple in the corner had stopped their romancing to listen to the revelry.

"I'd say now is a good time to leave, don't you think?"

He stood, holding his hand out for her. Tricia felt her cheeks flush with color as they moved toward the door. She called to her friends, waving for them to follow. With Harvey and the other men clamoring for them to remain, Tavia and Nancy blew kisses and curtseyed several times before bounding out the door and waving to the two musicians still strumming their mountain music. Ewan helped hoist the two girls, now laughing in wild abandon, into the back of the wagon, and assisted Tricia in climbing to the passenger seat beside him in the buckboard. Twilight was just beginning to settle into the mountains.

"Lawd have mercy, could there be a bigger cad out there than Harvey Bryson?" Nancy hissed under her breath. "I need a bath."

"He's an ass," Tavia offered, which brought a laugh even from Ewan, who gently shook the reins, urging the horse forward, and causing the girls to pitch backward across a burlap bag of potatoes. More giggles and loud complaining ensued when he asked about their evening.

"Yeah, great. Fantastic," Nancy reeked of playful sarcasm. "While you and Tricia here were exchanging civilized pleasantries and such, we were waist deep in Harvey Bryson's drooling and babbling about himself."

"I think I might have more teeth in my mouth than at least three of those old yokels put together," Tavia muttered, sending both girls into gales of laughter once more, as they leaned against one another in the back of the wagon. "Tricia, when do you think Lorene and Rachel are coming back for us?"

"Who cares?" Tricia responded. "But I can promise you this. When that broad least expects it, I will repay the favor, you can count on that. And it will be no small prank either. She's going to rue the day she messed with us."

"Now we're talking," Nancy laughed. "What do you have in mind?"

"I've been thinking," Tricia hesitated. A few things. One really deviously good thing. But I'm not quite sure how we could pull it off."

"Tell it, Sister!" Tavia raised her voice, sending Nancy into approving laughter once more.

Tricia glanced at Ewan, who now smiled at her from underneath the hat he had donned for the ride. She was glad to see him amused by the jovial feminine banter.

"Since I'm on the trip craft staff, I know the schedule for the overnight camp outs for every cabin. Which means I'll know when Lorene's cabin will be empty for a night." Tricia grinned. "Gosh, it would just be a shame if all her belongings ended up on the floating dock in the middle of the lake, wouldn't it? Her bed. Her trunk of clothes. Her lantern. Everything. Don't you think?"

The girls squealed with vigorous approval, vowing to find a way to make the deed happen.

"May I offer assistance, ladies?" Ewan spoke up. "I'd be happy to come over in a canoe one night and help you anchor the dock in the lake once you have all the rest in place."

Now Tricia stared at him, smiling.

"Why, Mr. Munslow," she teased. "You do have a sense of humor underneath that serious demeanor, I believe." Ewan tipped his hat and shook the reins once more. Nancy exchanged glances with Tavia, both grinning at Tricia, who gave them a silent plea to refrain from commenting.

"I love doing favors for folks," he said, smiling. "Especially deserving ones. Just let me know in advance. I'll work it out."

"Hey, Ewan," Nancy interrupted. "The men inside started talking about something that happened around here recently. A man was murdered after he tried to kidnap a local girl. Harvey Bryson kept acting like he was the hero, but somehow that doesn't square with the buffoonery we saw tonight. He's a big talker."

"That did happen," Ewan offered after a moment of thought. "The whole town, small as it is, has been talking about it. I would agree with your impression of Harvey Bryson, however."

"So, if Harvey didn't save that girl, who did?" Nancy continued. "And who would want to hurt her to begin with?"

"Good questions, "Ewan responded. "I would be surprised if Harvey had anything to do with being a hero."

"Well, what can you tell us about a man around these parts known as the Sin Eater?" Tavia asked, looking at Tricia. "They say he eats food off of dead people's bodies, like eating their sins."

"There is such a man." Ewan said. "In fact, there are a few such men in these mountains, scattered about western North Carolina. They would not harm anyone, I don't think. They perform their rituals only to help people, and to provide for their own families. Their identities are kept secret, because it is believed they harbor all of the sins they now bear. No one looks at a sin eater. In fact, they avoid him at all costs, if they should see him. But mostly sin eaters are just simple mountain folk doing the best they can, like everyone else."

"Harvey kept saying he could not identify the man that tried to take the girl because he had something over his face," Tavia added, "but he would not say for sure if he thought this person was the Sin Eater. The other men kept asking him if he thought the Sin Eater could have tried to take the girl and then killed the other man that was with Harvey. He said he couldn't be sure the killer was the Sin Eater. No one else goes around in a disguise, except maybe the Klan, but they usually wear white."

"I can't really say," Ewan hesitated. "The sheriff here will investigate. No one says too much openly about Harvey, as his father is the well-respected judge up in Highlands. Harvey has his own reputation with which to deal, so many questions remain. He is not as trustworthy as his old man. He dabbles in a bit of the lumber business on some land his father gave him. No one wants to accuse the Sin Eater, either, because many people around here need him, but no one can be certain of anything, I guess."

"What do you think happened, Ewan?" Tricia searched his face for clues.

"I don't know. At least I don't know for sure. But Harvey and Chester Graves, the man he was with that night, have never been known for their charitable actions, nor their bravery."

"Could they have been involved in the kidnap attempt?" Tricia asked.

Ewan stared ahead, looking at the road, as the entrance to Arden Woode came into view in the dim light of the growing darkness.

"I guess that could be a possibility." He gestured ahead of them. "Ladies, it seems we arrived before your friends have discovered you beat them at their own game."

"We can walk from the inside gate, I think," Tricia offered. "At least that way, we don't call much attention to ourselves, for those still here at camp."

"You made the evening quite memorable," Ewan mused, when the inside camp gate became visible. "May I suggest a different spot for you to go to experience some more appropriate mountain fun and culture?"

"By all means," Nancy intervened, smiling. "Would Harvey Bryson be there?"

"He does come on occasion to dance and make small-talk with women. But no alcohol is served there, so he usually doesn't stay long, or he goes outside to procure it."

"Is it far from here?" Tavia asked.

"No, not far at all, just down the road, actually, near the Inn. It's open once a month. Stopped during the war but getting ready to open again. Hannah's Barn, it's called. Local people and folks visiting Laurel Valley all come to buck dance and such and listen to local musicians. It's a lot of fun. You would like it. Safer, too," he grinned.

"That sounds fun," Tricia mused. "I would like to learn how to buck dance," she said, referencing the local clogging dance.

"I can teach you," Ewan smiled.

Nancy and Tavia punched one another, grinning at Tricia, as she was assisted in dismounting from the wagon.

"Maybe you could let us know when Hannah's Barn will have the next event?" Nancy said, as Ewan lent a hand to her and Tavia.

"I will definitely do that," he smiled. "I will be back here at Arden Woode in a day or so with some supplies. Perhaps I will see you all then."

"Ewan, thank you again for helping us." Tricia gave a heartfelt smile, brushing hair out of her eyes, and waving. "And we will let you know when we need an extra canoe, also, if you still want to help." Ewan smiled back.

"I wouldn't miss it. Goodnight, ladies."

Tricia watched as he rode out of sight. Nancy pinched her arm with a devilish grin. Tavia snickered out loud.

"What? What was that for?" Tricia demanded.

"Daniel Middleton might want to find himself another girl-friend," Nancy giggled.

Tricia was glad they could not see her blushing.

"That might be very true," she snapped, "but I doubt Ewan Munslow is trying to run him off."

"Oh please," Nancy laughed, "He can't stop looking at you! *May I have a word with you, Miss Grimball,*" she teased, lowering her pitch to mimic the smooth deepness of Ewan's voice.

"The bigger question is, how do you feel about him?" Tavia asked. "Is it a summer fling or could he be more than that?"

"Whoa, wait, you two!" Tricia held up her hands. "Good grief, I've only had one meaningful conversation with him." She stopped momentarily.

"But?" Nancy said. "But what?"

"But it was the most interesting and invigorating discussion I've had in a very long time, I have to say."

"Well, that was pretty obvious, even to us across the room, while we were enduring Harvey Bryson preening all over the place with his conceited, puffed up self!" Tavia said. "Speaking of him, I think Otha and Ewan are right. His character is questionable, at best."

"He definitely wants people to think he is a hero. Whether he had anything to do with the attempted kidnapping of Priscilla Parker remains to be seen," Nancy said.

"I have a feeling there is a lot more that remains to be seen," Tricia added. "Did he say anything important at all?"

"Yes and no," Nancy said. "He mentioned Priscilla a few times and wondered if she was here at camp and if she was remembering anything. He did seem more than a little interested in her. But of course, everybody is curious right now. We never let on that she was at Arden Woode. But he never said anything any more specific than that. He sure was curious, though."

"So now what?" Tavia asked, as they made their way across the game field in the quiet darkness to the front cabin line, where they would go their separate ways. "We know that the Sin Eater and Harvey are both involved somehow, but we have no proof of anything, and we can't ask Priscilla at all. Is it time to maybe tell Hugh or Dammie and Mary what we know?"

"Not yet. We still don't know enough and if they tell us to leave it alone, we'd have to honor that," Tricia said. "We have some thinking to do about what we know and what our next steps could be. Let's talk with Cyndi tomorrow." Tricia lowered her voice, grinning. "And once I check the trip calendar, we have another stealth mission to undertake!"

"Hey, I wonder how long it took Lorene and Rachel to figure out how we got home, or if they ran into Ewan on the way back into camp?" Nancy said.

"Keep them guessing. Don't tell Lorene a thing. Except what a fantastic evening we had," Tavia laughed. "We'll get her back when she least expects it! Speaking of Ewan, maybe we should talk with him? He seems pretty straight-up and honest. He might be a real help."

"I don't know," Tricia hesitated. "I'm not quite ready to trust anyone else with this right now. Ewan is probably alright, but I think we should be really sure that we could trust him. And don't forget, we have to keep Otha out of it."

"Well, there's a surprise," Nancy laughed. "I thought after tonight you'd be all for more involvement with the intriguing Mr. Munslow."

Tricia brushed off the gentle teasing.

"It's just that we don't know enough about him yet, either. He seems reliable and a good person, but I'd rather be careful, for now," she said.

"Okay, here's my stop. I'll see ya'll in the morning, I'm beat." Tavia waved as she creeped up the steps to Chatter Box.

"Something eating on you, Grimball? Anything you're not saying?" Nancy offered with care.

Tricia thought about all she and Ewan had talked about and how much she wanted to talk with him again. And how much she did not want to see Daniel Middleton.

"Nan, I'm so confused. I want to trust Ewan, and I want to see him again, but I just don't want to make a mistake, you know?"

Nancy stopped walking when they reached the area between their cabins.

"This is about way more than just Priscilla Parker and all, isn't it? You're really sweet on this guy, aren't you?"

"I do like him. I like him a lot. But I still don't know him. What I do know, after talking with him, and being here in this place, is that I'm not in love with Daniel and I can't marry him, even if it will disappoint my family and Daniel's. I just don't see me enjoying the life he wants. He's a better fit for my sister, Maddie, actually," Tricia laughed. "She's more into the society demands. I just want something different."

"What's wrong with that? If you don't love him, for gosh sakes, don't marry him. That wouldn't be good for either of you. Surely your folks would understand that?"

"They see Daniel as a step up for me. Marrying into money and having a secure future. I don't know how to explain it. It's like they think I should marry him and then learn to love him, because he has the means to take me off their hands. You know, because I'm not expected to have to take care of myself unless something happens to him. Who knows, maybe they don't even care if I love him. Anyway, they fight all the damn time, or either they don't talk to each other. I thought that was normal until just recently. Maybe it is and my expectations are wrong."

"What? No, not normal at all," Nancy stated with emphasis, frowning. "Old Adelaide and Dave might have a fight every now and again, but my parents love each other, and it's evident every day!"

Tricia smiled. She found the way Nancy referred to her parents by their first names somewhat amusing, but affectionate. She envied her friend, the big, loving family. Maybe she would visit the Baudette farm in Louisiana after camp was done.

"I've still got time to sort it all out before the summer is over and I go back for the last year at school. A lot can happen, I suppose."

"Indeed, it can my friend, it sure can! I have a feeling a whole lot is going to happen. Just don't worry. Proverbs 3:5, my favorite verse, go read it. Helps me when I'm all worried down with the blues. In the meanwhile, rest up. We're going to need it!"

Tricia opened the screen door to Du Kum Inn and smiled at the empty cots. She missed the youthful banter and silliness of her girls, their contagious effervescence. For now, she would rest, basking in the rare solitude and thinking of Ewan Munslow and all that had happened, and what the days ahead might hold. Opening the Bible that was given for confirmation, she read Nancy's referenced verse: *Trust in the Lord with all thine heart; and lean not unto thine own understanding. In all thy ways acknowledge him and he shall direct thy path.* Tricia smiled, as she finished her prayers. There was certainly a lot she did not understand.

Once again, the soothing night sounds of the mountains wrapped her in peaceful comfort, and she would sleep well. Tomorrow, her girls would return, ready to take on all that Arden Woode offered. There would be new challenges, more questions, more possibilities, and hopefully, more answers. Closing her eyes, she prayed for trust, certain that she would need it.

Chapter Nine

The dining hall buzzed with excitement as the campers who had been to the Laurel Valley Inn Family Night event streamed into the room, lit dimly by the morning light and the flickering fire in the great stone fireplace. Tricia's girls rambled on about the luxury and festivities.

"The place had electricity!" Chuck marveled. "With bright red carpet and big stairs. The adults ate fancy grown-up food, but we had spaghetti with these great big 'ole meatballs."

Chuck grinned, holding up her hands as if embracing a cantaloupe.

"There were some gooey brownies, too," Gaylen added.

Not to be outdone, Christa flapped her hands in anticipation of adding to the conversation.

"The best part was when a magician came out," she giggled, "and pulled a rabbit out of a hat and a quarter out of Chuck's ear."

Natalie gave Tricia a hug and warm smile.

"But we couldn't wait to get back here to camp. We missed you and our own little cabin. Did you miss us?"

Tricia glanced at the front doors in time to see Lorene Hogue enter with her crew. Making eye contact with Nancy and Tavia, she nodded toward the doors and turned back to Natalie.

"Oh, my sweet girls, you have no idea how much I missed your little selves! Du Kum Inn was lonely without you! But you're back now and I'm so happy! We'll catch up more at rest time. We need to talk about signing up for an overnight, too."

Lots of squeals ensued as the girls sat down to oatmeal, fruit, and bacon that Otha had prepared on the outside fire. Out of the corner of her range of vision, she took note of Lorene and Rachel sneaking glances in her direction throughout the morning meal.

When the bell rang signaling the end of breakfast and the warning for morning activities in the Castle, Tricia gathered outside in front of the docks with her friends. Cyndi crossed her arms in mock disdain.

"I leave you all for one little night and y'all have an adventure without me. So much for trusting Queen Lorene, I guess."

"Speak of the devil," Tavia nodded at the girls at the top of the dining room stairs now making their way down and past the intense gazes of the ones below.

"Hey, Lorene," Tricia called out, "We want to thank you two so much for the enjoyable time at Buford's Place. Really great guys there."

Lorene stopped moving. She gave a slow and deliberate perusal of the group.

"Well, I guess even mountain men have their standards at times." She smirked sideways at Rachel, who stood in silence with crossed arms. "Just a little friendly prank between friends, right? So, how much dough did you have to cough up for one of those old drunks to carry you back?"

"Not one thin dime!" Tavia interjected before Tricia could respond. "Such gentlemen, really. Gave us a spin around to some tunes, taught us some billiards, and saw us home safely. We ended up having quite the enjoyable evening. Perhaps we will go back sometime."

"Uh, that might be a bit of hyperbole," Nancy whispered over Tavia's shoulder.

Undaunted, Lorene waved them off, smiling as she made her way toward the Castle.

"Hey, Lorene," Tricia yelled. "So glad to hear that you like friendly pranks."

Smothered giggles erupted from her fellow counselors.

"Good one, Tricia," Nancy hissed. "Not that we really give a rat's ass what she thinks, payback is coming!""

"Rat's ass?" Tricia grinned. "Never heard that before."

"What, c'mon!" Cyndi laughed. "It's been around awhile. Back in the days of the plague, a bounty was put on rats to get people to kill them, as many as possible. To carry them all, they'd chop off the asses and keep them as proof that the rats were dead. A single rat's ass was worth almost nothing, as there were so many. So, not giving a rat's ass pretty much means that one doesn't care at all about something."

"Of course, Cyndi would know that," Tavia said. "It's perfect. Rat's ass! They will never know when we strike!" Tavia clapped her hands together as if snapping at a bug.

"Yeah, rat's ass is right! She'll give more than one when she sees her junk all out on the floating dock, whenever we decide to do that." Nancy muttered under her breath.

Tricia watched Lorene and Rachel disappear up the hill and faced her group once more.

"Cyndi, Hugh and I will get all your gear for the river trip down to the dock area after Castle time. Looks like a beautiful day for being on the water and in the woods. Y'all have a good one. Nancy and Tavia, see you two at lunch."

After morning announcements and Castle time, Tricia made her way toward the trip craft hut, arriving just in time to see Hugh Carson drive up with the back of the camp truck loaded with firewood plus additional supplies for today's river trip.

"Good morning, Tricia," he beamed, waving from the vehicle. "I was outside pondering, chopping wood last evening, and went on ahead with gathering what we need for today. Hop in and we'll head on down to the docks to get everyone packed up and load the canoes on the trailer."

Tricia hoisted herself into the truck, taking in the smell of mountain air and fresh pipe tobacco. Hala gave a quick bark and snuggled against her.

"Good morning, sweet Hala," she rubbed the thick fur and smiled at the beloved camp pet. "Hugh, I feel bad, you've done all the work today."

"Oh, not to worry, I'm going to let you take a look at the overnight trip calendar while I'm gone and fill in some spaces. Since the two counselors and I can handle these intermediate age girls for this trip, I need you to stay behind today. You'll have to go around and check with a few counselors who have not yet signed their cabins up for one. Check with Otha about needed campfire victuals. We are having to rearrange just a wee bit, what with the big Fourth of July celebration at the Laurel Valley Inn coming up on Friday night. Think you're up for that?"

"Absolutely." Tricia smiled, thinking of Lorene and the possibility of yet another adventure and prank. "Whatever you need me to do, I'm on it."

"I'd also like for you to check with Priscilla's cabin and be sure that they are paired up with a good match for an overnight. We want it to be a special time for her, especially." Tricia pulled a tiny notepad from her bloomers pocket and scribbled the aforementioned task. "Anything else?"

Hugh tilted his hat back and puffed repeatedly on his pipe, as he pointed the truck in the direction of the waterfront.

"Yeah. There is one thing. You and Lorene Hogue okay?" Tricia was caught off guard at the question and hesitated before replying.

"I'm not sure. I'm okay, yes. Just pranks on each other so far, but I'm not so sure why she seems to single me out."

"I know she and Rachel had asked to use the carriage vehicle to show you girls around a bit, since your campers were at the family night event at the Inn. But after I was doing my pondering last evening, I heard a few of you coming across the game field at one time, and then, a good bit later, I heard Lorene and Rachel walking back to their cabins before Taps. Anything amiss?"

"Honestly, Hugh, it all turned out just fine. Yes, they played a prank on us." Tricia knew she could have easily told him what happened but felt an odd urge to not tell all. "I don't know why she's chosen me to have it out for. But nothing has happened that we could not handle."

Hugh smiled and tapped his fingers on the steering wheel, reaching to pet Hala with his other hand.

"Well, I can only share some sage advice from my grandfather," he grinned. "When in doubt, ask. In the meanwhile, I love a good prank! Memories in the making, as long as they are safe."

"Thanks, I agree." Tricia felt somewhat relieved, just having a word from the venerable staffer. "May I ask you a different question?"

"Fire away." He puffed on his pipe once more, the smoke wafting into the summer air.

"What can you tell me about a man around these parts known as the Sin Eater?"

"Yes, there is one of those in this area." He stopped the truck in front of the docks. "I've never seen him, but I've heard about him. An old custom and ritual brought to Appalachia from Europe. Harmless, as far as I know. I imagine, with time, this too will change."

"Is it possible that he could have anything to do with what happened to Priscilla?"

Now Hugh stared at her with unabashed surprise.

"You mean hurt her? I guess anything is possible, but that's not the impression from the talk about the man that I've ever heard. What made you ask that?"

"Well, I've heard mostly the same as you. But I have also heard a few rumblings that he could have somehow been involved, whether good or bad."

"I'd say those rumblings are most probably rumors gone wild. Judging a man is something I try to avoid. How a man or a woman acts and treats people, day in and day out over time, says more to me than anything about character or nature of a person. From all I've heard about this strange phenomenon, macabre as it is, seems to me that the whole intent has been to help people, to reassure them that their loved one is redeemed."

"So, you don't think it's a huge con? That he charges money for a service that he certainly cannot guarantee?"

"Unlike a snake oil salesman, or huckster, the Sin Eater doesn't seem to have a set fee, nor is there obvious intent to deceive. A donation is a more accurate scenario. At least I've never heard that he charges anything specific. He also makes no promises of curing anything. As I've heard it told, he simply agrees to take on the sins of another so that the dead person does not go to Hell. He makes a little something off of it, yes, but I'd say hardly enough to make a living. I have no idea what this man really believes, theologically speaking. We all know that Christian people believe salvation is only through the Christ, correct?"

Tricia nodded, wondering where Hugh was headed with this.

"The Sin Eater is surely behaving in a Christlike manner when he is willing to take on the sins of another, is he not, if that is truly his intent? Could be he simply is providing a measure of comfort for the surviving family. Unlike the cunning, bombastic snake oil salesman, this man stays in the shadows, maintains anonymity, only comes when called upon. Anything is possible, I suppose, but that's what I see."

"I guess that makes sense," she said. "Hey, looks like everyone is here. I'll finish loading you all up while you're going over stuff with them and then I'll get right on the trip planning for the remainder of the summer. Have a great trip and will see you all this evening."

Waving to Cyndi and the excited cabins of campers going on the outing, Tricia loaded the trailer with the large inner tubes, packs of equipment and food, and waved the group on their way to a day on the nearby Tuckaseegee River. When the campers and all of the equipment disappeared around the corner, she made her way back to the trip craft hut and found the master calendar of cabin overnights, hiking, canoeing, and tubing trips. With a pencil she copied the calendar to a fresh piece of paper, found a clipboard and began the task of tracking down any of the counselors that were not already signed up for an overnight camping trip, or a day trip to one of the nearby local rivers to canoe or tube. Depending on their age or skill level, a variety of trips were available.

Making her way back to the Castle, Tricia decided to make Lorene Hogue the first stop of the many needed to complete the calendar. She found her going through dress up costuming, no doubt for an upcoming skit. Lorene stiffened somewhat, placing hands on her hips, as Tricia closed the door and approached her.

"What can I do for our hiking assistant today? Thought you had a river trip to go on? Hugh decide to leave you behind?" Tricia chose to ignore the implied slight.

"He needed the trip calendar firmed up for the remainder of the summer. Your cabin is not on the list yet. Thought you might want to take a look and choose a date and a destination." Lorene reached for the proffered clipboard and smiled.

"Seeing as how my girls are older and the most skilled, we definitely want a three-way trip. Horses, hiking, canoeing." Tricia remained silent, but smiled, as Lorene perused the calendar.

Good, the longer you're gone, the more fun the surprise will be when you find your stuff on the floating dock.

"Here we go, this one will work for us." Lorene wrote her cabin name on the calendar and marked off with arrows the weekend date in July for the overnight. "I'm putting Rachel's cabin on here with us, so go check with her to be sure it works, if you don't mind."

"Sounds good," Tricia offered. "I'm sure it will be a most memorable trip."

"You know, you could be my stand-in for when we are gone. Maybe see if you could manage to plan an evening program?"

"I'd just love to try, Lorene," Tricia could barely manage the disdain.

Queen Lorene thought she was handing out a difficult task for an underling to do. With a little planning, Priscilla's inspiration for Christmas in July would be the perfect activity. Even more fun would be the look on Lorene's face when she returned to camp to find her belongings on the dock.

"I'll try to make it as fun as your evening programs."

"Good luck with that," Lorene said with a hint of a sneer.

"Bye, now."

Tricia gave a dismissive wave as she sauntered out the door, quite pleased with the result of her meeting. She had thought about confronting Lorene in that moment about whatever it was that the girl held against her, but decided the timing was not right yet. Christmas in July would happen, and the queen would be publicly dethroned first. Now to find Priscilla Parker's cabin counselor, who also worked as the arts and crafts instructor. Making her way to the shack affectionately nicknamed the "Bang Shop" because of the jewelry-making tools there, Tricia found Jean, the instructor and displayed the remaining available overnight options.

"How about Toxaway Falls?" she suggested. "It's not overly strenuous, but a vigorous hike with beautiful views, and the girls can leave right out of camp to do the trip, if that sounds good to you? It would be a total camp experience for Priscilla especially, with hiking, swimming, too."

Jean agreed on the choice of destination, before deciding on a second cabin to include.

"You know Priscilla really likes your Natalie. They are both kind of shy and seem to enjoy the same activities. If you aren't already signed up for an overnight, would you consider doing that with us? I'd love for Nancy's cabin to come, too. Priscilla thinks she's really funny."

"Nancy is something else, for sure. If you've never heard her tell the story of Romeo and Juliet, Cajun-style, it's really funny. We will have her do it! So, all of our three cabins, right?" Tricia smiled. "Yes, I think they would love it. Natalie, of course, will be thrilled. Hugh would be on that trip also, so that would be a good thing, as an added layer of protection. We pack up Wilhelmina, the horse, with the heavier gear, so all the girls will enjoy that, too. Let me see if Hugh is fine with three cabins going instead of two."

"Tricia, I wonder if I should probably tell Dammie and Mary about this, but last night Priscilla woke up from a strange dream. At least I think it was just a dream. She said there was a man, covered all in black, that she could not make out his face. She was shaking when I woke her up. Do you think that's significant enough to report?"

Tricia's heart raced as she thought of the Sin Eater. Could Priscilla be recovering her memory or was this just a bad dream? If it were true, it once again confirmed that the Sin Eater was clearly in the midst of what had happened.

"Wow, that is interesting. Yeah, it might not be a bad idea to let them know. Did she say anything else, or mention what happened to her at all?"

"No, nothing specific about the mysterious man." Jean stopped momentarily. "Wait. She did say that she had been told that she was found unconscious, but that she doesn't remember anything about that evening. Just that she had been walking home with her brothers and they ran ahead of her, that's all. She knows that she woke up at the doctor's house, but not how she got there. That's all."

"Well, that's something, at least."

Tricia tried to sound casual, as if none of this news meant anything, but her head was brimming with theories about what might have happened. Was the Sin Eater the one that tried to hurt Priscilla, or did he try to save her, like Otha thought? What about Harvey Bryson and Chester Graves? Why was Priscilla attacked, to begin with, and was her attempted abduction connected to the disappearance of the others? So many questions still remained. She had to know the answers, if it took all summer to find them.

Chapter Ten

The mid-day meal at Arden Woode was often consumed in the outside kitchen and eating area beside the large dining hall, as it would be on this day. Otha and her helper had prepared an oversized pot of thick vegetable soup heated over a fire. Baskets of warm cornbread had been placed on the raised boards that served as the low group-size table, and apples and cold milk were handed out to the campers and staff seated on the ground with their camp-made woven mats. Tricia smiled as her campers gathered around in a flurry of activity. Word of their overnight trip had already circulated between the two participating cabins. As soon as the blessing was given, the chatter began.

"Did you hear, Sign of the Hemlock is going with us to Toxaway Falls!" Natalie's eyes were ablaze as she gave Tricia a bearhug. "And Linger Longer girls are going too."

"Of course, she already knows that, she's one of the trip planners, silly." Gaylen grinned, eyeing the cornbread as she took her seat.

"Hey, if anybody doesn't want their cornbread, I'll take it! Yummy! And, I'll take your apples to feed the horses."

"Girl, eat your own food," Chuck laughed, quickly taking a large bite of her apple and chewing with ferocity as Gaylen frowned in mock disapproval.

"Tricia, did you plan that trip for those cabins to go together?" Christa asked.

"Actually, I did not. Their counselor did. She said they wanted to go with us, and I agreed that it was a great idea. She asked for Nancy's too. Voila, it's done!" Tricia smiled at Natalie, who beamed with approval. "Happy, sweet girl?"

"I sure am! Can I sleep next to Priscilla and be her buddy, please?"

"I don't see why not. We can probably work that out." Tricia smiled.

"I will sleep next to Jessie!" Chuck grinned. "Are we gonna eat s'mores, too?"

"You know that will likely happen," Tricia smiled, enjoying the excitement the upcoming trip was generating. She glanced down the long line of smiling and laughing campers and counselors. Such a wonderful group of girls these all were. With a quick pang of loneliness, she envisioned what the last day of camp would be like. Happy and sad tears, no doubt. Forever friends and pen pals made in this special place. She pushed aside the disquieting thought. She had them all now and intended to enjoy each of them for as long as she could.

When the meal had ended, and noonday announcements were made, the gathering began the slow dispersal toward cabins for quiet time, rest, and letter writing, Tricia caught sight of Ewan Munslow rounding the corner in the buckboard with fresh produce and milk for Otha. He eased down from the seat and began unloading his delivery, but not before spying Tricia from among the girls, and tipping his hat to her. Nancy had seen the gesture as well, and winked at Tricia, mouthing the words, *Go talk to him!*

Before she could respond, she heard Chuck screaming from the side of the dining hall close to the lake. Two other girls were waving their arms and shouting, also in a frenzied attempt to get help. A dark-haired camper was seated on the ground, holding her hand and crying in loud waves of distress.

"Help! Help, hurry! Louisa got bit by a snake!" Chuck yelled.

Without hesitation, Tricia, Nancy, and two others rushed toward the girls, while several counselors kept the remaining campers away. Seeing the melee, Ewan reached into the back of the wagon for a large sack and rushed toward the frantic girls.

"Where is the snake?" He demanded with calm control. Chuck pointed toward the edge of the water. "It went somewhere along there. It's gone." Turning to face the ashen-colored Louisa, he knelt beside her and asked where she had been bitten, as the girls were all moved behind them, away from the lakeside.

"My hand," she whimpered, holding it up in the air. Ewan immediately grasped her hand and placed it on her knee.

"She went to get her apple that we were throwing to each other, because it rolled over there and it must have bit her," Chuck said.

"Louisa, is that right?" Ewan continued to keep his hand on hers, as he examined the bite and felt the area around the two fang marks with his finger. "I want you to keep your hand here, do you understand? Do not raise it up at all. Keep it on your knee. Take some slow, deep breaths for me, would you?"

He smiled at Chuck.

"Maybe you could sit beside her and breath slowly with her? That would help me a lot."

Tricia managed a tiny smile at the seriousness with which Chuck took her newly assigned duty, as she placed a hand on Louisa's back and began to breath slowly in and out, while instructing the frightened girl to do the same. Reaching into his bag, Ewan retrieved a bottle of greenish liquid, a small wooden bowl, and a handful of chopped mixed herbs and plants. Pouring some of the liquid directly onto the wound, then a small amount into the bowl, he handed the bottle to Louisa to drink. Making a paste out of the leaves and liquid, he began applying it to the wound, while talking to the frightened camper.

"You're a very lucky girl," he smiled at her. "I believe that this is mostly a dry bite."

"A dry bite?" Tricia asked. "What is that?"

"A dry bite is a snake bite that lacks the venom, or toxin, in it. Either because the snake was not significantly addled, or that it simply did not land a firm bite on her hand. But just to be sure, we are going to treat it as if she had a full bite. Did anyone get a good look at the snake, by any chance?"

"I think I saw it's tail. There was kind of a yellow tip and it was light-colored, what I could see," Chuck offered. "But I didn't see how big it was."

"That's actually quite helpful, young lady." Ewan smiled at Chuck. "It sounds like a young copperhead. They are venomous, but not so much in this case, I don't think. You girls stay away from thick vegetation like that, piles of wood, and such. Let your counselors and staff handle all that, just in case." He gave a big smile to Tricia. "There are a few poisonous varieties around here, but they are generally as afraid of you as you are of them."

"I should not have reached into there for the apple," Louisa grit her teeth in pain, trying to smile through her tear-streaked face. She looked up at Nancy. "You told us in the Nature Nook pretty much what he said about snakes. I guess you were right. It still hurts but not as much. I have a yucky taste in my mouth now."

"Louisa, I think we need to get you to the infirmary hut so that the nurse can keep an eye on you for a while, just in case." Tricia said.

"Let's put her in my carriage," Ewan offered, lifting the young girl from the ground. "Keep that hand on your knee, below your heart for another fifteen minutes or so, Louisa. You can stretch your legs out, but don't lie completely flat for a few hours. I think you are going to be just fine. How do you feel?"

"I'm okay, I guess. It scared me a lot."

"Chuck, why don't you go tell her counselor what happened, then go back to our cabin. I'll go up to the infirmary with Louisa, then find Mary or Dammie, and I'll see you girls shortly. How about you all start writing on your letters home, or just rest and chat til I get there."

"Ay, ay, Captain Tricia," Chuck saluted as she smiled and made haste to take on her assigned mission.

"I'll go to Louisa's cabin, too, to be sure her counselor knows she is resting at the infirmary so she can go up and see her," Nancy said. "You go ahead with Ewan, you know, to be sure the nurse knows we've done everything we should."

She grinned at Tricia, who tried hard not to smile back, as she followed Ewan to the carriage and assisted with getting Louisa in the back.

"So, Dr. Munslow," she smiled at him, "please tell me what you did, exactly, and where did you learn to do that? And by the way, your bedside manner was quite impressive."

Ewan gave the briefest of smiles as he shook the reins to guide the horse up the small hill to the infirmary.

"Well, you already know that I read a lot. Also, some of the Cherokee Indians still in this area who are my friends showed me how their ancestors made the poultice and elixir tea from witch hazel, plantain, and black cohosh. They still use the process today. It is very effective for bites from a variety of animals, with anti-inflammatory healing properties and such. More than once, I've had to make a quick spit poultice on the spot out in the woods or while gardening." At the look of confusion on Tricia's face, he added, "A spit poultice is made when one has to chew up the leaves to make the pasty application. Additional benefits can be obtained by chewing the leaves and absorbing some of the natural juices. After I did that a few times, I decided to create my own medicinal potion of sorts. It lasts for a few days before I have to make another. But, as you can see, it can come in handy at times."

"That's very impressive. Do the Cherokee make other kinds of teas or medicinal drinks?" Tricia asked.

"Indeed, they do. Blackberry, yarrow, ginseng, goldenseal, wild cherry bark, and one from a hemlock."

"Hemlock, isn't that poisonous?"

"Now I'm impressed, Miss Grimball." Ewan smiled down at her as he pulled the buckboard to a stop in front of the infirmary. "Yes, there is a very poisonous hemlock, so it's important to know which to use. The toxic variety grows from three to eight feet high and has many branches of smooth, purplish-spotted hollow stems. The leaves are sort of fern-like, with tiny clusters of small white flowers. Fortunately, it also possesses a foul odor that is quite noticeable when one is near it or crushes its leaves and stems."

"Thank you, Ewan. Really, we were very fortunate that you were around."

He stood close and held out his hand as she exited the carriage. Tricia felt her cheeks flush with warmth as his shoulder brushed against her.

"Perhaps you would consider a dance then, at the Fourth of July event, or at Hannah's Barn?" She blushed under his intense gaze, the coal-dark eyes penetrating hers.

"I would, yes. Remember, you said I could learn to clog or buck dance. I think you said you'd actually teach me."

"I did say that. And I always keep my word. I look forward to it, then."

"As will I," she smiled back at him, her eyes aglow.

She couldn't wait to find Nancy. There would be lots to discuss with her and the others, when they were all free to meet. Perhaps Ewan Munslow would be trustworthy after all. She made her way back to Du Kum Inn to find her girls resting quietly. Christa was asleep while Gaylen and Chuck were finishing their letters to home and drawing pictures together. Natalie was laying on her cot, holding her teddy bear and watching the girls. Tricia shared the good news that the injured camper was going to be all right and said that she was going to read some before rest hour was over. Before long, the slowed and gentle hum of sleep-breathing permeated the tiny cabin. Tricia closed her eyes, thinking of Ewan and all that he had said.

"Tricia, are you still awake?" Natalie whispered, clutching her stuffed teddy bear to her chest, lips trembling and voice shaking. Tricia sat up, rubbing her eyes, and brushing hair out of her face.

"Nat, what's wrong, sweet girl?" she whispered. "Here, sit down on my bed."

"I'm scared," Natalie whispered back.

"What's wrong?"

"Tomorrow, we are riding horses and they are going to let us go faster. Like a canter or a trot or maybe even more. They are so big. I'm scared of them." Big tears rolled down her cheeks, and a faint sob gathered in the back of her throat. Tricia hugged her close.

"You're afraid of going faster on a horse?"

"Yes. And I'm afraid that I'll be laughed at if I can't do it, or if I start to cry."

"I'm glad you told me what was bugging you. Thank you for telling me. That's a good first step, talking about what is bothering you, you know."

"It is?"

"Sure. It's hard to tackle something that we can't talk about. You've called out your fear of the horses for what it is. That's a big first step."

"So now what do I do?"

"What have you already done? Can you get on a horse and just walk with the animal?"

"Yes, I did that, but I was really afraid. They are so big."

"Did you tell anyone there how you felt?"

"No, I was too embarrassed. I kept it to myself."

"I see. And now you have to do something that scares you more. How do you feel about trying it?"

"I want to do it. I want to ride. I know my mother really wants me to learn how to ride, too. I just get scared though. I freeze up and panic."

"Okay. You know it's pretty normal to be afraid of something, right? I mean all of us usually have at least one thing that we are afraid to try or that seems hard or scary. For me, it's heights. I'm scared to go up a great big mountain. I've been working on it. And snakes, they scare me, too. And I don't like feeling closed in, you know. I've got some experience in feeling scared. I'm not an expert, but I can give you a few tips or things to think about, if you'd like."

Natalie dried her eyes and released the death grip she had on Tricia's hand.

"Okay, yes."

"Well, first of all, tell the riding instructor how you feel. Tell her privately, if you wish. That way, she will be better able to help you. Second – and this is important – picture yourself doing what you want to be able to do. Picture yourself enjoying it! Don't worry about being afraid. That's okay. And let yourself have little successes at a time. Maybe the first time, you will not do it perfectly or get as far as some of the others. Remember that here at Arden Woode, we help each other get better and learn."

Natalie smiled, leaning her head on Tricia's shoulder.

"Thanks, Tricia. Hey, maybe you can help me to help Priscilla with something she's afraid of."

Tricia felt the breath catch in her throat.

"What is Priscilla afraid of?"

"She's afraid of the water. That is, she's afraid of going under the water. She says it makes her feel like she's going to die, like she can't breathe. Today, she told me something weird. She said that when she tries to go under the water, even when she's holding her breath, she thinks she can smell something very strong and sweet. She said it was scary and she can't stay under the water because she's so afraid. She doesn't want anyone else to know but I can tell you."

"That does sound pretty frightening. Perhaps you could share some of the strategies we just talked about? Tell her to take it slow, and to share her feelings of fear with the swim instructor. Natalie, did she say where she thought this fear came from?"

"No, not really. She said she doesn't really know why it scares her so much. But it scares her a lot, I can tell."

"Keep being a good friend to her. Think you can rest a bit longer now?" Tricia gave her a hug, then stretched back out on her own metal cot. Priscilla Parker was beginning to remember something about what had happened to her. First there had been the man all in black that was most likely the Sin Eater. Now the mysterious scent that she was recalling when she was covered in the water. What could that have been? If only the poor girl could remember more.

CHAPTER ELEVEN

The Fourth of July brought myriads of fun and excitement to Arden Woode, from the blueberries and strawberries breakfast served with fresh cream on top of Otha's flapjacks, to the beauty of the morning sing-along on the banks of Emerald Lake. Campers and staff alike enjoyed an early morning swim, followed by singing patriotic songs with the greatest of fervor, loud enough for the patrons of the Laurel Valley Inn to hear them across the lake. The daily activities would give way to a longer rest period than usual, followed by the walk to the Inn to participate in the festivities of the evening that would include a barbeque feast, complete with fresh corn on the cob, watermelon, and peach ice cream that the campers could take turns helping to churn.

With the end of the Great War, along with the opening of the new girls' camp, a special fireworks display was planned to culminate the celebration before the campers would make their way back around the lake, exhausted and happy. There would even be a small orchestra to play appropriate tunes for singing and dancing. Along with the well-heeled patrons at the inn, anyone who held a position of importance in the nearby towns of Cashiers and Highlands would be invited to participate.

Tricia found herself wondering if Harvey Bryson or his father, the judge, might be there. Tavia and Nancy had both voiced the desire to try to elicit more information from Harvey, if he were in attendance and they could manage a conversation, while Tricia and Cyndi would make any contacts possible to discover more about the mystery surrounding Priscilla Parker. Of a certainty, Ewan Munslow would be present, assisting the staff at the Laurel Valley Inn, as needed. She smiled as she thought of him bustling around the grounds, seeing to the needs of others.

The girls of Du Kum Inn fluffed their hair and took turns preening in front of the tiny mirror in the cabin when rest time was over. Tricia smiled at the youthful giggling and the warm camaraderie that had developed among the cabin mates. Each had grown since the beginning of camp, in their ability to try new activities, their level of self-confidence, and in their willingness to encourage and help others. Even Natalie had finally galloped a horse. The accomplishment had spurred her interest in trying more challenges, and Tricia reveled in her blooming strength and character.

"Okay ladies, we need to go over the rules for the evening. What's the most important?" Tricia sat cross-legged on her cot and raised her eyebrows and hands in anticipation of their responses Chuck jumped on top of her own metal cot, thrusting a raised fist in the air.

"We stick together and stay with Tricia unless we have permission to do something else!

"We mind our manners!" Gaylen yelled.

"And!" Christa looked at Natalie, who cheered with her. "We represent Arden Woode and make everybody proud!" Tricia gave an approving smile.

"I think you've got it just right, my lovelies! Who's ready to have the best Fourth of July ever?"

"Me, me, me," they shouted, piling onto Tricia's bed, laughing and hugging one another in excitement.

"Tricia, can we spit watermelon seeds?" Chuck asked, grinning.

"Let's take our cue from the others there. I'd say not on the verandah, but perhaps out on the lawn. And please volunteer to take a turn churning the peach ice cream."

Campers and staff gathered on the game field, as Mary and Dammie led the walk to the Laurel Valley Inn, with Hugh remaining in the back of the large group. As they made their way around the curves in the worn path and neared the Inn, the orchestra music mingled with the voices of invited guests to create a festive, patriotic mood. As the Inn came into full view, the campers fell silent, staring at the sprawling Queen Anne style frame building that boasted bright electric lights. Now, it appeared almost ethereal with both lights and torches illuminating the early evening sky.

The structure loomed even more massive sitting atop a slight elevation overlooking Emerald Lake, where tables and chairs had been set up all along the lawn area. It was a two-and-a half story masterpiece, with a main block and additional rear wings. Three large singled gables, hipped dormers, and a magnificent three-story corner turret accentuated the elliptical windows and elegant lakeside stone verandah, where the orchestra played and a handful of yellow umbrellaed tables dotted the edge of the piazza.

A single Magnavox transmitter, or carbon microphone, was mounted for public address. The hotel, built by the Toxaway Company, boasted of high-ceiling rooms, red carpet in the main areas, and every possible amenity, including a bowling area, parlor, and tennis courts. Since its inception in 1898, it was reminiscent of a Swiss resort, and indeed the view was magnificent with the stark face of Bald Rock Mountain rising up from the gleaming cold waters of the lake.

Tricia took note of the prominence of the guests at the Inn, reflected in the clothing they wore. Casual, but the height of fashion, with the men in summer pinstripe or sack suits, two-tone shoes, stripe or paisley print neck and bow ties, and some sporty, stylish straw boater or gambler hats. The ladies were garbed in a variety of fresh summer dresses, some drop-waisted and feminine, many with matching hats, or in high-waisted casual skirts, with colorful, soft blouses and high-top shoes. Their hair and make-up appeared coifed to perfection.

She felt underdressed in the traditional Arden Woode gray middie and green bloomers and stockings but knew that all expected the campers and staff to be in their uniforms. Adjusting the green felt armband that denoted her status as a counselor and tucking a strand of dark hair behind an ear, she scanned the crowd of merrymakers for Ewan. She spotted him leveling one of the many tables out on the lawn. Though not dressed in the prevalent summer suit, he looked scrubbed and polished in his pinstripe shirt and dark pants. Some of the staff sought him out for direction and he pointed out where trays of hot barbeque and steamed corn and beans were to be placed. He waved as soon as he recognized her. The young campers took notice when she waved back at him.

"Oooo, Tricia has a boyfriend. Smoochie, smoochie," Chuck teased, as the girls nodded their heads in agreement.

"He is handsome, you should marry him," Gaylen giggled.

"Okay, stop it, ladies," she tried to tamp down on the silliness before it got worse. "That's the guy that delivers fresh produce and milk to Otha, remember?"

"He's also the one that saved Louisa when she got bit by that snake." Chuck said.

"Then you'd better marry him!" Christa added, as Natalie laughed out loud.

Mary and Dammie began directing the girls to tables on the lawn, while Hugh chatted with a dapper-looking man who followed him to where the girls were all seated. He was the manager of the Laurel Valley Inn and gave a hearty welcome to the campers, promising them slices of watermelon chilled in the pristine lake waters, and freshly churned ice cream after the sumptuous meal before them. Guests of the Inn had been encouraged to speak with the campers as well and began meandering among the Arden Woode girls with great curiosity and light-hearted conversation about the new camp and their endeavors there. They sipped on glasses of freshly squeezed lemonade with sprigs of mint that smelled as clean as the mountain forest that surrounded them. A few couples danced on the stone veranda as the orchestra played upbeat music for the occasion.

"Grimball, look over there." Nancy was beside her, pointing up to the veranda. "It's Harvey Bryson. You reckon that older man and woman with him are his parents? He kind of resembles the man." Tricia stared through the glistening sun that was trying to set behind the Inn. Harvey Bryson was dressed to impress and had already begun fraternizing with any female that walked by him. "What a sleazy guy, huh?"

"You got that right. Think you or Tavia can get a word in with him? I can watch your kids and I'm sure Cyndi would help us."

"Yeah, we'll figure it out and watch him a little bit. You see Ewan?"

"I did." Tricia smiled.

"I got your babies when he asks you to dance," Nancy gave her a playful wink.

"We'll see," Tricia smiled back. "My girls are already giving me a rash of stuff about him. They saw us wave at one another."

"Oh, lawd," Nancy drawled. "No turning back now, they're like vultures on the romance stuff. Let me attend to my girls before they gobble up all the barbeque."

Tricia returned her attention to her own girls in time to see Ewan Munslow approaching. A group of three older couples, no doubt elite guests, by the way they were dressed, listened with rapt attention to the girls' tales of camp. One gentleman in particular, with round-spectacled eyes of bluish gray and white blond hair stood with arms folded while Chuck regaled him with a story.

"Yes, we've learned all about the animals around here. We haven't seen any bears yet, but we did see a snake. Louisa went into the edge of some brush and it bit her. But this man saved her. That's him, right there. He said it was more of a dry bite, probably. You know, like the fangs didn't go all the way in." She pointed at Ewan, who looked surprised at the attention he had garnered from the gathering. The older man with the spectacles smiled at him.

"Well, young man, I'm intrigued as to how you treated the snake bite." Ewan reached across to shake his hand.

"It is indeed an honor to meet you, Dr. Halsted. I've read a great deal about your work. I'm Ewan Munslow and I farm for the Inn here and assist as needed." Tricia recognized the name of the doctor immediately as the physician who had cared for Priscilla Parker the night she was left on his doorstep. The others in the doctor's party smiled and laughed, as the well-coiffed woman on his arm patted his shoulder. Likely his wife, Tricia thought.

"William, I see your reputation as one of the world's best surgeons follows you even to local social events." The doctor ignored the comment, remaining focused on Ewan.

"I'd love to hear what you did, if you are inclined to share it."

Ewan took a deep breath before he began.

"Well, Sir, the snake was likely a young copperhead, from the description I was given by the campers. The bite did prove to be mostly dry, but I erred on the side of caution at the time and applied a poultice and gave the young victim a medicinal elixir, as well. Thankfully, she is fine. Certainly, we would have fared much better with your adept skills."

"A poultice and elixir of what, may I ask?" Dr. Halsted said, crossing his arms.

"The Cherokee and a few Creek Indians that remain in this area have shared how they treated venomous snakebites before modern medicine. Many plants and herbs around these parts have anti-inflammatory and even some anesthetic properties. Witch hazel, black cohosh, and native plantain provide a commendable blend of these. When one is out in the woods, a spit poultice may be made by chewing these and then applying to the wound that should always be kept below the heart for circulation purposes. I have found that both a poultice and a medicinal tea may be made somewhat in advance so that an individual may have the benefits of both internal and external treatment. Thankfully, providence intervened, and the girl recovered nicely." Tricia beamed at Ewan, knowing how much this chance meeting with the good doctor meant to him.

"Providence?" The doctor shook his head. "I don't put much emphasis on that, as much as I do good medicine."

"If you'll pardon me, Sir," Ewan spoke up, "I believe there is more providence in your work than you are willing to acknowledge. I know you are familiar with the ligature constriction work of Ambroise Pare and have quoted him. If I may be so bold, 'God cured her, I just assisted'. I believe you have said those words before, and I concur. I believe providence is at the heart of healing and helping others."

The entourage in the doctor's party smiled and gave Dr. Halsted hearty ribbing about Ewan's words.

"I believe the young man has indeed studied your work, Doctor," one of them said. "Very well said, young Munslow."

"Mr. Munslow wants to be a physician, and he would make an exceptional one, I believe," Tricia offered. "He is a very quick study and has been to school some, and of course reads voraciously."

At once, all eyes were upon her and the table became silent, though Tricia did not miss the smothered giggles from her campers, as well as the appreciative glances from Nancy. She could not read Ewan's expression, but wondered if she had overstepped her bounds.

"Where did you do your schooling?" The doctor studied Ewan with the intensity of one conducting an interview.

"I was able to complete two full years at Rutherford, in Brevard, before my father was killed in a mining expedition. I wanted to remain there, then pursue my academics in medicine, but felt compelled to help in my father's sudden absence. I took over his position here at the Inn and expanded it to include delivery to the camp and some to Zachary General."

"Munslow, you say you farm for the Inn, do you? I raise dahlias and do a bit of gardening and a little astronomy at High Hampton. Might you be willing to pay me a consultation visit of sorts?" Ewan's eyes beamed, but his demeanor never betrayed the thrill of an invitation to spend time with the famous physician.

"Yes, Sir, I would be honored to do so."

"Very well, then. Perhaps you could arrange to come by this week or week's end? Mrs. Halsted and I should be there. Anytime around the noonday meal hour, if you wish. We will set an extra place. Simple but delicious fare, you will find."

Without waiting for further response, the doctor and those in his party made their way around the tables of exuberant campers before returning to their own table. Ewan turned to Tricia.

"I have to help the staff awhile, but was hoping you might save me a dance later?" Gaylen and Chuck placed hands over gaping mouths and grinned at Tricia. Natalie and Christa exchanged excited whispers.

"Yes, that would be very nice," Tricia responded, "if I can get someone to watch my girls."

"Then, ladies, please excuse me," he said aloud to the table of campers. "I hope you enjoy the evening. And Tricia? Thank you." She watched him disappear into the crowd before turning back to her girls, who all stared at her with smiles as big as Emerald Lake.

"What? He's just a friend!"

"Sure, he is," Gaylen laughed. "Tricia is sweet on Ewan. Tricia has a sweetheart!"

"Whoa, now, girls, I told you he is not my boyfriend, don't you start! No ice cream or watermelon for you fabricators, I think!"

Groans and protests erupted from the playful campers, as Tricia squeezed between them at the table to partake of the feast that the Laurel Valley Inn had provided.

The festivities continued, as Arden Woode girls and inn guests alike partook of the meal and began to enjoy the watermelon, while the delighted campers took turns with the ice cream churn. The smell of ripe peaches and vanilla wafted through air, as the orchestra played music that encouraged more dancers on the verandah. Tricia smiled as Tavia and her girls, along with the campers in Nancy's cabin, gathered about on the patio and frolicked to the music. She saw Nancy make her way over to Harvey Bryson and the older couple, chatting with animated friendliness, shaking hands, and exuding her Louisiana charm. Her dark brown hair brushed to and fro in the gentle breeze, as she directed her attention to the group. It was not long before she and Harvey Bryson were engaged in a dance. Tricia smiled. Nancy was working that bayou magic of hers while Tavia kept an eye on all the girls.

"Can we go dance, too, Tricia?" Natalie breathed with excitement.

"Sure, why not? Let's show these folks how it's done!" Tricia accompanied the girls to the area beside Tavia's group, where they made a circle, holding hands and jumping about in wild abandon. Out of the corner of her eye, she saw Ewan watching them from out on the lawn. He spoke to one of the workers, then made his up the stone steps.

"Excuse me girls, do you know how to buck dance or clog?" He smiled at the young campers.

"Is that a dance?" Chuck asked.

"Indeed, it is!" Ewan answered her, his smile broadening. "It's a folk dance that we do in the mountains here. I told your counselor that I would teach her, but I can teach you, too, and you can teach it to your friends, if you'd like."

"Yes, yes," they clamored, clapping their hands, their eyes wide with excitement. Ewan glanced at Tricia as he began to instruct them in the striking of the heel and toe on the floor on the downbeat of the music to create the audible rhythm of the local dance. They picked up on the rudimentary motion and laughed with delight at the noise they created. When the rollicking music slowed to a more intimate pace, he offered a hand to Tricia, and faced her girls.

"Would you all mind if I borrowed Miss Grimball, here, for a dance?"

More giggles and affirmative nods, as Nancy, who had finished her mission with Harvey, motioned the Du Kum Inn campers to sit with her girls. They missed none of the details as Tricia placed a hand on his shoulder, while he offered a hand to her, resting his other hand on the small of her back, as they began a gentle sway to the soft music.

"It seems I owe you a huge debt now," he said, his dark eyes staring into her hazel ones. "Dr. Halsted is one of the most renowned surgeons in the world. Thanks to you, I have the opportunity to get to know him."

"I remember what you told me about him. I didn't mean to intrude. But I didn't want to let a good opportunity pass, either. And, speaking of opportunities, thank you so much for teaching my girls some dance steps. They will be over the moon with their new skills and will teach others, I have no doubt. So, how do you think your conversation with Dr. Halsted will go?" Ewan shrugged his shoulders, smiling.

"It's hard to say. He has a reputation for taking strong candidates under his wing, I've heard, but he also expects dedication and lots of knowledge. I hope I can measure up, given my lack of formal schooling."

"You can't be serious, of course you can!" Tricia smiled up at him, a smile tugging at her lips. "I saw how much attention he was paying to your snakebite healing. He knows you are a natural and that should mean a lot. What you don't have in formal education, you make up for in the drive to educate yourself, which requires the highest of self-discipline. He'd be a fool to not see your integrity."

"Halsted is anything but a fool. His aseptic surgical techniques are quite impressive, and he is most interested and knowledgeable about anesthetic technique as well, especially for women who require surgical procedure for breast cancer."

"Anesthetic technique? You mean medicines that can keep a person from feeling pain or perhaps even being awake during surgery?"

Tricia remembered what Natalie had shared with her about the sweet, strong smell that Priscilla Parker was remembering and wondered if a possible explanation now presented itself. She would have to find a way to ask the good doctor.

"Yes, exactly." Ewan lowered his voice. "It's been whispered that Dr. Halsted's good friend, the wealthy Harvey Firestone, knew that he had become addicted to the drugs cocaine and morphine, as he did many experiments on himself to test their efficacy as anesthetic agents. It's been said that Firestone had him abducted and sent to Europe, which took two weeks for the journey, and dried him out a bit. But he came back and rumor has it that the personal use of these anesthetic drugs continues today. He has a keen interest in chemicals that might be used as anesthetics." Ewan smiled, leaning close to her ear and whispering. "I hear he still sends his dress shirts to Paris to be laundered. As you can see, he dresses impeccably."

"That's incredible," she smiled. "I wonder if he ever had any children?"

"No, I don't think so. He and his wife – who was his very skilled operating room nurse – reside here in the summer at their High

Hampton home, raising dahlias and pets and such. They are said to be a bit eccentric, but very nice. They do a great deal for the people around here. I've heard that he has personally sent a child or two to Johns Hopkins for treatment." Before Tricia could respond, the music stopped, and Ewan guided her back to her smiling youngsters.

"Thank you all for allowing me a dance with your counselor. Miss Grimball, I hope I will see you again before the evening is over. I need to go help elsewhere now and get ready for the fireworks." He made a slight bow to all and made his way back to the busy staff that were bussing the spread of tables. Nancy cupped a hand to whisper in her ear.

"Does Daniel Middleton stand a snowball's chance in hell? Ewan Munslow would be a hard act to follow."

Tricia winced.

"Nan, I don't know. It's so easy to talk with Ewan. But I'll never see him after summer, so what's the point?"

"What's the point?" Nancy repeated. "The point is what you think and how you feel. The point is what you want. You, Tricia. You're so busy trying to please everybody. This is your life, you know. Hey, we need to try to get together with Tavia and Cyndi to touch base. 'Ole Harvey Bryson was with his parents. Lord have mercy, he's just been spoiled rotten. I think his folks want him to amount to something good but know he's too lazy to make a buck honestly. He asked about Priscilla Parker again. How she was, if she was here tonight. Of course, he was also busy chasing anything female. But he made it a point to ask how she was and if she remembered anything. I told him I had no idea about her. And," Nancy hesitated, "know what else? I mentioned the other missing young people and he acted like they'd just run off on their own. But he was beyond curious about Priscilla. I thought that was kind of weird."

"I agree, it is. Hey, watch my kids just one minute more, Nan? I need to go ask the good doctor a quick question if I can get his attention. It's important and might help us."

"Yeah, sure, go on. We're good here with ice cream until fireworks time." As Tricia made her way to the verandah, she was unaware of Ewan Munslow watching with great interest as she approached the doctor and his party.

"Excuse me, Dr. Halsted? My name is Tricia Grimball."

Everyone at the table turned to look at her. Tricia felt small and insignificant as she momentarily held her breath in the presence of the doctor and his distinguished friends. "Would it be possible for me to speak with you for a quick moment about a medical concern?" The doctor wiped the corners of his mouth with a linen napkin as he rose from his chair, seeming only mildly taken aback at her intrusion. He motioned her a few steps away.

"How might I be of assistance, young lady?"

"Oh, not for me, specifically. I heard you are an expert in the area of anesthetics. Is there one that you know of that smells strong and sweet, by any chance? That could be used to render someone unconscious?" Dr. Halsted studied her face for a moment before giving an answer.

"In fact, yes. Oleum dulce vitrioli. Sweet oil of vitriol. Medical folks know it as ether. It is used for surgical anesthetics."

"Ether? Is it easy to obtain? I mean, could anyone buy it and use it?"

"Yes, one can purchase it. In Europe, and even here in America, ether has been diluted with sugar or perhaps cinnamon, honey, and cloves, and drunk as an alternative to alcohol. One must surely know how to administer it with care, however."

The doctor smiled and winked.

"Revelers rarely notice the bumps and bruises they acquire while out frolicking in the pubs. It's actually quite easy to make a crude version. Heating ethanol, or grain alcohol, with sulfuric acid will work quite nicely. I'm curious as to what provoked such a curious inquisition from a young woman."

Tricia froze, unprepared for his questioning.

"Just one of our girls," she offered. "She had to have an infected tooth extracted and could not remember what was used on her. She kept talking about a very strong, sweet smell. It certainly sounds like ether. I was just very curious, is all. Thank you for helping me."

"My pleasure." His expression was quiet and more intense. "I do hope we will have occasion to discuss your young lady again, perhaps?"

"Yes, Sir. That would be very kind of you. Thank you for your time."

"Miss Grimball." He leaned toward her. "You might find it interesting to know that I recently treated a local young lady that was attacked by someone. She remembered not one detail about what happened at the time. I do hope that the poor girl will recover her memory. I may be able to assist her, without the power of suggestion, if she has difficulty recalling details. There is a most interesting procedure that might help her." Tricia stared at the doctor, momentarily unable to speak. Did he guess that she was talking about Priscilla? Was he trying to offer help in some way?

"Yes, of course. I hope she does, too. Please excuse me."

From his station on the grounds of the Laurel Valley Inn, Ewan Munslow could not decide whether to smile or frown, as he watched the interaction. What was Tricia Grimball up to now?

CHAPTER TWELVE

The dark walk back to Camp Arden Woode was filled with a blend of quiet night-time reverence and contented youthful spirit, as camp songs were softly sung, and happy exchanges about the evening abounded. Tricia had waved goodbye to Ewan and informed her counselor friends about the conversation with Dr. Halsted. Nancy, too, had given a quick assessment of her few minutes spent with Harvey Bryson and his father and mother. Now Tricia walked with her young charges, listening to their delighted giggles and smiling at the jovial silliness and camaraderie they had developed while at camp. The evening had been everything she had hoped it would be, culminated by the beautiful fireworks from the banks of Emerald Lake that had illuminated the lush summer greenness of the mountains. In her head, she replayed the conversations of the evening, especially that of Dr. Halsted.

"Tricia, I hear you had a marvelous time and even got a dance with Ewan Munslow." Hugh Carson appeared by her side and spoke in his usual pleasant voice.

"Yes, I did," she smiled. "It was a wonderful evening. He taught my girls and I a little about clogging. I think they plan to teach the rest of the camp, or so I hear."

"Ah, yes, a little local culture is an excellent option for them. I hope they do teach the others. We ought to see if Lorene would include that as an evening program."

"My girls would love that," she said, trying not to sound sarcastic at the mention of Lorene. "They are so excited about the newly acquired skill."

"So, are there some sparks there with Ewan Munslow?" Hugh asked. "I think everyone has noticed the attention he gives you." Tricia felt herself flushed hot with embarrassment, even in the coolness of the night air.

"Oh, I don't know about that. He is a very nice person though, and I enjoy talking with him when he's at the camp. I am fond of him."

"Well, he is a hard-working and honorable man, in my opinion. I think he has seen the inner character of an Arden Woode girl and made a nice choice," Hugh smiled. "There's more time to the end of summer. Let your heart do it's job."

Tricia remained silent as the thought of her family and Daniel Middleton clouded her head.

"I'm sorry, did I say something wrong?" Hugh was gentle in his asking.

"Oh no, no. Not at all. I do like Ewan very much. It's just that, well," her voice trailed off. "It's just that I'm practically engaged to marry someone else perhaps next year, at least according to my parents. I honestly don't know what to do about my feelings. I shouldn't like Ewan so much, if I'm engaged, should I? It's confusing." Hugh smiled and rubbed his chin.

"I need a pondering pipe for this one," he quipped, adding at least a small bit of levity. "Tricia, what really matters is not what is proper, because of the expectations of others, even your family. What matters is how you feel and what you want. I'm sure you know that, on some level. You are the only one who can decide about your life, now that you are a young woman. Think on it. Make your own honorable and wise choices. And they may be hard for others to grasp. But you can't let anyone dictate what your life will ultimately be, if you are going to be true to yourself. That's between you, the Almighty, and the person you decide that you love and want to go through life with."

Tricia smiled.

"You sound like Nancy. And Tavia and Cyndi."

"I rest my case. Arden Woode girls are ladies of distinction and intelligence. You'll figure it out." Tricia shook her head, laughing.

"Hugh, you really are the camp daddy, as I've heard others say. Thanks a lot."

"Camp Daddy, huh? I like it. By the way, I saw you speaking with Dr. Halsted. He's quite the renowned doctor, you know." Tricia hesitated. Should she tell Hugh everything? Maybe just a small part, for now.

"I was talking with him because he has invited Ewan to visit at his home. Ewan has always wanted to be a physician, perhaps even a surgeon like Dr. Halsted. But he did mention Priscilla Parker indirectly, and not by name. Just that he had treated a local girl that had been attacked. He said that she remembered not one detail about what happened. I said that I hoped she regained her memory. I never acknowledged that she was with us."

Hugh chuckled to himself.

"What surprised me was that he mentioned a new procedure that might help her, that could be done without giving her the facts about what really happened. He said he could do it."

"Did he, now?" Hugh raised his eyebrows. "Well, I'm quite sure that the good doctor is fully aware that she is at Arden Woode and he is, I'm also certain, concerned for her safety and recovery, as well. But you responded appropriately, and just as we instructed, so good for you."

"Thank you, Hugh. And thanks for the guidance."

"My pleasure. Let me go visit on up the line. More camp daddy duties," he smiled. "I sure could use my pipe on a night like this," he mused aloud, waving. Tricia held her lantern, as did the other staff members, so that the worn path into the camp was more visible. Looking up, she saw Cyndi approaching, walking against the flow of campers headed back to Arden Woode.

"Hey, who's got your girls?" Tricia asked. "Everything okay?"

"Tavia has them, and yeah, it's all good. But I've been thinking. Something has stuck in my craw now for a while."

"Oh, lord, Cyndi's thinking, so something's up," Tricia teased.

"No seriously." She lowered her voice and looked about to be sure no one was listening to them. "You said tonight that Doc Halsted said Priscilla didn't remember anything about her attack, right?"

"That's what he said, yes. How come?"

"Remember when you told us what Otha said about what happened to Priscilla?"

"Yeah, I remember, why?"

Cyndi grabbed her arm and whispered.

"You said that Otha said that the only thing Priscilla remembered was something being put over her head." Tricia stopped walking as Cyndi held onto her arm.

"Good lord. Yes. Yes, that is what she said!"

"So, you know what that means?" Cyndi breathed, her voice steady and low.

"It means that Otha knows more than she's saying. Oh my God, Cyndi, you're a damn genius!"

"I think it means more than that," Cyndi said with quiet confidence.

"What do you mean?" Tricia's eyes widened. Cyndi grabbed both shoulders and gave her a tiny shake.

"It means," she whispered with intensity, "that Otha saw it all. Tricia, she had to be there. She knows exactly what happened to Priscilla Parker and is too scared to say."

"Oh, my God," Tricia whispered back, her voice filled with reluctant realization. "You think so? How can we be sure? Do we flat out ask her? What if she shuts down on us, then what?"

"I don't know," Cyndi admitted. We need to think, weigh it all out and look at what we know and what we don't know."

"What have we gotten ourselves into? This is beyond crazy. If she knows who did this evil thing, we have to get her to tell someone that can help do something. Hugh. Mary and Dammie. Somebody!" Tricia rubbed her eyes. "You know, Otha has taken up for the Sin Eater pretty much, and she has no use for Harvey Bryson, or that dead Chester Graves. Do you think she's been maybe trying to feed us information all along, so that it gets solved without a colored lady being involved? She has been very adamant about keeping quiet."

"Yeah, maybe, that all makes good sense," Cyndi agreed. "Harvey or the Sin Eater is guilty. Or maybe both. Except for one thing. One hugely big thing."

"Which is?"

"We didn't see any of it. Otha did. If she is the only witness, and if that word got out, she's in even more danger than Priscilla Parker. Remember, right now, Priscilla doesn't know much of anything. Nothing she could say could condemn a man, unless she knows it for sure. She can't guess about it."

Tricia felt sick. Because of the selfish desire for adventure and excitement, her beloved Otha could be in the most danger of all.

"This is all my fault. We have to do something to protect Otha. But there's even more to consider." She shared her conversation with Dr. Halsted about the ether and the possible procedure, watching as Cyndi shook her head, and thought some more.

"It all makes sense. If you're right, Tricia, if someone sneaked up on Priscilla and used ether to knock her out, it would not only explain her recollection of that sweet, strong smell that scares her so, but it would also explain why she doesn't remember anything at all about being attacked. She may have never seen her attacker."

"Right, exactly. But why? Why would someone take her? And why the others, the girls and the boy? My God, Cyndi, what in the hell is going on here? And where are the missing, if they are even alive?"

"I don't know," Cyndi shook her head once more. "It's a terrible mystery. We have to do something soon. We have to. And we have to know for sure before we accuse. Let's talk, just our group, when we can get a moment. In the meanwhile, we have to be very careful. It's too dangerous now. For all of us. Someone out there is hell bent on doing evil."

Tricia bit her lip that quivered in the chill of the night. She felt sad, having to acknowledge that her meddling might have placed Otha in extreme danger.

"Hey," Cyndi interrupted her thoughts as if she could read them. "Tricia, this is not your fault. Don't forget, Otha wanted you to know. It was you she trusted enough to tell. She could have kept safe by keeping quiet. Instead she told you. That took a lot of courage. No small thing."

"She knows that -right or wrong- most white folk aren't going to believe her. She even said so. She told me because she likes me, and she knows I'm her friend. I feel like I've betrayed her now."

"But you haven't!" Cyndi insisted. "We are the only ones that know, and we aren't going to let her get hurt. I truly think she told you because she knew you were genuinely interested in the whole story and that your heart is in the right place. Otha knows you care for her and want to do the right thing."

"I sure hope so. I feel awful, just the same."

"Tricia, listen to me! She was willing to risk telling you. Through you, she can help to get justice for Priscilla and the others but keep herself safe."

Tricia thought about Cyndi's words for the remainder of the trek back to Arden Woode. Knowing her friend was right in sentiment was a comfort, but she could not shake the gnawing in her soul for having any part in placing Otha Moses in the deadliest of situations. Worry would follow her for the remainder of the evening.

The familiar night sounds she had come to love, that filled her mind with peace and wrapped her body in the deep lull of restful sleep, evaded her on this night. Every nocturnal noise seemed an intrusion, something to fear. Dark images floated in her mind. The Sin Eater, staring at her from beneath the hooded anonymity, a hurt and angry Daniel Middleton at what would be her rejection of him, the disappointed expressions of her parents. The face of Otha Moses stood out among them all, cried out for help. And in the midst of it all there was Ewan, who consumed her every thought. Could she trust him? Tricia closed her eyes, but sleep would be a long time coming.

CHAPTER THIRTEEN

The arrival of Sunday morning at Arden Woode found Tricia more than ready for the pace of a relaxed day and schedule, after the weekend of festivities and the opportunity for time to finally meet with her friends during extended rest hour. Chapel time found campers and staff alike in tired, but happy reflection. The campers in Du Kum Inn were grateful for extra quiet time after lunch to play cards, read, and visit with one another. Counselors, too, were thankful for the extra hour, as the staff could all take turns at supervision duty and extended free time to socialize with their peers. Tricia and her friends had agreed to meet at the hut, a small stone-hewn covered structure located by Emerald Lake, just below the outdoor chapel area.

"Alright, let's summarize what we've got so far and sort this mess out." Cyndi rubbed her hands together and stood leaning against the stone wall. "For sure, Otha knows more than she's saying, and we are all in agreement that it sounds like she was likely a witness, somehow. The Sin Eater and Harvey are also involved, and we think Harvey and Chester Graves are probably the guilty parties."

"But we don't know that for sure," Tavia added. "I mean, remember that Priscilla has recalled a dark, mysterious man that sure sounds like the Sin Eater."

"True," Cyndi agreed, "but we don't know if he saved her or hurt her. The evidence so far says he may be the good guy. But, no, we don't know for certain. Priscilla also has some kind of recollection about a scary strong, sweet smell, which we think could have possibly been ether. According to Dr. Halsted, anyone could buy it or make it, so we don't know the details there either."

"Yikes," Nancy said, tapping on her knee. "Sounds like there's more that we don't know than what we do. The biggest questions being why, and are the missing people connected to the attempted snatching of Priscilla and where are they?"

"Tricia, you haven't said anything. What are you thinking?" Cyndi looked at her. Tricia sighed aloud, shaking her head. The mystery was a mind-numbing mess.

"I'm trying to think about where we go from here. How do we find out the truth about Otha, is the biggest question for now, perhaps? She may or may not hold the key to a lot more information, especially if she is a witness. Also, if Harvey Bryson is the remaining guilty party, how do we prove it? And the last big thing? At what point do we include Mary, Dammie, and Hugh with what we know?"

"I have a question." Tavia looked at Tricia. "It's pretty obvious that Ewan fancies Tricia and seems to be a really nice person. Should we consider trusting him to help us?" No one said a word, but waited for Tricia, who considered the possibility.

"My gut tells me we can trust him," she said with slow deliberation. "My head, on the other hand, says we ought not to rush it, because of Otha. I feel hugely responsible for her, not to mention, it would be good to know her role, first."

"I agree with that," said Cyndi. "But I do think we can likely trust him. Otha seems to, so does Hugh. He's given us every reason to, thus far. And, we know he is not a friend of Harvey's, so he gets a lot of points from me, there."

"Okay, how about this? Nancy and I have an upcoming overnight with our girls and Priscilla Parker's cabin. She could recover some more of her memory, perhaps by then. Also – and I bet you all had forgotten about this – but payback time is coming up soon for Queen Lorene."

"Lawd, lawd, here we go!" Nancy cackled. "What are we going to do?"

"You know the Christmas in July event is also coming up, right after our overnight to Toxaway Falls. It's no accident, of course that it is scheduled for the weekend that Lorene's girls are going on their overnight that Friday. The main event, with our gift-giving and Christmas meal will be Sunday, so her cabin will be back Saturday and here for all of that. But since she will be gone Friday, that will be the perfect time to execute our plan." Tricia grinned. "Hugh told me that Ewan plays the fiddle some at Hannah's Barn with some other local people, and we have a piano here in the Castle, so I was thinking of having the musicians play, have my girls demonstrate how to clog, and then sing some Christmas carols."

"What a great and fun idea!" Tavia clapped her hands, as the others voiced approval.

"Yes, I'm kind of proud of it, myself." Tricia beamed. "But ladies, the best part is that, after the evening program, Ewan will be here to help me get Lorene's bed and locker out to the dock. By then, we will hopefully know more, maybe have more information from Otha and Priscilla, too."

"So, Grimball, are you thinking that you could possibly ask him to help us that night?"

"Yes, maybe, if all goes well."

"That sounds reasonable," Cyndi said. "And a lot could happen between now and then too. What do you think about saying anything to Otha about what we suspect?"

"I think we should wait a bit more, even on that," Nancy added, knowing how reluctant Tricia was to further jeopardize the adored camp cook. Tricia gave her a grateful wink.

"So, there's just one more question, then," Tavia put on a serious demeanor. "Tricia, how do you feel about Ewan? You know you have to dish some for us, c'mon." Tricia found herself not wanting to hide her feelings for Ewan any longer. In a way, it was the most liberating of emotions.

"Ewan is very special to me. I have strong feelings for him, and I do want to know him even better. He's the most interesting man I've ever been around."

"And Daniel?" Cyndi asked.

"Who?" Tavia joked. "Ewan wins! Rat's ass!"

Tricia grinned. What wonderful friends she had made here,

almost like sisters was their bond.

"Grimball, what are you going to do?" Nancy said in the most empathetic tone possible.

"Yeah, it's time to do something here, I know. Even if nothing ever happens with Ewan but just for this summer, I know I could never have the feelings for Daniel that I do for Ewan. I can't decide whether to tell Daniel or my parents first. And how? I don't want to do it in a letter, but I don't want to wait all summer either."

"I agree with you that an in-person conversation would be best." Cyndi said. "But you aren't going to be able to do that until the end of camp, and that's not fair to you or to Daniel."

"Well, I think you should write the best letter you can to your folks and also to him." Nancy interjected. "Send them at the same time. Let 'em down easy. Thank your parents for raising you well. Hey, they won't be as disappointed if you toss them a bone, right? Besides, this really is your decision, Tricia. Better to be honest now, let Daniel move on and your folks get used to the idea before you get back home."

"And," Tavia jumped up from her perch on the stone bench, throwing her hands in the air and smiling, "then you are free to really follow your heart and be in the best place for you, whether that's with Ewan or no!"

"Yes, lawd, amen!" Nancy laughed aloud, pointing at Tavia. "Proverbs 3:5-6 will never steer you wrong, Grimball, I told ya. Can I get a witness here, or what?"

"Hallelujah, sweet baby Jesus, yes!" Tavia held up her right hand, as if giving a court testimony, as the girls embraced the levity of the moment.

"I heartily concur with the distinguished representatives from Louisiana and Florida," Cyndi added. "I think we're done here."

Tricia walked with Nancy back toward the line of cabins that dotted the front of Emerald Lake. The soothing balm of a good, though hard, decision had lifted her spirits and given her soul the clarity it needed to move in a healthy direction. She had finally removed the ball and chain that had rendered her immobile.

"Baudette, how about your love life these days? Are you still getting letters from that guy back home? Johnny, the one that has been a good friend?"

"Grimball, I have the exact opposite problem from you. I didn't realize how much I cared for 'ole Johnny until the last letter I got from one of my sisters." Her voice began to waver. "He's engaged to be married." Nancy wiped tears from her eyes as Tricia's mouth opened in surprise. "Honestly, he may as well have just slugged me in the face."

"Oh, Nan! Oh, my friend, I am so sorry!" Tricia paused. "Want me to go stomp his behind?" Nancy smiled through the hurt and hugged Tricia back.

"Aw, no, not his. Mine, maybe, for being so stupid. I should have told him how I felt when I had the chance. But you know what?" Nancy hesitated before continuing. "I have to follow my own advice to you. If it's not Johnny Whitman, then the good Lord has bigger and better plans for me. But damn, in my mind we were gonna raise smart and beautiful Cajun babies and live a good life back home on his family's farm, at least in my mind. Oh well, I have to let it go, now."

Tricia marveled at the inner fortitude of her witty and wise best friend. Always true to her own morals, never seeming to waver in her faith or self-confident dignity, even when life handed her sadness. Nancy was a solid beacon of light.

"Well, then God is truly busy making you a man that is deserving of you, and it might take a while!" She stopped walking and spread her hands wide, as if opening a grand work of art. "Picture it, Nan! He'll be as wonderful as Douglas Fairbanks or Charlie Chaplin, perhaps!"

Nancy finally smiled.

"Grimball, I don't know. Maybe I'll just be an old spinster."

"Well, whatever you're going to be, it's going to be the best one ever, and you are going to do important work in this world, Nan, so don't forget that!"

"Okay, time to move on then and quit giving a rat's ass about something I can't control, right? So, this overnight that we're doing to Toxaway Falls, think it might give us the chance to find out more from Priscilla Parker?"

"I don't know, maybe. If she keeps having these little bits of memory recovery, then yes. She shares things with my Natalie. They are a lot alike – tender, sweet. The one I'm hoping to do a little gem mining from is Otha Moses. I think there's much more there, and that maybe I can gently dig a little without scaring her. Otha's no fool, though, she can spot a fake a mile away, so I have to be careful and honest."

"What's the deal with her family, do you know?" Nancy asked. "Does she have any, and do they live around here?"

"I know her husband died a few years ago. Otha has been doing whatever she could to raise her son Samuel and a niece that is the daughter of one of her husband's sisters who lived in Chicago." Tricia added, "She doesn't talk about them much, but I've met Samuel once when he was helping Otha out in the outside cooking area. A pleasant sort, kind of quiet. He and the young niece live in Otha's place down the road while she is here at camp. Hugh says she came highly recommended by locals as a hard worker and excellent cook, and that the Arden Woode staff did not care at all that she was colored. Hugh says she is fairly indigent. Samuel now does odd jobs for people to help out, I think, but it's not much."

"Tricia, I have an idea." Nancy's eyes were wide with excitement. "What if we – I mean the Arden Woode girls – could help her out?"

"How do you mean?"

"Well, I've never seen where she lives, and I know you haven't either. What if we could help fix her place up? Or maybe, if it's too run down, maybe find her a new place?"

"Wow, it's a great thought and idea. I can run it by Hugh, to see what's possible. I know he and Dammie and Mary are always wanting to help those who truly need it and encourage our girls to always give back. What better way than to help one of our own? Wait, Baudette!" Tricia flapped her hands back and forth as an idea gelled in her head. "What if we used the Christmas in July event to help Otha? The girls could make her some art and trinkets for her home, even craft a few pieces of jewelry in the Bang Shop, and perhaps even sew her some items for her house or weave some, make presents for her son and niece?"

"That's a brilliant idea! Yes, talk with Hugh. We're gonna make the best of the summer yet!"

From a sizable distance to the Emerald Lake docks of Arden Woode, a small nondescript canoe floated in aimless fashion, as many frequently did from the Laurel Valley Inn. From his spyglass, the lone viewer could see the exuberance on the faces of the two young counselors. Scanning the shoreline, he took in the sights and sounds, the location of structures closest to the water, the line of cabins. He made a thorough sketch of the layout he saw. It would all be useful information. But no sign of the one for whom he was looking. Not this time.

CHAPTER FOURTEEN

The day of the overnight trip to Toxaway Falls dawned with a cooler, crisper feel to the dewy mid-July morning. The Du Kum Inn girls could barely contain the thrill of a wilderness camping experience and the hike that would be both exhausting and challenging, but a memorable break from the daily camp routine. The cabin was tidied up in record time, as Tricia checked each camper for proper attire, canteens, bandanas, and shoes. Natalie in particular was happy that Wilhelmina, her favorite horse, would help carry the packs and gear needed for the overnight. Tricia had kept up with her equine progress with great interest, since much of the young camper's feelings of self-worth had been embedded in her ability to overcome the fear of riding with speed. Now, she seemed more self-confident, less scared of attempting other new challenges, as a result of her riding achievements. Tricia smiled, knowing how happy she would be when Hugh selected her to guide Wilhelmina for the first leg of the trip.

Otha had prepared a wonderful hot breakfast and offered seconds of oatmeal to the chattering young sojourners, while listening to their good-hearted pleas for her to accompany them on the trip to cook the evening meal of hobo stew.

"Now, you chillun' know 'ole Otha ain't goin' on no mountain climbing trip, not this day or no other day, no. Tell you what – there will be a big steaming pot of beef and potatoes and vegetables when you get back. Here come Mr. Ewan now, bringing me some fresh victuals."

Tricia leaned back in her chair to catch a glimpse of Ewan as he pulled the reins to stop the buck wagon in place. There was jovial energy, a happiness in his motion, from jumping off the carriage seat to heaving baskets of newly harvested produce to the outside dining table. He gave Tricia a hearty wave from his perch in the wagon, pulling in front of the dining hall to return to the Laurel Valley Inn, and stopped to jump back down when he saw her descending the stone steps.

"He sure enough seems mighty happy today," Nancy commented, grinning at Tricia. "I'll let you two chat a bit. See you at the Castle. I'm gonna walk by Lorene shortly and butter her up a bit. Make her think we've forgotten all about what they did. Lawd, I can't wait for the reckoning, huh?"

Tricia laughed, watching Nancy approach Lorene as Ewan made his way toward her, a smile as big as Bald Rock Mountain spread across his face.

"Tricia, guess what?"

"Hello, Ewan, do tell!"

"I made that visit to see Doc Halsted on Sunday for lunch!" Ewan grabbed both of her shoulders in his excitement. "Three hours he spent with me! His wife, as well, you know she was his nurse. We talked about medicine, his dahlias, astronomy, more medicine!"

"Oh, Ewan, that's wonderful!" Without thinking, she hugged him, then quickly withdrew, but not before her campers waved and smiled with delight, giggling as they scrambled up the steps of their cabin.

"He invited me to come back and wants to see the farm at Laurel Valley. And," Ewan paused, his eyes wide. "He asked a great deal about my formal education, as well as what I had been able to learn from my own reading. He said he thought I had a natural proclivity for the field of medicine and surgery."

"Ewan, I couldn't be happier for you," Tricia breathed, smiling up at him. "It could be the start of fulfilling your dream."

"I don't know about that," Ewan smiled back, "but I hope that it will be just the beginning of good things to come. You know, it would not have happened, had you not spoken on my behalf. I owe you a great deal, Tricia."

"No, you don't." She gave his arm a light tap." You clearly have both drive and knowledge and the esteemed doctor can sense that. All I did was try to push that meeting along a little because," she hesitated, "I think you are very talented and have a lot to give. Hey, I'm sorry I can't talk more, but I have to go now. We are going on an overnight to the Toxaway Falls area, and I need to help Hugh and my girls also."

Ewan smiled down at her, his steel gray eyes exuding affection.

"Until you get back, then. Be safe, Tricia Grimball."

"I will, Ewan Munslow."

She felt the color rise in her cheeks as she turned toward her cabin. All of her mischievous young charges were seated on the steps, bandanas tied around their heads, ready to begin their adventure, staring at the flirtatious exchange.

"Bye, Ewan," they waved. "Hurry back to see us. I mean, Tricia," Gaylen yelled, as the other campers guffawed, not even trying to hide the playful teasing.

"Count on it, ladies," Ewan made an elegant bow. "You'll see me again. So will Miss Grimball, here."

The girls squealed in delight as Tricia mounted the steps, shaking her head.

"All right, you all. Show's over. Let's go, we have a hike to get on with! Grab your gear, head to the front of the dining hall. Everyone will be ready to go!"

The assembled group of campers in front of the Adirondack-style dining hall could not hide the effervescent enthusiasm among them. Natalie found Priscilla and grabbed her hand, both girls giddy with anticipation. Hugh was in a jovial mood, greeting all by name and Hala bounded from one camper to the next for cuddles and attention. The remaining girls had paired off with a camper from another cabin and were sharing all of the known exceptions to camp rules that were allowed on an overnight.

"We can have coffee at breakfast and Hugh gives us candy, too!" Gaylen said to one of Nancy's girls, whose eyes widened with excitement.

Tricia loved this aspect of Arden Woode that allowed each girl to develop relationships along with their best selves. She felt as if she had benefitted from this nurturing environment as much as any camper.

Two and a half enjoyable hours on the Toxaway Trail passed without much interference other than a brief water break and rest for Wilhelmina, who was guarded by both Natalie and Priscilla Parker with great maternal care. The three cabins of energetic girls were mindful of nature's observations along the way, as Hugh provided periodic commentary about the flora and fauna they encountered. "Mother Nature" as he playfully referred to Nancy in her capacity as the Nature Nook instructor, stopped to weigh in with a question to see who had been paying attention during camp nature activities.

"Here we are at our lunch and rest stop," she announced, as the group entered a beautiful shaded area with a cool running mountain stream. "Who can tell me the precautions we take when out in the woods, especially near water that we play in?"

"Watch out for poison oak and ivy," a high-pitched voice yelled from the back of the cluster of campers. "Be careful where you put your hands."

"Lookout for snakes, especially the four poisonous ones in the mountains," Chuck smiled, fully knowing the effect her comment would have on some of the girls.

"Yes," Tricia jumped in to add, "we know they are about in the summer, but are afraid of us and don't bother people unless they feel threatened. Always use care in the woods."

"No running off to explore. Stay with the group, so no one gets lost." Hugh added.

Tricia motioned all to be seated in the clearing and helped Hugh pass out sandwiches, oranges, pickles and crackers, which were consumed by the voracious hikers before they waded and played in the nearby creek. Hugh checked his watch and spoke to the three counselors, still relaxing in the coolness of the day.

"I figure we will leave here around three or so, hike for another good hour, then stop at the Old Toxaway Inn ruins, where we will gather firewood, set up for the night, and have our hobo stew and toasted marshmallows. 'Ole Wilhelmina was kind enough to carry my guitar, so we might even sing a few camp songs out here on the dusty trail."

"Hugh, what exactly happened to the Toxaway Inn, why is it deserted and run down now?" Nancy asked.

"About three years ago, two or three bad hurricanes came through the area at about the same time. Very strange. The developers of this inn – same as the ones that built Laurel Valley – built a stone and clay dam, a masterpiece of sorts. It created the huge lake that used to be here. When that final storm came through, the French Broad River, the Swannanoa River, all the rivers around here crested, the lake was overflowing, and the flooding was massive. The dam finally collapsed. When it did, the ground shook like an earthquake and all the soil and trees were decimated, all the way down to the rocks. Crops were washed away, farms ruined, and Lake Toxaway was gone. The Toxaway Inn also fell into a state of disrepair and never reopened. Our girls have signed their names on some of the inside walls, as we will let this group do." Hugh stopped to puff on his pipe. "They love going inside the building to explore."

"So, what happened after the flood?" Tricia asked. "The area looks like it has never been developed, like it is in a natural state, except for some downed trees, perhaps."

"Lumber business in these parts now, pretty much."

"Lumber?" Tricia repeated. "Is it owned by locals?"

Harvey Bryson and his lumber business leaped into the forefront of her thoughts.

"I suppose a few locals are involved. Mostly the very wealthy, the same folks that built the resorts to begin with. I'm sure a lot of money was lost that year in the flood, and lumbering is a good recoupment. They could have sold some land to a local, I suppose." Nancy glanced at Tricia, then at Hugh.

"I met a judge from Highlands the other night at the Laurel Valley Inn. I'm pretty sure I remember his son said something about milling lumber?"

"You must be talking about Judge Bryson," Hugh said between after-lunch pipe puffs. "By all accounts, a stand-up sort of guy, I'm told. Don't know much about his son or his lumber dealings, although I hear he was one of the men that attempted to rescue Priscilla."

Nancy ventured another attempt at gleaning information.

"I overheard a few wagging tongues there. They said what you did, Hugh, about the judge, but kind of hedged a little bit on the son. One woman even said he was no-count. He kept asking me questions about Priscilla."

From the fleeting expression of concern on the face of the trip director, Tricia and Nancy sensed that they had his rapt attention.

"Yeah, he kept saying he had heard she was at our camp and

would I point her out, tell him how she was doing." She stopped to take a bite of her sandwich and a large gulp from the canteen. "I never let on that we had her, but he kept asking if I thought she remembered anything."

"Well," Priscilla's counselor spoke up, "so far, she only remembers a distinct smell, a feeling of not being able to breathe. She did say something one day about a man covered in something dark."

Nancy stole a sideways glance at Tricia. Hugh had recovered from any semblance of surprise and spoke with calm.

"I imagine she will eventually remember, with time. It had to be a very frightening experience for her. Thankfully, there was no evidence of any injuries, so the thinking thus far has been that her lack of memory is largely emotional, rather than physical."

"Hugh, are there any theories at all about who might have tried to take her, or why? Do you think it's someone local?" Tricia asked.

Hugh gazed toward the stream where Hala played with the frolicking campers.

"Sadly, I do tend to think that it was someone who lives around these hills, as Judge Bryson's son has told folks that a man was there that was all covered up somehow. It fits with what Priscilla is saying."

"How does that indicate he is local?" Nancy asked.

"I figure if he is the man who is responsible for the death of the other man, and the attempted kidnapping, he covered himself so no one would recognize him. It appears to be quite planned. The only place where we really have outsiders is the Laurel Valley Inn, and those folks don't tend to venture into the tiny scattered villages much. It could have been someone else, but a stranger on the road would be much more noticeable, as everyone knows everyone around these parts. I think he knew that young Priscilla came from a poor family, who is not well-connected enough to mount a sizeable search for her very fast." Hugh took a last puff and gazed at the campers and Hala. "Ladies let's round up the troops and hit the trail for the last leg of the trip. These gals will be tired by the time we get there, do a quick visit to the ruins, and gather up some wood for the campfire."

The last hour proved to be as Hugh had known to predict from his prior excursions there. They arrived at the camp site tired, sweaty, and hungry, after the quick tour of the old Toxaway Inn ruins, but all were eager to help gather firewood, knowing that hobo stew, campfire baked apples, and chocolate were soon to be theirs. Before long, a blazing fire was aglow with the sound of endeared camp songs and surrounded by laughing campers, filled from the meal and the toasted marshmallows and chocolate bars that Hugh always brought on the overnight trips.

"There's just something about eating a hot meal prepared out-doors. Delicious. And singing camp songs with these kids here in the woods, too. Just so peaceful and right, you know?" Tricia smiled, watching her own girls in carefree banter. "Natalie has been so excited about being able to buddy up with Priscilla for this trip. I think those girls are becoming fast friends."

"That could work to our advantage, you know," Nancy whispered.

"Yeah, I thought about that. If Priscilla tells anybody anything, it would likely be Natalie." Tricia whispered back. "They've already asked to be in the same tent tonight. I asked Hugh if I could be assigned to that tent, so we would be sure to have some ears at the ready, in case she does decide to talk or share information."

"Good idea, Grimball. Of course, they're going to be so tired, they may go right to sleep as soon as they hit the sack."

"Oh, I think there is still a lot of chatting and giggling still to do," Tricia smiled. "You never know. Are you up for sitting out here for a little longer after they've all settled in for the night?"

"Yeah, I'm good for that. Something on your mind?"

"A lot of things, I guess. I'll meet you back out here. We won't make it late since we will be rising early to eat and then hitting the trail back."

After Hugh had played every camp song requested, and told an engaging tall tale or two, the girls were hustled through teeth brushing and preparations for sleeping. Each of the three tents held four girls and a counselor, with Hugh and Hala in a separate smaller tent. Tricia listened as the remnants of chatter fell prey to the rhythmic breathing of needed sleep. Only Natalie and Priscilla remained awake.

"Can we talk a little bit before we go to sleep, Tricia, please?" Natalie begged.

"I don't see why not. Just do it softly, so no one else wakes up. Nancy and I are going to let the fire die down some and talk, too. We won't be long. We'll all need rest before tomorrow. Goodnight, you two." Tricia closed the flaps of the tent and found Nancy wrapped in a blanket in front of the fire.

"Lawd, my girls didn't talk long. Once their heads hit the ground, they were all gone, exhausted, the best kind of tired. Yours all asleep?"

"Just Natalie and Priscilla are still awake. But I don't think they will be much longer."

"So, what all is on your mind? I could probably guess, though, with everything we have going on." Nancy gave a quiet laugh.

"You're really going to laugh. With all of this mystery and craziness, even all of the camp stuff, Lorene and all, you know what I'm thinking about?" Tricia hesitated.

"Daniel Middleton and your folks?"

"No, I've actually made my decision there and have the rough draft of the letters ready. I used to dread telling my folks, risking their disappointment, but I can't marry someone I don't love. It's Ewan Munslow I can't stop thinking about. Honestly, Baudette, I surely wasn't looking for this to happen, but he's special. I get the feeling he feels the same way. But I'm only here for the summer, so it may not matter anyway."

"Why not? If it's meant to be, it will be. If it isn't, it won't."

"That's what I love about you, Baudette. Always positive, always a faithful answer. Dr. Halsted has taken an interest in Ewan and I hope it will be beneficial, since he has always wanted to become a physician. At some point, he could be invited to study elsewhere, so there are a lot of unknowns here."

"Well, take it from me," Nancy offered, "if you think he is special, he needs to know, or have the chance to tell you, too."

"He's coming for one of our Christmas in July nights and then we will move Lorene's stuff, so we will have some alone time then."

"Trust your heart, girl, you got to. Just let things be for awhile longer. But don't count anything out."

"How about you, Nan? How are you feeling these days?" Tricia smiled at her friend.

"I'm gonna be okay, Grimball, I am. Now that my old flame has gone completely out," Nancy made a face, "I'm thinking I need to follow some of the advice I gave you and tell my parents what I want to do."

"Which is?"

"Travel around. Live and work somewhere for a bit, then try someplace else. I'm not so sure old Adelaide and Dave will like the new plan, but I can teach anywhere, you know? With five brothers and sisters, I got to be independent more than most. I love where I live, but I want to see the rest of America. I know it's frowned upon for women to travel much alone, but things are changing. Once I'm married, at least I hope, we will raise our kids in one place, have a good home, all of that." Nancy grinned. "Then, I'll cook lots of jambalaya and etouffee."

"Women have more opportunities each day now, Baudette. If that's what you really want, then, yes, take your own advice and do it. But we have to keep in touch, don't forget. We can write each other and plan a visit."

"Of course, we will. Hey, if things don't come together with Ewan or Daniel or whomever, you could come, too, and write about all the travels. Two women of the world branching out!"

"My parents are going to be so disappointed over my decision about Daniel, I may have to," Tricia quipped. "They might disown me."

Without warning, Hala begin to growl, low at first, then louder. From out of the corner of her eye, Tricia saw Priscilla and Natalie emerge from the tent, hugging their respective stuffed animals and looking frightened.

"Tricia, someone was outside our tent! Right outside! We're scared!"

"What's going on?" Hugh leaned out of the front of his tent, restraining Hala, who struggled to get out. "Everything okay?"

"The girls said they heard something outside their tent and got scared." Hugh crawled out of the tent, buttoning his overcoat and carrying a lantern, with Hala close in tow.

"Oh, it's more than likely just a few night critters out and about, but I'll go back there and look around, so you girls can get some sleep. Go ahead and settle back down now."

Nancy smothered a smile as the girls crept back inside. She mouthed the words, *Wampus Cat* at Tricia.

In a few minutes Hugh made his way back to the last of the campfire light. He was not smiling.

"What's wrong?" Tricia asked as he seated himself beside the girls and began tapping his fingers together, then stroking Hala's soft fur.

"I did find some tracks back there." He paused. "Footprints. A set larger than mine, coming from the woods through the grassy area and right up to the back of the girls' tent. Not sure when they were made. It could be nothing. Maybe leftover from a local that maintains the area for us." For a moment no one spoke. Hugh pursed his lips. "I think perhaps, given the circumstances, we ought to take turns on watch tonight for a few hours and let Hala sleep in the tent Priscilla is in. I'll take her there now. The girls will sleep better and so will we."

"Well, I'm definitely not sleepy now," Tricia declared, as they watched Hugh move toward the tents.

"Neither am I." Nancy responded.

"Tricia," Nancy stared at her friend. "I think it's time to tell him everything."

"Not yet," Tricia began, her voice lowered. "If we say anything now, they will call us off of everything. We will be dead in the water."

"We may all be dead, regardless, Grimball!" Nancy sputtered, trying to remain quiet. "What are we waiting for? Someone may be here, may still be out there tonight!"

"Maybe. But what was he going to do with all of us here? Sixteen of us, one of him. Even if there was someone, my guess is he's listening for whatever he can hear." Tricia lowered her voice even more. "All we have are a bunch of conjectures. No proof of anything, not for sure. We need to find out more, somehow. And soon. We'll be gone in a few weeks, and we'll have to tell them before we go. But we still don't know anything for sure."

"Except that someone doesn't want Priscilla to remember or to talk. We know that! And maybe someone knows we were coming here, away from camp."

"Okay, yeah, we do know that much. But we don't know why, or what is going on, do we? There's so much we still don't know. And no proof. At least let's wait until after Christmas in July. Maybe by then we will have some answers."

"We're running out of time, Grimball." Nancy whispered.

"I know." Tricia answered. "I need to talk with Otha. That's one thing. And if I can trust Ewan," her voice trailed off, before she whispered, "Nancy, he knew we were coming here tonight."

"You can't possibly think that Ewan is part of all this, do you? C'mon, Tricia, a blind man could see he's sweet on you and he seems like a straight shooter to me. Anybody could have overheard someone talking about a trip. Maybe Hugh mentioned it at Zachary's General Store or something. Or Mary or Dammie said something in passing. Or those tracks may be from earlier in the day even. Quit trying to find something wrong – wrongness will always show itself eventually. Give the guy a chance. It's not like he can really court you proper, you know."

Tricia stared into the flames that leaped about the chilly night air. Nancy was right. They were running out of time, with few clues to go on and no clue as to why Priscilla was attacked and others were missing, or even if the events were related. She would have to speak with Otha soon. And perhaps confide in Ewan Munslow.

When she at last entered her tent, having turned the night watch duties back over to Hugh, she crept with care not to wake the sleeping campers. She listened to the nocturnal sounds of the mountain creatures in the wee hours of the night, until sleep finally overtook her. In her dreams, she danced once more with Ewan, his piercing, soulful eyes looking deep into hers, and his dark hair brushing against her forehead. In her heart, Tricia knew what she had not yet told anyone. It was growing inside, no matter how hard she tried not to acknowledge what was happening. She was falling in love with this man in a way that she could never be with Daniel Middleton.

CHAPTER FIFTEEN

The hike down the mountain and back to camp proved to be grueling after an almost sleepless night, compounded by the earlier- than- usual wake-up call. Hugh had not shown any outward signs of concern, though Tricia did observe him walk a slow circle around the tents, scrutinizing all he could. Natalie and Priscilla had all but forgotten the night before, shaken off any residual fear, and now raced laughing and shouting with the other campers to see which cabin would enter the grounds of Arden Woode first.

"Lawd, I'm so tired, I swear I could sleep standing up," Nancy quipped, fighting off a yawn, and rubbing her neck. "I plan to take full advantage of quiet time after lunch today with the longest nap I can manage."

"Me, too," Tricia added. "If I can get my girls to settle down and sleep. Or just be quiet and read or write letters home. But I did a lot of thinking all night long."

"Of course, you did," Nancy laughed. "So, what's the plan for now?"

"I definitely need to talk with Otha by myself. She'll respond better if it's just me and her talking. Maybe I can get her to tell me what she knows about the night in question. I don't know, she may also be angry with me for getting so involved."

"I think Otha wants everything to end well, and the right things to happen," Nancy said. "But, yeah, she definitely has good reasons for not sharing all she knows and how she knows it. I think you're going to have to go easy on the old girl to get it out of her."

"I'm too beat to do it today. Can't think straight. Maybe before dinner, if I can rest and recover my sensibility. Or tomorrow. Then, there's Ewan. I have to decide if I can trust him. I guess there's only one way to find out. I'm not going to mention anything about Otha, though, just in case. I know he cares about her welfare, but I could never forgive myself if she got into trouble because of anything I said."

"We need to talk with Tavia and Cyndi, too," Nancy added. "Fill them in on what happened on the trip and see if anything else has changed. You know, circle the wagons and come up with another plan. How about we try to meet at the Ark tonight or tomorrow, depending on how we recover?"

"Right now, I've barely got the energy to drag my behind to the dining hall for lunch. Rest hour today will be so sweet! After we unpack and get some food, we can check in with the others about tonight. Later, Baudette!"

Tricia found her Du Kum Inn girls outside the cabin, taking turns holding their cumbersome sleeping bags while shaking and beating out the residual debris, and still cackling about the night before.

"Tricia, want us to do your sleeping bag, too?" Christa offered.

"Why, I certainly do!" Tricia smiled at her brood as she set the pack on the ground. "As always, you girls are the best! I'm going to go inside for a moment, be right back."

"Can I talk with you for a minute?" Natalie had scrambled up the wooden steps behind her. "It's about Priscilla," she whispered.

"Sure, of course you can, sweet girl. Here, sit by me." Tricia sat on her metal cot, and pat the space beside her, as a distraught Natalie wrung her hands and shuffled uncomfortably, finally settling into a cross-legged position on the bed and biting her lower lip.

"Priscilla told me what happened to her," Natalie breathed. Tricia said nothing, trying not to reveal any emotion.

"I don't understand. What happened?" Natalie glanced about to be sure no one else could hear them.

"She told me she is the one that got attacked. She said that's the real reason she came here to camp because her family could never afford it otherwise."

"I see. What exactly did she say?" Tricia held her breath.

"She said she was told that she was attacked, but she can't remember much else. She knows she was walking home with her brothers, but that's all. She said her momma told her somebody took her to the doctor who lives at High Hampton, and she remembers waking up at his house, but that's it."

"Has she told anyone else besides you?" Tricia asked.

"No, no one. Not even her counselor. But she remembered how you helped us both get over some things we were afraid of. At least she's getting better about going under the water. I think she sort of wants to talk with you, but she's scared."

"What exactly can she remember?" Tricia ventured in the gentlest tone she could muster.

"Just that strong, sweet smell. And she kind of remembers a man in dark clothes, but she can't see his face and doesn't remember anything that he did or said. She said whenever she thinks about him, she feels afraid, but she doesn't know why, really."

"Priscilla must really value your friendship, Natalie, to confide in you this way. I'm very proud of you, sweetheart." Tricia gave her young camper a hug. "It sounds like she is trying hard to remember what happened that night. How can I help?"

"If I can get her to talk with you, would that be okay?"

"Yes, I would be happy to talk with Priscilla. This must be very hard for her."

"She has had so much fun at camp. She said she feels safe here with us, but she misses her folks, too. Sometimes she said she feels like someone is watching her."

"Well, I'm not surprised that she feels that way. I think I might feel that way, too, if I were in her shoes. How about if you just tell her that you mentioned to me that she might want to talk about some things that were on her mind? You don't have to tell her that you told me much. But I will leave that up to you."

"Thanks, Tricia. I'll tell her today." Natalie smiled as she slid off the bed and bounded out the door to join her friends.

"Hey, it's almost time to eat, so you girls might want to finish up out there before we see what Otha has for us today. I think I remember her saying something about stew beef and vegetables."

After braiding her hair into a soft ponytail and washing her hands and face, Tricia followed her campers up the steps to the dining hall, where Otha greeted them all,

"There are my babies, all back from the woods! 'Ole Otha's got some beef stew and cornbread fixed up for my chillun'."

The happy cook gave a broad smile as the bevy of youth expressed great enthusiasm over her food preparation prowess.

"Grimball!" Nancy tugged on Tricia's arm. "I saw Cyndi and Tavia. They are both free this evening after lights out, if you and I can get some rest."

"Sounds good. Let's see if we can make it happen. There's a new development, too." Before she could elaborate, Hugh Carson announced the blessing, much to the chagrin of the two counselors, as Nancy's eyes widened in anticipation of more information that would now have to wait until after the meal.

As if an answer to prayer, the skies began to look angry and gray toward the end of the noonday dinner, and ripples of wind started among the trees and spread across Emerald Lake in waves. Dammie, Mary, and Hugh could be seen talking among themselves and gesturing past the windows and front porch area. Hugh stood to address them all.

"Well, Arden Woode ladies, it looks like one of those summer storms might be upon us fairly soon. We're going to give everyone some extended rest and free time in your cabins today, perhaps an extra hour."

A mixture of groans and giggles came from the campers. Tricia caught Nancy's eye, who gazed skyward with affection, folded her hands as if in prayer, and mouthed the word *hallelujah* back at her, as Hugh continued.

"Counselors, please be sure everyone gets a little needed rest time, and then you are free to enjoy the extra quiet time inside as you wish. We will ring the bell to alert everyone first, then ring it about fifteen minutes later to resume our regular camp activities. Enjoy this nice reprieve, everyone!"

Campers and counselors alike began to scramble as the first quick flash of what Tricia's grandmother referred to as heat lightning lit up the outside for a brief moment.

"I don't think I've ever been so happy to see some bad weather," Nancy quipped as they descended the stairs and headed down to the front line of cabins.

"Same here," Tricia said. "We're going to take full advantage of this time. I'm hoping my gals will let me take a long snooze. This will make it easier to spend some time at the Ark later."

"Okay, Grimball, that sounds like a plan. Rest up, we got a lot of ground to cover this evening, don't you know! Here comes the rain!"

The Du Kum Inn girls made it to the cabin just as the droplets of rain began to fall faster and harder from the thick gray clouds. Tricia gave a silent smile as they flopped like mountain trout on their respective cots and remained quiet as Tricia lowered the last of the canvas roll-ups to both darken the cabin and prevent any torrential rains from blowing inside.

"Sleep well, my lovelies." She ruffled the hair on each of their heads. "Let's enjoy the great sleeping weather. Whoever wakes up, just read, write letters, or talk softly. Let everyone sleep as much as they want. We've had a busy couple of days. Love you, girls."

"Love you too, Tricia," they each responded, with the exception of Christa.

"She's already asleep, can you believe it?" Chuck giggled.

"Yes, I can," Tricia smiled back, "because I'm getting ready to join her. Sleep tight, don't let the bed bugs bite."

"Eww, that gives me the creeps," Gaylen grinned, making a face. "Bed bugs, I hate them."

"Girl, you know you have never seen a bed bug!" Chuck teased.

"I have, too!" Gaylen shot back. "They look like this." She pulled her lips away from white teeth and bared them at Chuck, wide-eyed.

"Alright, you two, let's close it down for now. No bed bugs. None. At all."

She shook her head at the playful girls, who smiled at each other before finally settling down. Stretching out on her own cot, Tricia pulled a light blanket over her and tucked it beneath her chin. Within minutes, she was oblivious to the rain that now fell in soft sheets as the accompanying low rumbles of thunder lulled her into a deep and peaceful sleep that would sustain her for the remainder of the day's agenda.

The Ark was occupied by several other counselors after lights out, so the four friends made the move to sit on the porch benches at the top of the stairs to the dining hall and whisper to each other in the open-air space.

"Okay, so what have we got so far, just to catch us all up?" Cyndi asked, after Tricia and Nancy had shared the events of the overnight camping trip.

"We have Priscilla, who still cannot tell us what happened to her," Tavia offered. "We have three other missing people that we know of, two girls and a boy, who don't seem to be connected, other than they are all missing."

"And we are fairly certain that Harvey Bryson and the Sin Eater person are involved, and that Otha is a likely witness to it all but is staying quiet to protect herself," Nancy added. "We also know that Harvey Bryson has some kind of small lumber business somewhere near here."

"We also have good reason to believe that someone may be watching the camp pretty carefully, or at least trying to watch Priscilla, now, right?" Cyndi said.

"Yes, and there's one more important thing." Tricia lowered her voice even more. "Natalie has shared with me that Priscilla has confided in her that she was attacked."

"That's huge, Grimball!" Nancy gaped at her. "What did she say?"

"Unfortunately, not much. She knows she was walking home with her brothers, and that someone took her to Doc Halsted's place, at least she has been told that much, and she remembers waking up at High Hampton. She has talked about the strong, sweet smell – that I believe could have been ether, maybe – and she has mentioned recalling a man all dressed in dark clothes and a hood that upsets her, that could be the Sin Eater."

"But she doesn't know anything else, right?" Cyndi asked.

"No, but she may agree to talk with me, according to Natalie. If she does, I will let you know, of course. And that means that, pretty soon, we're going to have to tell Hugh and Dammie and Mary. We can't keep it under wraps much longer."

"So, what are we waiting on?" Cyndi asked. Nancy glanced at Tricia.

"Well, I'd like to try to talk with Otha by myself, if I can, to see if she will share anything else with me about that night," Tricia said. "And, I want to enlist Ewan's help, but I don't know." Her voice trailed off as the she looked up at the others.

"She's not sure if it's okay to trust him," Nancy added. "I think it is."

"We could use some outside help for sure, and Tricia, he's obviously pretty taken with you. He seems like a gentleman to me." Cyndi noted, glancing at the others. "Why don't you trust him?"

"I think I can – but, I feel responsible for Otha and I promised her I'd keep her confidence."

"Okay, so just don't tell him that part!" Cyndi said, "You could do it that way. Talk with Ewan first, then Otha."

"Well, you know he will be here the next weekend for our Christmas in July event that I've been working on, since The Queen and her sidekick are going to be on an overnight trip that Friday." Tricia hesitated. "He and a couple of guys are going to play some carols and such on the fiddles and piano for us. Then, Hugh and Cyndi and I will play Silent Night on the guitars."

Tavia clapped her hands. "The kids are gonna love that!"

"We hope so – don't tell, it's a surprise." Tricia said. "At any rate, after that is all done, he is going to help me move Lorene's things to the floating dock. Payback, remember, for that lovely night at Buford's Place."

"Oh, lord. Damn straight, pay her behind back. Rat's ass!" Tavia hissed.

"Shhhh, girl you gonna wake the dead," Nancy laughed.

"Alright," Cyndi interjected. "Tricia, are you saying you want to talk to Otha and Ewan maybe by then, first? I think that's a good plan, but I do think we have to tell someone what's going on pretty soon."

"Yeah, me too," Nancy added. "We can't keep them in the dark much longer."

"I know, yeah, y'all are right. Let me do those things and hopefully talk with Priscilla too."

"There's one more thing," Tavia said, smiling at Tricia. "What's the deal with you and the intriguing Mr. Munslow, anyway?" Tricia's grin got even bigger.

"I think about him often, and I find myself looking forward to the times he visits here. I feel like I've shared more of who I really am with him than I ever could with Daniel. Speaking of him, I've decided to send those letters to my mother and to him, regardless of whatever happens with Ewan. I can't marry Daniel, I just can't. At least not feeling the way I do. I'm going to tell him that I'm just not ready to be married."

"You have to do what you think is best, no matter what," Nancy said. "You won't be happy in life if you don't."

"You don't have to suffer the wrath of Abigail Grimball, either," Tricia made a face, crossed her eyes, then frowned. "But seriously, I'll get it all worked out, somehow."

"Let your heart and head guide you. Pray on it. You'll know." Nancy added.

"I've been praying about a whole lot of things," Tricia shook her head. "This is all either going to end really well, or really badly, and I feel like I don't want to mess up."

"We'll all pray, storm those pearly gates," Tavia smiled. "And we will all be ready for whatever the next step is."

"I'm so glad you all are here," Tricia whispered. "This has been such a summer. Honestly, I don't think I've ever felt more alive than I have here in this place with you all."

"Aw, doggonit, Grimball, don't make me cry," Nancy grabbed Tricia's hand. "Sisters, always, friends? No matter where life takes us?"

"Absolutely, yes, no matter the time or space between us," Cyndi added. "Now, to see if we can find all the answers to this insane mystery before camp is over."

Indeed, Tricia thought to herself. *The lives of others could be at stake here – we have to see this to the end.* Sleep would finally come again, but not before she had thought of all the scenarios possible to address in the coming weeks. She knew her friends were right. They would have to tell someone something and soon.

CHAPTER SIXTEEN

"Are you ready for tonight?" Nancy grabbed Tricia's arm as they made their way down the steps of the dining hall after the evening meal. The much- anticipated first night of the Christmas in July weekend was finally here. Tricia could hardly wait for Ewan and his friends to present their musical performance. Her girls had been practicing the clogging moves that he had taught them and, much to her surprise, had been able to keep that part of the evening a surprise. Ewan had gone out of his way to seek her out on his supply runs to Arden Woode, often engaging in conversation as time would allow, or giving her a book to read, or engaging in playful commentary with her girls, who had all come to love his visits. She was elated at the thought of extended time with just him later in the evening when they would carry out the plan for moving Lorene's belongings to the floating dock.

"There's the loaded question of the week, how's this going to end?" Tricia mused. "You know Lorene Hogue has gone out of her way to try to look helpful while not actually doing a darn thing to make this event any easier, right? I should have known her wanting me to plan this while she was off camping was so that she would look good. I can't wait to see her reaction when the queen and her crew come paddling back across the lake tomorrow morning and every single thing that she owns is on that dock!"

"It's definitely going to be fun to watch, especially her reaction," Nancy said, laughing.

"Hugh had suggested I talk with her, you know. But if I had tried to bury the hatchet then, this wouldn't be nearly as fun now."

"Well, I've really got to hand it to you, everything has come together well! The tree in the dining hall smells wonderful, with the dried orange and lemon slices, the beautiful pinecones with beads and sequins, and the popcorn strands. I can't wait to see all of the candles on it lit up on our Christmas morning. It was a great idea to do a tree in the Castle, too."

"When I got the idea for all the campers and staff to draw names to exchange handmade presents, I knew we had to have a tree there, too. Hanging all the paper stockings in the Castle for the girls and staff with compliments from everybody was actually Hugh's idea, but I loved it. Truth be told, I think it will be a highlight of the weekend."

"Did you ever mention the possibility of making some things for Otha?" Nancy asked.

"I did. He and Mary and Dammie wanted to be sure that all staff members were equally recognized for this event. Oh, but you're gonna love this! They did like the idea of a camp service project and tossed around the idea of trying to involve the town in the renovation of the abandoned shack down the road – you know, the one where we parked when we went on our big adventure to see the Sin Eater. I felt bad, having to pretend I had no idea where that was." Tricia smiled, glancing toward her cabin of girls. "Thanks for bringing them up to the Castle for me. I'd better head back up there to be sure they are finished setting up."

Making her way up the steps to the Castle, Tricia smiled as she saw the candles glowing on the tree already, no doubt lit by Hugh, as Mary and Dammie talked with Ewan while his friends arranged the piano and staging area as they preferred. He was dressed as he most often was in his work clothes, but with a clean, polished edge to his appearance. His dark hair and intense eyes, juxtaposed with the crisp white shirt he wore, the sleeves rolled up to just below his elbows, and the well-tailored black pants only enhanced the outdoor rugged-ness of his male pulchritude. Tricia tried to brush off the feeling of warmth that rushed over her when she saw him. As soon as he spied her, he made his way in her direction, amid the chattering campers that had begun to file inside.

"Good evening, Miss Grimball," he smiled. "Are you ready for a fun evening?"

"I can hardly wait, Mr. Munslow," she teased back. "I'm actually full of Christmas cheer this evening. I appreciate your doing this. You are a man of many talents, playing the fiddle too, and a clogging expert."

"Hardly anywhere close to expert, but they both bring me a great deal of enjoyment. It will be a good evening. I have no doubt. I love the Christmas tree, complete with candles." Leaning closer to him,

Tricia whispered, taking in the fresh woodsy scent of him.

"And I am beyond excited that you are helping me with the plans for later."

"As am I," Ewan gave her a mischievous grin. "I've been looking forward to the entire evening. Perhaps we might have some time to talk, if the hour is not too late for you. I have something to show you. I'd better go now, since it looks like we are close to getting started. Until later, then."

Once Dammie had addressed the group and welcomed the guest musicians, Tricia introduced Ewan and his friends, then all of the campers and staff, as she wanted to set the tone for the evening and remainder of the weekend.

"As you all know, we are most fortunate to be able to be here at our beautiful Camp Arden Woode. It is the most special of places, where young women are nurtured and challenged to be their best selves, to encourage one another in that effort, and to celebrate our joyful achievements. It is in that spirit that I would like to recognize and thank our newest member of camp, Miss Priscilla Parker, who came up with this most excellent of ideas for an evening program. May we all be messengers of the spirit of Christmas, with faith, hope, and love for all."

Tricia glanced first at Ewan, who raised his hands in vigorous clapping, then at Nancy.

"I would also like to give a word of thanks to Lorene Hogue, who is on an overnight trip with her cabin and Rachel's. Lorene graciously allowed me to plan this event in her absence. They will be back for the Saturday gift exchange and Sunday Christmas meal and campfire time. Enjoy the program tonight!"

More clapping ensued as Ewan winked at her, now standing by her side, and Nancy, Tavia, and Cyndi all shook their heads, barely able to contain knowing smiles. Tricia moved from the staging area to sit with her campers, who could now barely contain their excitement at being able to surprise the onlookers with their dancing. A hush fell over the gathering, as Ewan addressed them, amid appreciative stares, especially from the counselors.

"Thank you all for having us this evening. We will play a few Christmas carols for you, then we have a small surprise in store." Tricia's campers giggled in anticipation. "As you may know, many of the carols we sing today have their origin in Europe, where I am from. Even the fiddle, as my Celtic one here, most common in our mountain music in these parts, has origins as far back as the Byzantine Empire, from its ancestor, the bowed string instrument called a lira. Please feel free to sing, as you wish."

Moving close to his friend at the piano, and joined by another fiddle player, Ewan began to play an upbeat version of the opening solo lines of "God Rest Ye Merry, Gentlemen" before the other fiddle and piano joined in. The sound was so pure and magnificent, no one moved or sang, but sat enrapt with the beauty of the music. Only when the performers began to sing, did the audience join in. The soft minor sounds of "What Child Is This," followed by the well-known "O Come, All Ye Faithful," were works of art, with the joyful singing of happy voices blended into the seasonal music. Tricia was pleased that the evening seemed to be a hit with all of Arden Woode.

Ewan motioned for the girls of Du Kum Inn to join him on the stage to demonstrate the art of the local clogging dance. Tricia beamed with pride as all four of her young campers slid their feet and stomped their way through the demonstration, before inviting everyone to rise and try out the dance moves for themselves. After the cheering and clapping subsided, the girls took their seats on the stage and Ewan addressed the Castle gathering once more.

"Before the very last carol this evening, we would like to play an old Irish tune for you. The melody begins rather slowly, with the tempo gradually increasing to that of a good clogging number. At the appropriate time, these girls here will let you know when it's time to join in. We hope you will enjoy this one." Ewan took a step toward the center edge of the stage and began to play. The melody was haunting, with low notes held long and blended with staccato ones that enhanced the dramatic timbre of the music played. His face was intense; his body bent and swayed with each stroke of the bow as the muscles in his arms worked to create the melodious sound. In all of her imagination, Tricia had never heard anything as captivating and evoking of intense emotion. Ewan had told her he would play one of his favorite pieces that was instrumental. *Words would detract from the magic of the music*, he had said. He was right. She felt her cheeks flushed and tears rose in her eyes as she watched him begin to quicken the pace, with the other musicians joining in. He smiled at her, a loving glance that none of her friends missed. Nancy's eyes grew wide as she caught Tricia's attention and gave her a thumbs-up signal.

Before long, everyone had risen to their feet and were moving and dancing to the rollicking and joyful tune that had reached a frenetic crescendo. With the last dramatic stroke of his fiddle, Ewan pulled the bow across the strings in a quick, deft motion and raised it in the air in a finishing flair. He and the musicians took a bow, then motioned for the dancers to follow. Hugh Carson took the stage, thanking everyone and noting the work Tricia had done to make the evening possible.

"For the last number tonight, we invite you to join us in the reverent singing of "Silent Night," which was originally written for and played by guitars one Christmas Eve in Austria, when a river flood had damaged the church's organ. To commemorate that incredible night and the miracle of Christmas, we ask that when we are done, for everyone to please leave the Castle quietly with your cabin, and don't forget to give thanks for this time together and for one another. In the words of Tiny Tim, 'God bless us, everyone!' We will now play and sing this beautiful hymn. Tricia and Cyndi, if you will join me on stage with your guitars please?"

The campers clapped softly as places on the stage were assumed and the first strains of music were strummed and picked. Campers and staff alike linked arms and sang in whispers, as Tricia sang the first verse aloud, her voice clear and sweet, with Cyndi adding lovely harmony for the second verse, and Hugh underscoring the piece with even more depth for the final verse, as the campers all maintained the melody. At the end of the song, campers and staff alike moved in near silence, filing out of the building into the quiet dark, with counselors holding lanterns held high and campers whispered to one another in an effort to keep the almost spiritual mood. Hugh stopped beside Tricia as she assisted in helping the guests pack up their instruments and belongings.

"Ewan, we can't thank you all enough for sharing your time and talent with us tonight." Hugh shook his hand and turned to Tricia. "My dear, that was truly an incredible evening. Congratulations on a job well done. Mother Nature and I are going to walk your girls and hers to their cabins and let them get settled in until you get there. You go ahead and see our guests off, if you will." He gave a broad smile to Tricia. "That way, Hala and I can enjoy an evening pipe down by the water for a few minutes before I retire for the night. Good evening to you both."

"Tricia, would you walk outside with me to the carriage? I've got something for you to read that I want to be sure to give you before the evening gets away."

"Of course, can I carry anything to help you? Perhaps your hat and jacket?" She reached for the items mentioned and moved toward the steps while Ewan motioned to the musicians who were still speaking with Dammie and Mary. "Where would you like me to put these?"

"Just lay them on the front seat for now, will be fine," he answered. "Let me grab my fiddle and say goodbye to the camp folk and round up the others."

Tricia eased down the steps to the horse drawn buckboard that was secured at the end of the building and searched in the dark for something to grab in an effort to hoist the jacket and hat into the raised passenger seat. Her hand brushed against a box perched just underneath the bench seat, knocking it over onto the floor. She reached to pick it up, as the lid fell off, and its contents tumbled out. A wooden bowl and utensils clattered down, resting with a gentle thud at her feet. She had seen them before. Waves of nausea and horror flooded over her as she bent to retrieve the crude items. Her hand shook as she reached into the box that now laid sideways on the floor of the carriage, the dark clothing that had been folded inside now exposed.

"Tricia."

Ewan Munslow stared at her clutching the disguise of the Sin Eater, and taking a deliberate step away from him, her eyes filled with sadness and disbelief.

"You! It's been you all this time!" She whispered, a sob threatening to escape from deep in her throat.

"Tricia, please! It's part of what I wanted to share with you. Please give me the chance to explain," he begged, moving toward her.

"Don't!" She whispered, the tears creeping out of her eyes and sliding down her cheeks. Struggling to take a deep breath, she fought for composure, having been blindsided by what had just happened. "You don't care about me at all, do you? All of this attention, pretending to like me. You knew it was me that night, didn't you?"

Ewan made no attempt to come closer, but she could see the hurt in his eyes and hear it in his voice, now low and deep.

"Tricia Grimball, whatever else you think of me, know this: I have never cared for anyone as much as I do for you. Please say you'll at least give me the chance to explain."

Dammie and Mary, along with the other musicians, appeared at the top of the stairs, still engaged in amiable conversation, unaware of the storm brewing below.

"Tricia, please." Ewan whispered in desperation. "At least hear me out before you find me guilty. Meet me on the dock in an hour after I leave. Please say you will."

Tricia relaxed her grip on the black clothing and shoved everything back in the box. She turned to face him, saw the pain on his face.

"Alright. I'll meet you in an hour. But you'd better be honest with me."

"I will, I promise. I'll tell you everything. I'm so sorry you found out this way."

"I have to go now."

She walked past him, wiping her eyes and looking away from his, escaping as quickly as she could toward the line of cabins on the lakefront before the fresh tears began to fall. None of this made sense. Ewan did not fit any of the descriptions she had been given of one who would take up the macabre ritual of sin eating. Worst of all, he was surely involved in some way with what happened to Priscilla Parker. On second thought, that wasn't the worst part. What was devastating was that she had grown to love him, believe in him, trust him, and ached to tell him. She couldn't decide how she felt now amid the myriad of emotions that tore at her soul. Betrayed, hurt, sad, confused. In this moment, she felt as if she were drowning in a sea of overwhelming loss. Not even the soothing night sounds that she had grown to cherish could console her.

"Grimball!" Nancy called to her, as she and Tavia rushed to catch up with her. "Your girls are all tucked in and settled down. So, a great night so far, right, with the best part coming up!"

Tricia stood in silence, staring out over the lake, her words momentarily adrift with the night breeze. She fought back yet another round of tears.

"What's wrong?" Nancy demanded. "What in the world happened?"

"I'm still in shock. Quite by accident, I found something out that I wasn't supposed to know. This changes everything, ya'll. Everything."

"What? What in the world are you talking about? Just say it." Tavia insisted.

"It's Ewan." She gave a helpless glance toward the sky, then whispered, barely able to articulate the odious words. "Ewan Munslow is the Sin Eater."

Nancy's eyes grew wide with disbelief. She grabbed Tricia's shoulders. "Bloody hell, what did you say? Are you sure?"

"I was helping load stuff in the wagon and accidentally knocked over a box that had his disguise and food utensils in there. I recognized them immediately. It was awful. He said he was planning to tell me tonight. He begged me to let him explain it all. I'm meeting him on the dock in an hour. I don't know. How can I trust him now?"

"I don't even know what to say," Nancy stared at her. "I'm stunned. He comes across as such a great guy. What in the world?"

"Okay, wait. Wait a minute. Hold up here. You are going to let him have his say, right? Tricia, this man has not given you one reason until this to doubt his sincerity or his character! It's pretty clear how he feels about you," Tavia spoke up. "There has to be a reason."

"What if it was just a ruse? He's involved in all this now! And why on earth would he do such a thing? It makes no sense at all."

"Okay, you know what? Tavia's right, he at least deserves a chance to tell his side. I'm surprised, too. But you two are crazy about each other. Anybody can see that. He has been more than honorable in every way. Hugh likes him. Otha likes him. And you know Otha can spot a fake and a bad seed a mile away. I admit, I'm baffled. But if you do care for him – and I know you do – you have to give him a chance to hear his side of all this."

"I did agree to listen. I know I should. It just isn't making sense."

The three young women stood in silence just long enough to breathe in the night mountain air, letting it wrap them in quiet calm.

"Tricia, this right here is what happens in life. It gets messy sometimes, no matter how hard we try to act in good faith. You said you wanted to see and know about real people, about their lives and stories, right? So, find out! If he's half the man we all think he is, there's a reason why he's doing this." Nancy squeezed her hand. "I mean, look at it this way, too. Now that we know who the Sin Eater is, we have an advantage here."

Tricia looked up at the crest of Bald Rock Mountain, looming over them like a sentry, through the stars that now appeared in the darkening sky. Nancy and Tavia were right. These hills were laden with far more than just the natural beauty that encompassed them. They were also infused with humanity through the ages, from the ancestral Indians and immigrants that first settled these woods, to the hard-working folk who now chose to make this land their home. Ewan Munslow was part and parcel of it all, a living embodiment of both the past and present, and had been more than a gentleman to her thus far. If she truly loved him, she had to trust that there was a reasonable explanation.

"God love you, ladies, I sure do!" She hugged her friends, smiling and wiping away the residual tears. "I guess I owe him an apology for the rush to judge. It's just that I've grown so fond of him and the man

I thought he was, that it felt like a slap in the face to me to find out this secret that he's kept. And I wondered for a brief moment if he cared about me or was just trying to get close to me because he knew I saw him and heard him that night."

"I'm betting he is still the man that cares for you and that there is another layer to all of this." Nancy was firm in her declaration of faith in Ewan.

"I guess I'll know soon enough. Let me go check on my girls. See you in the morning."

"Don't worry about your girls. They know you will be close by and that Tavia and I will too. Hey, take the whistle, just in case!"

Tricia eased up the steps of Du Kum Inn, opening the cabin door as quietly as she could. Christa and Natalie were already asleep, no doubt exhausted from the busy day. Gaylen and Chuck remained awake, talking in low whispers across their cots.

"Tricia, we had so much fun tonight!" Chuck said, sitting up and shaking her head full of curls.

"Yeah, were you proud of us?" Gaylen grinned.

"Oh, you have no idea how proud I am!" Tricia sat on the edge of Gaylen's cot and whispered back to the girls. "You performed perfectly, and everyone loved it! It will forever be one of the best moments of the summer."

"Tricia, can we tell you something?" Chuck squinted at her, cocking her head to one side.

"Of course, sweetie, what is it?"

"We asked Ewan what he liked about you the most." Chuck giggled under her breath, as did Gaylen.

"You did? Oh, my, girls! Well, what did he say?"

"He said that you were a woman of great integrity and courage." Chuck said.

"What does that mean, exactly?" Gaylen asked.

"It means that I think he likes me for the right reasons." Tricia smiled. "Okay, it's time for us to get some sleep. Another fun day tomorrow! Good night, my precious ones!"

CHAPTER SEVENTEEN

From her seat on the dock, Tricia strained her eyes to see the lone figure in the rowboat that glided through the murky waters of Emerald Lake. A breeze brushed across the gentle waves that shimmered in the low fog and light of a partly clouded moon. Ewan Munslow was like an apparition floating on the lake, much as he had been the night she saw the Sin Eater, and finally coming into clarity before her. She felt for the whistle that Nancy had insisted she take for precautionary measures and stood, reaching for the rope that he tossed to her and securing the boat against the main dock.

"I owe you an apology, Ewan," she began, "I was surprised – overwhelmed, truly – and I reacted badly, without giving you a chance. Please forgive me."

He stood close enough to make her blush, staring down at her, his gray eyes intense, before spreading the blanket that he carried and motioning for her to sit beside him.

"You owe me nothing. I have wanted to tell you for a long time, so that you would know everything about me. It seemed the right moment and time never happened. I am so sorry, Tricia, for any discomfort and mistrust that I have caused. I would never intentionally inflict a moment of pain for you." He hesitated, then moved closer to her, crossing his legs and looking deep into her eyes. "Everything I have told you about me is true. If you will do me the kindness, I will tell you the parts that have been left out until now."

"Of course, I will listen. I want to know all about you. Tell me everything."

"My uncle, Richard Munslow, who was my father's oldest brother, lived with his wife and four young children in Ratlinghope, a small, sparsely populated village in Shropshire County, in England, which is next to Wales in proximity. He was a successful farmer, of good social standing. They lost four of their young children, with three of them dying in one week in May of 1870, from the ravages of Scarlet Fever, I'm told.

"What a devastating thing to happen to anyone." Tricia murmured.

"At the time, the practice of sin eating was largely intended to allow those who died before they got the opportunity to confess their sins, a chance to be able to go to Heaven. It also insured that the sin-plagued dead did not walk the earth as spirits, which is why a sin eater prays over a body by saying, 'I give easement and rest now to thee, dear one. Come not down the lanes or in our meadows. And for thy peace, I pawn my own soul.' It is said that Richard was so overcome with grief that he took on the role of a sin eater so that no one else would ever have to lose a loved one and not believe that they were received into Heaven with Christ. He died in 1906 when he was seventy-three years old. I was just a boy but loved him very much. And his death crushed my father."

"I'm so sorry, Ewan." Tricia reached for his hand, holding it briefly before withdrawing hers. "If I may ask, didn't the church frown on this practice? I mean, I know my priest back home would say that only Christ could forgive sins."

"Yes, the church very much disapproved, still does, but they largely turn a blind eye to it, as long as folks come to church and believe. A sin eater came to the home of the deceased the night before a funeral or either just before the funeral took place. It was, and is, considered bad luck to ever look a sin eater in the eyes, so they were avoided in every possible way, and no one ever knew, or cared to know, exactly who a sin eater was. It was always assumed that he was a person of little means or social standing."

"So, what your uncle did was a very selfless sacrifice, of sorts, literally for the souls of others, then, is that right?"

"Very much so. The practice of sin eating appears strange and macabre at first glance, and it will eventually die out, I'm sure, but the roots of such have their beginnings in Christianity. Just as Christ gave his life for all of humanity, sin eaters willingly sacrifice their souls to cleanse and purify those of the unforgiven dead." Tricia frowned, sweeping the hair out of her eyes that a soft breeze had tousled.

"There's one thing I still don't understand. Even a sin eater or priest cannot cleanse a person's soul. Only Christ can."

"Yes, and I believe that, too. But Christ tells us to forgive one another, doesn't He? Are we not supposed to forgive, so that our own sins may be forgiven? The willingness to take on the sin of another is an act of love, just as Christ did that for us."

"Then, what happens to the sin eater at the end of his own life?" Tricia whispered. Ewan looked out over the water before returning his gaze to her.

"Not to worry," he smiled. "I pray daily for the forgiveness of sins, mine and those I took on. I try to live the best life I can. Hopefully that will count for something, right?"

"What made you decide to follow in the path that your uncle took?" Tricia asked.

"That's another part of what I wanted to tell you. When my father died, I knew that his own faith was well-grounded. But the wife and children of one of the men killed that day in the mine were beyond distraught because they were unsure of his salvation. A young son had gone with him and perished also, so they were sick with grief. They were embarrassed to attend church after that, as well. Because of my own rule of life, I made the decision to meet them where they were – to relieve a lot of their grief by taking on their deceased family members' sin. I resurrected – I guess that's an appropriate choice of words here – the disguise my uncle had worn. No one in Laurel Valley knows that the Sin Eater and I are one in the same. The money that I make, I give anonymously to those who need it the most.

"What is a rule of life? What is that, exactly?" Tricia frowned.

"I struggled with the loss of my father, who was the only family I had left. For a while I retreated into my own shell, I suppose, not much good to anyone. The vicar at The Church of the Good

Shepherd in Cashiers gave me a book about creating a rule of life. Around the fourth century or thereabouts, after the emperor made Christianity legal in the Roman Empire, a group of men and women sought solace in the deserts of Syria and Egypt. Their goal was to find God and be grounded in their work, prayer, and Scripture, and to grow and mature in spirit, while helping others. They all created a specific plan, if you will, called a Rule of Life, to help them live more intentionally and with joy. Creating my own rule has been invaluable to me, as well."

"What is the rule? It sounds punitive." Tricia observed.

Ewan smiled, his body relaxing.

"Quite the opposite. It isn't a rule, or even just one rule, in the traditional sense. In fact, the origin of the word is from a Greek translation that means *trellis* or *scaffold*. So, it is meant to be more of a support, a guide, or a rhythm to actually liberate rather than constrain. When one formulates a rule of life, it is meant to be individual, realistic and simple, to help infuse the love of God into one's life. And it can change over time as people grow. I take a day to examine mine each year, to refine or change it, perhaps."

Ewan reached into the canoe for the tattered satchel that he had left on the seat. Pulling out a book, he handed it to Tricia.

"This is the book that the priest gave me. As St. Benedict once said, '*He should first show them in deeds, rather than words, all that is good and holy.*' When the woman that lost her husband could not get past the idea of his not having confessed his sins, I knew that she could not find a measure of peace until she could deal with that. I knew I had the means to help them all in that moment." He stopped talking long enough to take Tricia's hand. "I need to tell you what happened that night like I said I would."

Tricia nodded, not saying a word, but squeezing his hand in return.

"I was returning from the home of a family up the road a good way from Laurel Valley. It was twilight and I was on horseback and had not removed my disguise as the Sin Eater. As I said before, people totally ignore a sin eater, even move away from one, but there are rarely people on the road after dark, anyway, so I did not expect to see many people. I heard a commotion around the corner from where I was. Chester Graves was holding a young girl who had a large burlap sack over her head. Harvey Bryson was by the wagon. I could not tell what he was doing. I dropped my voice down as low as I could and told Chester to leave the girl alone. He let her drop to the ground and lunged hard at me. I had my knife, but he could not see it. It happened so fast. I stabbed him and he fell to the ground, never got back up. Harvey, the coward that he is, grabbed the reins of the wagon and took off as fast as he could. I removed the burlap sack, carried the girl to my horse, then down the road to Doc Halsted's place. I never saw any blood or other evidence that she had been hurt. She had only just begun to show any sign that she was conscious when I banged on the door. Of course, I did not want the Sin Eater involved in any possible way, so I left as soon as I heard the doctor coming to the door."

"What does the law around here believe about what happened?" Tricia asked.

"As far as I know, Harvey has only said that he couldn't tell about the strange man covered up in dark clothes. Which is of course a lie, but he knows that the Sin Eater does not want any attention and Harvey doesn't want anyone to know what he was actually doing. I think he has been up to no good for a long time and is involved in something bigger. As you know, he is rather enjoying his imagined role as hero, and rescuer of the girl. The young girl, I hear, remembers nothing that could absolutely convict either him or the Sin Eater. So, right now, everything seems to be hinging on what she remembers, if anything." Ewan grew quiet as he studied her carefully.

"Tricia, I have to ask you. What made you come to Chester Grave's house that night, and why did you tell me that you didn't think I wanted to hurt him?"

"I had heard tell of a sin eater and I was curious. I was told that he would likely be at Chester Graves's home the night before his funeral." She blushed, remembering all that had happened. "I was spying on you through the open window. I heard and saw everything. And then I fell. Which, I guess you remember." Ewan smiled at her, still holding her hand.

"I most recall being surprised by your tenacity and courage. And I was quite taken with how beautiful you looked. Then, I met you at camp, and you were smart, interested in books, too. When you and your friends came into Buford's that night, I could barely take my eyes off of you in your soft dress and your pretty hair, as you tried to talk your way out of a difficult situation. You were quite entertaining, as well." Ewan smiled. "Then, the way you spoke on my behalf with Dr. Halsted – no one has ever done anything like that for me. Tricia Grimball, surely you must have an idea how I feel about you."

She took a deep breath. Looking up into his handsome face and intense eyes in the soft moonlight, she no longer felt doubt.

"The truth is, Ewan Munslow, that I think you are the most intriguing man I have ever known, and I dread leaving this place and you."

Ewan stood, pulling her to her feet and held her so close that she could feel his heart pounding in his chest, his arms not wanting to release her. With one hand, he tilted her chin up, then slid his hand underneath the hair around her neck and kissed her. In all of her imagination, Tricia had never been kissed with as much tenderness and passion.

"Then we will figure it all out somehow," he whispered, kissing her once more before adding, "Do we still have a mission to accomplish this evening?"

Tricia laughed, trying to keep her voice as soft as she could. In the intensity of the moment, she had almost forgotten about the clandestine prank to play on Lorene.

"Yes, we do. I think we can get it done in two trips to her cabin. Ewan, when we have more time, I want to talk with you more about the night they attacked Priscilla. Parker. I'm sure you know she is here and safe. I believe there may have been a witness that night that can help us. That's all I can tell you for now."

"Tricia, I trust you in every possible way, and I want you to trust me. Whenever we can be together or talk about this more, that's what I want."

Ewan kissed her once more before the two made their way off the dock to the path that lead to the line of upper cabins. Neither said a word, remaining as quiet as possible as they navigated their way through the camp.

It was no matter.

The figure known as "The Wolf" stared at them, his feral eyes now fully adjusted to the night as he crept in silence from his hiding place in the deep woods. He had heard enough for now.

Chapter Eighteen

Tricia awoke to the laughter of her girls, still reliving the excitement of the night before. She couldn't help but feel the same way, still reeling from everything that had happened with Ewan. She gave a quick glance toward the floating dock, now anchored slightly outside it's usual overnight location by the stationary dock. Lorene Hogue's cot, trunk, and a small bedside table that had held her lantern waited to be discovered by the rest of the camp. She turned back to her lively crew.

"Ladies, I still cannot get over how amazing you were last night. The dancing was perfect, and I have never been so proud of you! Everyone loved it!"

"We want to keep doing it!" Gaylen exclaimed, tossing her pillow in the air. "Could Ewan and his friends come back and teach us all some more?"

"Yes, we all want to keep clogging!" Christa added.

"I can ask the staff if we can plan something like that again. It was great fun. Okay, we need to get moving! Another big day."

The dining hall bell had just begun to ring for breakfast as the Du Kum Inn girls made their way down the cabin steps to meet Nancy's girls, who ran toward them.

"Look out there! Look at the floating dock!" One of the girls yelled. Screams and loud giggles erupted from a crowd of campers headed to eat.

"Lawd have mercy, would you look at that!" Nancy proclaimed in mock surprise, waving an arm toward the lake and winking at Tricia. "Someone played a huge trick today!"

Cyndi and Tavia caught up with them, smiles big as the sunrise over Bald Rock Mountain. Cyndi whispered to Tricia.

"Nancy said it was important that we all talk today, somehow. You have to tell us what's going on!"

"A lot happened last night. There's lots to tell." Tricia whispered back. "Maybe during swim time or tonight at the Ark, if we can." Tavia eased her way between Cyndi and Tricia.

"Well, friends, I just have to say it. A great big 'rat's ass' to us. Is this the best prank ever, or what? I can't wait to see Lorene Hogue's face when they come paddling back across the lake. When do you think they will get here?"

"Should be soon," Tricia noted, grinning, "and I'm getting a seat facing the windows so I can see and hear her."

The dining hall was bustling with jovial banter as Tricia and her girls sat near the crackling fire in the great stone fireplace. Tricia positioned herself so that she could see the lake as well as the entrance to the building. This was one show she intended to see from start to finish. The cloudless morning sky was a beautiful shade of bright azure, with the sunrise sending rays of sparkling light cascading over the top of Bald Rock into the water below. *The perfect backdrop*, Tricia mused, as Otha and a cabin of older girls placed bowls of steaming oatmeal and pitchers of milk on the tables, along with plates of fresh grapefruit slices. Nancy caught her eye and nodded her head toward the lake, a big smile creeping across her face. A handful of canoes paddled with vigor across the smooth morning waters of Emerald Lake.

"Hey! What in the world?" Shouts erupted from below and the sound, which carried with ease across the open water, wafted up the stairs to the dining hall occupants, who now strained to see the commotion outside. "I'm gonna kill whoever did this! They are gonna pay!"

Lorene's voice rang out amid the chatter from the girls in the canoes. It didn't take long for a red-faced young woman to come bursting into the dining hall, demanding that the perpetrators of the prank identify themselves. As soon as she spotted Tricia, she flew to her table, as ripples of laughter spread across the room behind her.

"I know you're involved in this, somehow! Aren't you?" She hissed in quiet anger.

Tricia wiped her mouth after a big gulp of the chilled milk.

"Whatever in the world are you babbling about, Lorene?"

"You know exactly what I'm talking about! My personal belongings all out on the floating dock. I know you did this! I'm sure I could guess who helped you."

Lorene sputtered, looking around the dining hall for Tricia's friends. The Du Kum Inn girls tried hard to smother giggles as they watched the exchange.

"Really, Lorene, I was way too busy planning the Christmas in July event. It's gone rather well, so far, I must say. But I seem to remember your saying you liked pranks, especially between friends, so I'm sure it will all be okay, won't it?"

Lorene's eyes narrowed and her lips pursed. "You just wait. Just wait."

"We did, Lorene. At Buford's Place, remember?" Tricia saw Nancy, Tavia, and Cyndi doubled over with laughter at their tables. "Would you like to tell everybody about it?" She whispered with a smug smile.

Lorene glared at her again before spinning on her heels and walking to the table on the other side of the room that her girls and Rachel's now occupied.

"Tricia," Natalie stared at her, eyes wide. "Did you put her stuff out there?"

"Now, what makes you say that?" Tricia grinned and winked at her young charges who stared at her with surprise and admiration.

"They are going to play more pranks on us, now," Chuck said, her curly head of hair bobbing up and down as she laughed. "Like the time they tied string around our chairs at breakfast."

"But we got them back when we put red gelatin powder in the showerheads," Gaylen laughed. "That was the best."

"Until this," Christa gave Tricia a big smile. "This is the best, for sure."

"Okay, my clever ones," Tricia interceded before the gloating grew, "Let's go get ready for Castle time and the rest of our day. Remember, the best pranks are done in silence, right? Let the deed speak for itself. Mum's the word!"

"Ay, ay, Captain!" Gaylen saluted as the young campers gathered their plates.

Hugh Carson ambled over to Tricia, as did Cyndi, Tavia, and Nancy amid the clatter to return dishes to the service area for Otha and the cleanup crew of girls.

"I'm guessing Lorene will need the camp wagon and Wilhelmina to get her belongings back up the hill to her cabin, perhaps?"

"Perhaps." Tricia replied, smiling at him.

"I'm thinking that whoever masterminded such a brilliant plan might give consideration now to calling a truce, or at least keeping the level of pranking to amateur? I'll see you at the trip craft hut shortly, Tricia. Ah, it's another glorious day at Arden Woode, isn't it? Good day, ladies."

They waited without a word until Hugh and most everyone else had exited the dining hall. As the last staff member closed the door on the way out, a collective burst of laughter broke the sudden quiet in the hall.

"Did you see the look on her face?" Nancy cackled. "I'd pay good money to have a photograph of her reaction!"

"I just have one thing to say," Tavia said, reaching her hand out in front of her and waiting for the others to follow suit. "Rat's ass, ya'll! That was the prank to end all pranks!"

"So, let's get serious for a moment." Cyndi interrupted, changing the mood. We have to talk tonight. Tricia, Nancy gave me the news about Ewan. I'm shocked to say the least. You will have to give us the details. But at least tell us now, do you still trust him? Is everything okay between you two?"

"Yeah, it's all good. I know all about him now, why he does what he does, and he is everything I thought he was and more. I'd trust him with my life. And he has promised to help us in any way that he can. I'll fill in the gaps tonight."

"Whoa, wait. C'mon, you have to spill this much. Did you two finally tell each other how you feel?" Tavia demanded. Tricia could no longer hide the blushing grin.

"We did," she said nodding her head, then whispered, "and Daniel Middleton could never kiss me the way he did." Excited screams erupted from them all.

"Get out, I knew it!" Tavia exclaimed. "Thank goodness, the suspense was killing me, and it was about time, I might add!"

The remainder of the day up until dinner time seemed to pass in a rapid succession of routine camp activities and fun. Tricia had assisted Hugh in preparation for a few more overnights and the last rounds of boating trips and was headed to see Otha about meal supplies when Nancy came careening around the corner of the outside dining area, carrying a large white piece of paper and shaking it at Tricia.

"This does it!" she yelled. "See what was left on my cabin door, Cyndi's, Tavia's, and of course, yours. My girls are all bamboozled now, thinking that someone is going to get them."

Tricia took the proffered paper from her friend, who now stood, arms akimbo, an expression of angry defiance on her face.

"Beware, the Tajar is watching you!" Tricia read aloud. The Tajar was a mystical legendary creature of the woods, indigenous to Arden Woode, that was imagined to be a cross between a tiger, a jaguar, and a badger. It was said that he was mischievous; that if a camper looked at him once, she would forget what he looked like, but if she looked twice, she would forget to forget what he looked like, which could be deadly. It was said that the Tajar knew everything that went on at camp. All of the campers knew about the Tajar as well as the Wampus Cat.

"I'm fixing to put a good, old-fashioned Loooosiana voodoo root on that *heifer*," Nancy said, emphasizing the last word. "It's time to end this with her! Tonight."

"Seriously, Baudette, what do you propose we do?"

"Besides kick her behind back up to the backwoods, wherever she's from? I think it's time we have a woman-to-woman chat with her and bury the hatchet."

"I'm all for it," Tricia said. "I'm sure my girls will be a bit rattled, as well, when they see the sign on our door. What did you have in mind?"

"I've already talked with her. She wouldn't admit anything. Said something about you stepping over the line."

"Me?" Tricia was indignant. "She's the one that drew first blood!"

"Yeah, I know, I know. So, I told her you wanted to meet her at the Ark tonight after lights out, to apologize."

"You told her what? Nan, she's the one that owes the apology first! Why'd you do that? Damn."

"Look, we have to get her down there. I knew she'd come if she thought you'd apologize."

"Well, I'm not apologizing first! She started this whole mess, and I don't even know why she's had it in for me since the first day of camp."

"Tricia, come on, you can put that Southern girl charm to work. You know how to get people talking, you know you do. A lot of these kids come to you when they have a problem. For heaven's sake, say you'll do it! We'll add the terms of agreement to the treaty they just signed in Versailles. World peace hangs in the balance!"

"Oh, good lord! Okay, I'll do it, geez. I hate it when you actually make sense. Besides, Hugh is all over this, too, as you know."

"Since Cyndi's cabin is up there near Lorene's, she's offered to take Lorene's line duty for a little while before we talk. Do you have it tonight?"

"I should say yes, and make your Cajun derriere do it for me, but no, mine is tomorrow night."

"Your mama will be proud." Nancy cajoled.

"My mother is going to pitch a screaming tee-total fit as it is, and you know it. She will never forgive me for refusing the advances of her future lawyer son-in-law. My father might have her committed to an asylum after I tell her about Ewan."

"See, then, this can only help, right?"

"Go on, Baudette, you're killing me with all your Louisiana logic. I'll see you after I'm done with the Queen."

"Atta girl, I knew you'd come through."

"Go away before I change my mind."

Throughout the evening meal and especially during the home-made gift exchange that evening in the Castle, Tricia caught Lorene staring at her, a look of discomfort on her face. Nancy had surmised that the girl was just feeling bad about all that had happened and was perhaps somewhat jealous over how well the whole Christmas in July event had evolved thus far. Everyone wanted to do it again the following year and the administrative staff had praised Tricia's efforts in organizing it. In her heart, she knew that her friend Nancy was choosing to remain positive about the upcoming meeting, but something told her that the task was going to be challenging.

After lights out, Tricia notified the counselor on line duty that she was headed to the Ark. Nancy and Tavia were waiting at the door for her, along with two or three other counselors.

"What are y'all doing outside? Why aren't you going in?"

"We're gonna go sit in the outside chapel, now that you're here. Lorene is there waiting for you." Tavia reached for the door, motioning Tricia forward. "Give it your best shot, Ambassador."

Tricia made a face, drew a deep breath and stepped inside. Lorene was lounging on one of the worn sofas, feet propped on an old coffee table. She twirled a piece of light brown hair and crossed her legs, the green middies bunching up around her knees. Tricia thought she was trying to appear relaxed but looked nervous.

"I was wondering if you were going to show," Lorene mumbled, a hint of disdain in her tone.

"I said I would. I always try to keep my word."

"Well?" Lorene raised her eyebrows.

"Well, what?" Tricia said.

"You're here to apologize. Let's have it."

"I'm curious to know what exactly you'd like to have me apologize about."

"I knew it." Lorene's voice dripped with sarcasm. "Of course, since I came, you aren't going to apologize, are you?"

"I was hoping apologies would be offered from all sides," Tricia said. "I mean if we are truly going to fix whatever has been eating at you from the start of camp, I need to know what it is you have had against me all this time."

Lorene bristled, still glaring.

"Please, like you don't know! You've tried to be the favored one since you been here." Lorene sat up, planting both feet on the floor and glaring at Tricia. In an overly exaggerated Southern belle voice, she pretended to mimic her. *"Why, I'm from South Caruhliiiiina, I'm a day student in college, no less, and I have a lawyer fiancé, even though I have been throwing myself at another man. My momma wants me to give fancy garden parties and all."* Lorene flipped a piece of her hair upward, sticking her nose in the air. *"And I'm Hugh Carson's favorite because I'm his assistant."*

For a moment Tricia said nothing, then took a seat on the other worn sofa across from Lorene. She leaned forward, resting her elbows on her knees and looked down at her feet before looking at Lorene once again.

"That's what you really think? That's how you see me?"

"I think I was pretty clear."

Tricia dropped her head, shaking it to and fro, and laughing.

"What's so funny?"

"This whole crazy thing, that's what" Tricia made eye contact with her nemesis. "All this time, I've thought the same thing about you. That you thought you were God's gift to Arden Woode, because you were from just down the road somewhere, a true mountain girl, and you knew more about this area than anyone, and that you were practically running this place because you were the evening program director."

"I wanted the job you have!" Lorene sputtered. "I do know more about outdoor stuff than you, I'm sure."

"I simply took the job I was assigned. I didn't choose it." Tricia said, with quiet firmness. "But surely you know, Lorene – your evening programs have all been spirited and fun, and good – very good. And you have me about as wrong as possible."

"What do you mean?" Her tone was still guarded but softened.

"I'm the first person in my family to go to college. We are not wealthy by any means. We're as middle class as middle class can be. My father is no doctor or lawyer. And I'm not even sure my folks even like each other anymore, the way they fight. I admit – my mother wishes I were a debutante, but we're not one of those blue-blood families. Her aspirations for me are to marry into that part of society in which no one in my family has ever been a part of, including her. She does want me to marry the man that everyone thinks is my beau. But I don't love him." Tricia hesitated. "I'm crazy about someone that cares for me for all of the right reasons."

"The farmer, Ewan?" Lorene asked. "The guy that gave you a ride back to camp from Buford's Place?"

"Yes." Tricia smiled. "The farmer. Guess I should thank you for that now. He wants to be a physician, perhaps one day. It's not going to be easy to ruin my mother's dreams for me. She can be pretty formidable when upset. But I'm going to have to do just that. So, what's your real story? Since I've apparently figured you wrong, too."

Lorene shifted in her seat on the sofa, pulling her knees to her chest and wrapping both arms around them. Her demeanor was dismissive, sad, Tricia noted, watching her mood change.

"My old man is a lumberjack during the day. Drinks some at night, starts rambling about his sister, my aunt, the only one in the family to really make something of herself, by virtue of who she married. I think my folks embarrass them, as the only time we see that part of the family is around Christmas. A reminder of our lowly, poor white trash circumstances each year. Anyway, my father goes wherever he can to find work or any kind of odd job. My mother came undone after one of my brothers died with the Spanish flu. She'll never be the same. My sister married just to get out of the house. Me, I'm here for now. At least it's a little money. I hear the Inn may be looking for people."

"I'm sorry, Lorene. You've had it tough. But you're here, you are more than capable, and you are going to make it. I wish we had gotten off better at the start of camp. Might have saved us the agony of a prank or two." Tricia smiled at her.

"Yeah. About that. I gotta hand it to you. The floating dock thing was pretty genius."

"Truce?" Tricia asked, smiling. "Please say yes, so Hugh will stop giving me a rash of grief for not working things out with you."

"Funny, he's been giving me down the country about you, too."

"Guess the rest of camp will be happy, to know we've worked it out." Tricia added.

Smothered laughing came from behind the back door of the Ark to the lake side porch, and foreheads, then eyes begin to appear in the bottom of the windows across the waterfront side of the Ark.

"Word travels fast around here," Lorene muttered. "I guess by breakfast in the morning, we'll be the talk of the remainder of your Christmas in July event, huh?"

"No doubt, a Christmas miracle," Tricia laughed, then faced Lorene with a serious expression.

"Merry Christmas, Lorene. I hope this one is the best for you."

"Merry Christmas, Tricia." Lorene smiled back. "May there be blessings all around."

Clapping sounds wafted in through the now open door, and happy counselors slipped inside to join the revelry.

"Hallelujah," Nancy smiled. "Finally!"

"About damn time," Tavia added, grinning.

When Lorene left to resume her line duties and the other counselors returned to their cabins, Cyndi joined them. The group of four remained in the Ark to hear about Ewan Munslow's history and the evening before. Tricia took great care to answer their questions to be sure that all information was perceived with accuracy and compassion.

"I say Ewan is a really caring man, like his uncle obviously was," Nancy said, with firm resolve. "He is willing to help others let go of their loved ones and maybe – in their own time and way – come to an understanding of what salvation and forgiveness are all about."

"And he risked his life to help Priscilla," Tavia added.

"So, we have some critical pieces to this wild puzzle," Cyndi said. "We now know who the Sin Eater is and that he acted in self-defense and to save Priscilla, who still doesn't remember enough to help us. We believe that Otha saw it all and can confirm who the guilty party is."

"Except that Otha is not going to say a word to anyone because she's terrified." Nancy interjected.

"How about Ewan telling the sheriff everything? And maybe then Otha would feel like she could tell what she saw also." Tavia asked.

"In a perfect world, that would make good sense," Tricia said. "Except that Harvey Bryson's word is more likely to be believed by some than that of a sin eater, even if it is Ewan, or of a colored lady. And don't forget that what Priscilla can remember right now is more damning to Ewan than it is helpful. She remembers a dark, covered up man, and she remembers being scared. Ewan would most likely lose everything and so could Otha. Dammie and Mary would not get rid of her willingly, but the pressure from Laurel Valley folks could be big and perhaps affect the camp in many negative ways."

"What do we need at this point to help us?" Tavia asked.

"Proof from another source," Cyndi said, "or at least evidence of some kind that Harvey Bryson and Chester Graves are guilty of trying to harm Priscilla and likely the others. But why would they be trying to grab not only young women, but a boy, as well?"

"Ewan has a possible theory, after a conversation he had with Dr. Halsted. Really, it's the only thing that makes sense, as terrible as it is." Tricia offered. "Since the Laurel Valley Inn and a few other similar resort type places have been built by the Toxaway Company, this area is not so isolated anymore. Railroad lines and spur lines are now close to these parts, along with the advent of the automobile. More people, especially those of means that are foreigners, are now coming here or coming through here, or engaging in business here. In the big cities, Ewan says that young women, mostly those wanting to get away from their circumstances, or those who are of lesser means, have disappeared from ice cream parlors, train stations and such, even dance halls. They have been called the 'ante-rooms to hell'."

"Why are they being taken, does he think?" Nancy asked.

"For immoral purposes. Like forced prostitution. Legal brothels were on the decline, and in 1910, they enacted the White Slave Traffic Act, or Mann Act, that made it a federal crime to transport women for such. Although the law is also invoked to prevent black men from entering into relationships with white women, or vice versa, it's intent was to criminalize what we might be seeing here."

"But not all of the missing kids are white," Cyndi said, ""and one of them is also a young boy."

"I said the same thing." Tricia added. "Ewan says he thinks it's highly possible that Harvey and Chester Graves were enticed by the lure of big money and were willing to kidnap anyone that someone might want for all kinds of illicit purposes. It's slavery in whatever form they choose."

"Ew," Nancy exclaimed, as Tricia continued.

"Ewan thinks Harvey is using his lumber venture to front the illegal business he's involved in."

"Well, if that's true, then we still need some kind of proof or evidence that it's going on, don't we?" Tavia asked. "How in the world would we get that?"

Cyndi jumped to her feet and began shaking a finger at the others.

"I think I have an idea." She looked at each one of them. "A dance hall, you say, is one of the places that the women disappear from? A dance hall like Hannah's Barn maybe?"

"Yes, I suppose so," Tricia responded. "What are you thinking?"

"Hear me out. Harvey knows who all of you are, right? But he has never met me. And he likes women a lot, especially ones that flirt with him."

"What in the world are you talking about?" Tavia asked. "You aren't thinking about being the bait for this guy?"

"Not exactly. If I were dressed up to look like a woman of means – a woman who might be looking to procure some help for a business of some sort, and needed some warm bodies, I might could get him to open up to me."

"Aw, geez, I don't know, Cyndi!" Nancy was adamant. "That sounds kind of dangerous and risky. You been around Tricia too much."

"I agree with Baudette, our distinguished representative from Louisiana, on this one." Tricia grinned at her friend. "Risky, for sure. But I also think that it just might be our only option for now. Unless anyone has a better idea? If we could get Ewan to be present, and that shouldn't be hard since he plays his fiddle there a lot, we would have some help if things got out of hand."

"Okay, wait, hold up," Tavia said, pressing a hand in the air. "So, we need some evidence or proof, and if this is a way to get it, what else do we need?"

"I think I still need to try to talk with Otha, just to be sure of what she saw and that we have it figured right. Also, I would like to get Dr. Halsted to tell me or Ewan more about the process he was referencing that might help Priscilla recover her memory."

"We have to tell Dammie and Mary and Hugh what's going on." Nancy shook her head, a concerned and skeptical expression on her face. "This is getting more serious each day."

"I know, "Tricia said. "Okay, let's say we tell them tomorrow. What would likely happen? Would they shut down our plans with Cyndi, or no?"

For a few minutes, the group fell silent, each pondering the possibilities.

"How about we tell them a part of it, for now? We'd have to have their help and permission from Priscilla's parents for any interaction with Dr. Halsted, so we could tell them that she has begun to remember and wants help. But we can't betray either Ewan or Otha, and we would be doing that, if we told them anything more."

"You're saying for us to tell them about Priscilla for now, try to get some evidence, then we'd be in a better position to tell them more?" Tavia asked.

"Exactly." Cyndi responded. "That would buy us some time, which we don't have much of anyway, and at least we would be telling them a little something. Tricia, can you talk with Hugh tomorrow, since you are the one closest to him?"

"Yes, I think so. And Ewan will know when the next event is at Hannah's Barn. It's apparently pretty close to the Inn, but I guess we've never really paid much attention, since it's only open once a month and set back off the road a little."

"Okay, then we have a plan." Cyndi said. "Be thinking about how my part in all of this could best work. See if Hannah's is within walking distance of the Inn for me. We better get back to the cabins before it gets any later, Morning comes pretty early around here."

Laying in her bed, Tricia pulled the blankets up over her shoulders and settled into the soft warmth. Sleep would soon overtake her, but not before she had given thanks for the events of the past few days. They were getting closer to finding answers. As the soothing night sounds lulled her toward the realm of dreams, she felt a deepening contentment. She was happier than she had ever been here at Arden Woode.

Answers – and more challenges – were coming for her, too. Of that, she was certain.

CHAPTER NINETEEN

Sundays at Arden Woode were always more relaxed after breakfast and the outside chapel service. Everyone wore the requisite
white uniforms which added an air of spirituality and calm to the day.
After rest hour, the campers all enjoyed an afternoon of canoeing
and swimming in the chilly waters of Emerald Lake. Tricia sat on the
floating dock, the summer sun warming her back as she watched her
girls frolicking and splashing about.

"Good afternoon, Miss Grimball." Ewan Munslow called to her
from his own canoe as he glided toward camp from the Laurel Valley
Inn area. Tricia found herself blushing at the sight of him in just an
undershirt, the muscles in his bare arms working to paddle closer to
her. His dark hair brushed about his face as he pushed his hat back to
greet her, laid both oars inside the boat, and retrieved the gray work
shirt from beneath his feet. Before she could respond, her campers
had recognized the familiar man in the canoe and climbed up on the
dock beside her, waving and laughing.

"Hello, Ewan! Have you come to see Tricia?" Gaylen yelled, shaking her head of wet hair, while the other girls giggled beside her.

"Good day, ladies," Ewan tipped the brim of his hat. "I was merely out enjoying some leisure time. But seeing all of you and Tricia has made my day that much better. It looks like you are having fun."

"We are!" They shouted back to him, as Priscilla Parker climbed onto the dock and stood next to Natalie.

"This is our friend, Priscilla," Natalie said, putting an arm around Priscilla's shoulder. "She's not in our cabin, but we are good friends."

"Pleased to make your acquaintance, young lady." Ewan tipped his hat to Priscilla, then smiled at Tricia. "And how are you this sunny afternoon, Miss Grimball?"

"Very well, thank you."

"I've been well, too, actually. Dr. Halsted came to visit the farm at Laurel Valley, and we had another amiable conversation. Perhaps I can share it with you later."

"I would like that, yes," Tricia smiled back.

"Good. You ladies enjoy your swim. See you first of next week, then!"

She watched as Ewan maneuvered the canoe across the lake toward the Inn. All of the girls except Priscilla and Natalie jumped back into the pristine water.

"I know Dr. Halsted," Priscilla whispered to Tricia as Ewan paddled away. "He is a nice man." Tricia thought twice before responding to the young girl.

"Yes, he seems very kind. He helped me once with something while we were at the Fourth of July Celebration, but I don't know him well."

"Priscilla wants to talk with you, Tricia?" Natalie asked. "Can she do it now?"

"Of course, you can, sweet girl, any time. What's going on?"

"I have a secret," Priscilla said in the softest of whispers, squeezing out the water that dripped from her long blonde strands.

Tricia thought about the waifish appearance of the young girl when she'd first arrived there and how she had become more vibrant and confidant since coming to Arden Woode. She whispered back to her, affectionately tugging on a lock of the wet hair.

"You can tell me whatever you want, Priscilla, and I will do the best I can to help you, I promise." Priscilla looked down at her hands, then back up at Tricia.

"Someone tried to hurt me," she murmured. "But I don't remember it much. That's why I'm here at Arden Woode, so I can try to remember and not be scared."

"That took a lot of courage for you to share, didn't it? I remember hearing a little about what happened to an unnamed young girl around here. I admire you very much."

"Dr. Halsted, he is the one that helped me. Someone took me to his house and he and Mrs. Halsted took care of me until my folks could come to fetch me home."

"Who took you to his house?" Tricia asked, taking care to not press too hard.

"That's just it, I don't know. I think I remember a sweet, very strong smell. It's what I remember when I go under the water and I can't breathe. And I think there was a man, but he was covered all up with dark clothes and a hood. He was scary looking."

"This man, did he say anything to you?"

"No, I don't think so. I just remember him a little."

"Priscilla, I'm so sorry that such a terrible thing like this happened. But I'm very glad that Dr. Halsted helped you and that you are here, and that you trusted me and Natalie enough to tell us. You have made good progress and I bet that whenever you feel comfortable and ready, you might remember more."

"I want to remember, so they can catch the bad man that did it."

This was the perfect presentation of opportunity, if ever one existed. Priscilla asking for help was the best possible scenario.

"Doc Halsted told me that he helped a girl, but he never said it was you. He did say that he might know of a way to help recover memory and ease the fear that one would most surely have after experiencing what happened to you. Does that sound like something you might be interested in doing?"

"Maybe. I don't know. Would I have to have a shot or take medicine?"

"I can't think of a reason why you would, but I don't know for sure, either. With your permission, I could ask him. I don't know if he is back from a trip he had to make, but I could find out. It might take a week or so, would that be alright?"

"Okay, you can ask him. Could I talk with him, too?"

"Certainly, of course." Tricia smiled at her. "There is one thing, though. I think we would need to be sure that your parents would give permission, once you decide you want to do it."

"I think they would let me do it if it might help. My father wants to find the man that tried to hurt me. I want to remember, but I'm also scared to remember."

"That makes perfect sense to me, sweet girl. I tell you what. Let's take this one small step at a time, so that you feel safe and can make the best decision. I will find a way to talk with Dr. Halsted."

The young girl hugged Tricia before the two campers jumped back into the cool waters of Emerald Lake and swam toward the other campers.

Tricia sat for a few minutes more, watching the girls play, thinking about what to do next. Ewan or Hugh could likely make the connection with Dr. Halsted. The administrative staff here would have to be consulted also. Then, there was the matter of Otha Moses and getting her to talk, not to mention finding out more from Harvey Bryson. But the proverbial clock was ticking faster, now that their time at camp would be drawing to a close in a few short weeks. Tricia stretched her legs to brave the dive back into the mountain lake after the sun had thoroughly dried her bathing suit. Hugh was standing on the shore next to the lake with Hala, who was retrieving a ball tossed in the lake by exuberant campers. If she could catch him for a few brief minutes, it might be enough to get this process started sooner than she had imagined. Hugh waved as she approached him.

"Ah, hello there, Tricia. I see Priscilla Parker has indeed overcome her fear of going under water and has become a fast friend of your Natalie."

She shook the excess water off her body and disentangled a strand of the floral gook from the bottom of the lake – endearingly referred to by campers and staff alike as *gunga runga* -from around her ankle.

"Good afternoon, Hugh. Yes, I think progress there is being made, and I need to inform you about some of that, if you have a minute?"

"Sounds like a pipe conversation." He smiled, pulling out the treasured pipe for a quick smoke. "What's going on?"

"Well, for starters, Priscilla has confided in Natalie, and now me, about what happened to her."

"Has she, now?" Hugh looked only moderately surprised. "What has she shared?"

"She doesn't remember much, other than a strong, sweet smell, seeing a man all covered in black clothes, and waking up at Doc Halsted's. She wants to remember more. Actually, I think it's all rather confusing for her. She is scared to remember but wants to. She did say her father especially wants to know who hurt her."

"Don't blame him one bit. Understood on many levels. Anything else?"

"No, and she has not told anyone else, other than me and Natalie. Do you remember my mentioning that Dr. Halsted might be familiar with a process that could conceivably help her in recalling more details about what happened?"

"I do recall that, I believe."

"Natalie said that she liked the doctor and his wife, so I asked if she might be interested in that kind of help, provided it was approved by her parents, of course. Do you think it might be possible to speak with Dr. Halsted about this?"

Hugh stared out over Emerald Lake, taking in the swimmers and surrounding area before responding to her.

"You have really taken an interest in this whole situation with Priscilla and the local goings-on around here. Is there anything else I should know right now?"

Tricia felt sure she did not adequately hide the look of panic and surprise at Hugh's words. She was certain he could sense her discomfort, see through her conflicting feelings.

"Not right now, no. But I promise that my intentions are honorable, and that I would let you know immediately if there were anything that I should tell you."

"I have no doubt that you would," Hugh said, after a pause. "By the way, I hear that you and Lorene are to be commended for your laying aside of the big rivalry."

"You heard, huh? We had each other pegged wrong, I guess."

"It happens to the best of us. I have all confidence in you, Tricia."

"Does that mean you think it would be possible for us to speak with Dr. Halsted about this process, then perhaps with Priscilla's folks?"

"Let me discuss it with Dammie and Mary. I think it would be a lovely idea to have the good doctor here as our guest for dinner, perhaps. He might even agree to be our chapel guest and speak with our girls about his tenure at Johns Hopkins and the medical field. His wife, too, is quite knowledgeable. She was his surgical nurse at one time, you know. We could arrange for that, I would think, and find some time for us to talk with him."

"Thank you, Hugh." Tricia breathed a relieved sigh.

"I wonder if there might be some benefit in having Ewan Munslow attend with him?" Hugh flashed a smile at her. "Since I hear that he has an affinity for medicine, and rumor has it that the esteemed Dr. Halsted finds him to be a promising young man. We could even ask Ewan to play a hymn on his fiddle."

"Really?" Now Tricia made no attempt to hide her pleased reaction. "I would really like that. Thank you."

"I've found that even good character and intentions can sometimes use a helping hand. Always here, if you need anything."

"I won't forget, Hugh. I promise. I'd better go 'round up my girls and get us ready for dinner and campfire at the Council Ring. See you soon."

The evening meal of hearty stew and rice was filling, and the jovial chatter of young campers filled the dining hall with an air of the special camaraderie that was Arden Woode. Tricia studied Otha with care, trying to decide if the mood was right to approach her after dinner, before the campfire started. The day had gone well thus far. She waited until the last of the girls assigned to cleanup crew were gone.

"Otha, I need to talk with you. I need your help."

"You know 'ole Otha gonna help you any way I can. What can I do?" Tricia stepped closer to the woman and spoke with quiet confidence.

"When you first told me about what happened to Priscilla Parker, you said that all she remembered was a sack or something being put over her head, do you remember?"

"I reckon I recall that." Otha shook a freshly scrubbed soup ladle out of the wash pot and dried it with a dish towel.

"You know I want to help find out who did this, right? And you know I am your friend always and would always stand by you." Otha set the ladle down and stared at her.

"This here sounds serious."

"Otha, I believe you told me all this because you wanted someone else to know." Tricia softened her tone of voice before continuing. "I don't know any other way to say this, so I'm going to just say it. I think you somehow witnessed what happened to Priscilla and you are afraid to tell it."

"That's some foolishness there. Why you think that?" Otha bristled.

"Because according to Priscilla and Doc Halsted, she has never said that she remembered anything being put over her head at all. You are the only person who said that." Before Otha could speak, Tricia added, "And I know you to be the most caring soul on this earth and I think you risked reaching out to me so that you could help Priscilla but remain safe."

Otha stared at her for the longest time, arms crossed, lips set in defiance.

"Please, Otha, tell me. Let me help."

"No," she finally said, "No, it ain't me that saw what happened to that girl."

"Otha, please," Tricia pleaded. "You're the only one who has said anything like that."

"I said it ain't me!" Otha turned her back to Tricia, her shoulders trembling and voice shaking. Tricia stood in silence, not sure what to do next.

"I'm so sorry. I didn't mean to upset you. I want to help! I believe you are carrying this terrible secret and I understand why you are." The grief-stricken cook turned to face her once more.

"No, you don't!" The tears began to slide down her cheeks.

"Miss Otha, I would die before letting you get hurt! You trusted me, trust me now!"

"I said it ain't me." Otha paused, wringing her hands. She took a step toward Tricia, the pain in her eyes even more evident. "It's Samuel," she whispered.

"Sam? What do you mean?"

"He the one that seen it. Not me."

Tricia let a hand rest on Otha's shoulder. No wonder the venerable cook was scared to share what she knew. She was protecting her son.

"He was walking home that night from helping Mr. Zachary in the general store. My boy done seen it all. But ain't no one gonna ever know that. Not ever."

"So, now you know. Now what?" Otha looked at her with sad, tired eyes.

"I'm not sure," Tricia admitted. "But I tell you what I will never do – and that is let you or Samuel get hurt in any way. You believe me, don't you?"

"I believe you mean the best you can. But you can't stop people who would kill a decent Negro boy or woman over a no-count white man."

"My granddaddy would call that kind of man 'white trash'. Otha, you've trusted me so far. You are loved here. That means Samuel is loved here too. He's a good boy and you have raised him well. Just give me some time to think on all this. A lot has happened, and I believe that the missing people you have told me about are all connected to the attack on Priscilla, somehow. If we can figure this all out, there are a lot of people that would be grateful to you and Sam both."

"Maybe. But you see the world a lot sweeter than it is. It's different here in this place, people kind and helpful. But even here, the only girls that can come here are white girls. Even in this place, and I love it, and all my girls in it. But my niece can't come here, even if I could afford it."

"I know that's true right now," Tricia acknowledged, "but what kind of life will we all have if we are afraid to help each other? We can beat each other into submission, but the only way to stop ugliness is to cover it in light, with all the love and honesty we can. You have faith and I do, too. I know there are people who will help us. We have to act on that. You don't want Samuel or your niece to live in fear forever, do you?"

Otha stared at her for what seemed an eternity, wiping her face and hands with the stained apron around her waist.

"My husband died in Chicago. Went up there where his sister lived – my niece's mother – to find better work and a new home for us and to help her out when she took sick. Folks said things was better up there, since the black man and the Indians around here didn't have it so good. He died after a man attacked him. Said he was trying to rob a store but my Jeremiah ain't never done nothing like that. Not ever. He was a God-fearin' man. And they killed him."

Tricia wanted to say she was sorry but sensed that she should not interrupt. It was much the way she felt when her own mother or father, or Daniel Middleton, didn't hear her, or think she needed to be heard.

"You know them riots that been goin' on in the streets up there and other cities?"

"Red Summer, they are called because of the bloodshed? I know of them."

"Just the other day some colored kids drifted into a 'white only' swimming area. Same place, Chicago. Not the South. One of 'em was killed. Things ain't no different up there. People just hide it a little better underneath all that fancy education and culture. After my Jeremiah was killed, we just stayed here where we at least have friends and know who evil and who ain't."

"Otha, I know we can't change all that overnight, the ugliness that's been in humanity since the dawn of time. I don't know why people do the things they do, or why they try to hurt one another. I know there's good and bad in all of us and it seems like some just want to control others through fear. Maybe we can just make it so that Samuel and your niece, and Priscilla don't have to be afraid. Let me, Nancy, Cyndi, and Tavia have some time to see what we can find out to verify what you know. Maybe we can get the proof we need without you or Samuel ever having to be involved. What did Samuel see?"

Otha motioned Tricia to follow her into the deeper confines of the empty dining hall.

"Priscilla was walking home with her brothers. My Sam was walking home too, but from the road that run into the one they was on. It was getting dark and them boys left her behind, just to taunt her some, like chillun' do sometimes. Harvey Bryson and that Chester Graves was on horses with a wagon and come up on that poor girl. Chester done grabbed her first and held something over her mouth. Then Harvey, he come over there and put a burlap sack over her head.

Then he went back to the wagon for something. She was all limp like a ragdoll then, Samuel said. Out of nowhere, a man came walking, all covered up in a black robe and a hood, he come up on Chester and told him to leave her be. Chester, he done dropped Priscilla on the ground and attacked the man. Then the man stabbed him with a knife. 'Ole Chester laid there his own self, bleeding. When the man turned to face Harvey, that piece of trash took off in that wagon like the sorry coward he is. Left his own friend, and that poor girl, too."

"So, the man in the hood took Priscilla to Doc Halsted's?" Tricia asked.

"Picked her up, carried her to where his horse was and took off. Samuel was hiding in the woods. We didn't know til later that the man done took her to Doc Halsted's."

"Otha, was the hooded man the Sin Eater?"

"Yes. At least I think so. There's only one of them around here but there are one or two in nearby places, so I can't say for sure which one it is. But most likely the one around here."

"I promise you, Otha. You know we are going to do our best to figure this out and make it so that Harvey Bryson pays for what he did. Please, you have to trust me. What if we could convince the sheriff, would you agree to talk with him then?"

"No! I ain't puttin' Samuel in harm's way, no! Otha rubbed her forehead, tears emerging once more. "I can't risk anything happening to my boy."

"I understand, Otha. I do."

"Them missing kids – you really do think Harvey and Chester tried to take them?"

"I do think so, yes. Now, we have to prove it. Maybe we can get the Sin Eater to help us."

"A sin eater don't want nobody to know who he is. He the lowest of the low and he know that. He gonna stay safe, too. No self-respectin' sin eater gonna come out in the open."

"I know. Give me some time to think. I have to go now, or I'll be late for the camp- fire. Otha, you have my word and Cyndi, Nancy, and Tavia's, too. We are going to do everything to see this end well. Please, may I at least have your permission to talk with the head staff and then we can talk all together?"

"No," Otha gave a heavy sigh, her eyes welling up yet again, the soft tears meandering to her chin. "Not yet. But if you find some proof, then maybe."

"But we have to keep you all safe. That means Samuel and your niece, too." She grabbed both of Otha's weathered hands in hers. "Otha, please! You know that your babies could be in serious danger, and you, too, if Harvey ever found out any of this!"

"But he don't know it right now." Otha closed her eyes and folded her ebony hands, as if in prayer.

"We all love you! Rest assured, you and your family will have a home here forever, if we can find those missing kids and end this nightmare! I know it!"

"You be careful," Otha warned. "Harvey Bryson and his kind is just low life dangerous riff raff, underneath all his charming ways around women."

"I will, Otha. I promise." Tricia hugged the older woman as hard as she could before making her way out of the dining hall and down the steps toward Du Kum Inn. Nancy and her girls were waiting in front of her cabin.

"We thought you'd never get here," Nancy smiled. "All okay?"

"Yes, all good," Tricia said. "Let's head over to the Council Ring for some singing and fun!" The campers all skipped just ahead, happy for the evening activities. Tricia motioned for Nancy to lean in close.

"I know it all, Baudette. Everything. It wasn't Otha who saw what happened. It was Samuel. She's protecting her son. Harvey Bryson and Chester Graves are the ones that tried to take Priscilla. Otha said that the Sin Eater, who we now know is Ewan, is the one that saved her. But there are a couple in other villages not far away, so she's not sure which sin eater, exactly."

"Good lord," Nancy shook her head. "Now what?"

"I don't know," Tricia replied. "See if Cyndi or Tavia can meet in front of my cabin tonight. I have line duty, so I can't come down to the Ark. Or you could talk with them."

"This is crazy. You know Harvey Bryson would not hesitate to do something to any of us that tried to expose him, right?"

"Yeah, I know. This is becoming more dangerous by the minute. But we have to have real proof, or we have nothing, despite all we know."

"We are going to have to tell Hugh and them what's going on."

"Otha won't give me permission to talk with them. Or the sheriff. She's scared to death for her family. I gave my word that I would honor that and try to protect them. And I have to protect Ewan, too."

"Right now, they and Priscilla will be in the most danger, if Harvey gets wind of what we know! This is too big now, Tricia!"

"I know. I know it is. But I can't betray them. I can't say anything without their permission. If we could just find some proof, something! I'm not too keen on Cyndi's plan, either, but it really is all we have. Ewan can't come forward, as the Sin Eater. It would be his word against Harvey's, and you know people would be quick to judge him or turn on him. Otha won't help because of Samuel. We are in the craziest position ever. We know so much, and yet we have nothing."

"Then, I guess we really are stuck between the 'ole rock and a hard place," Nancy moaned. "It's Cyndi's plan or nothing."

CHAPTER TWENTY

"What are you doing in here?"

It was an honest question from Lorene Hogue, who maintained the items in the Castle for her evening programs, and she asked it without condescension, Tricia decided. She knew her unannounced presence here in the room where all of the dress-up accoutrements for skits were kept would look suspicious to Lorene.

"Hey, I didn't mean to intrude. I guess I should have found you first. I was just in the area and decided to stop while I was here. Cyndi is looking for a costume for something, but her schedule isn't as flexible as mine is, so I told her I would look. Can you help me?"

Lorene paused, regarding her with casual amenity, but Tricia could sense the underlying disbelief.

"What is it you're looking for exactly?"

"She needs a particular kind of outfit and look. A high-class woman of means, so nothing too cheap or old. It needs to really look

239

the part, so nothing funny or obviously out of place. It needs to look like the real thing."

Lorene was still, crossing her arms and regarding Tricia with an air of skepticism.

"You said we were friends now, right?"

"Yes, and I meant it." Tricia responded. "We are friends. I hope by the end of camp, we will be even better friends."

"You do, huh?" Lorene smiled, moving to stand closer to her and eyeing the open trunk of clothes. "Well, then you can start by telling me what you're really up to. Maybe I can help. Deal?"

Tricia was caught off guard by the accurate intuition coming from her once nemesis. Lorene was from somewhere in these mountains. She had lived in the area all of her life. If she could be trusted, her assistance might indeed prove helpful. Tricia took a deep breath. Maybe her own intuition was reinforcing the decision to include Lorene. Telling even part of the detailed saga required a level of trust that she had not been prepared to engage. She made a silent prayer that she was making the right choice by allowing Lorene into the fold.

"Okay. It's a deal." Tricia sank cross-legged to the wood floor and motioned for Lorene to sit beside her. "I know you know about Priscilla Parker and that someone attacked her. Are you familiar with other cases around here of missing people?"

"You mean the girl from Franklin and the young colored girl and her brother from the train in Dillsboro?" Lorene's eyebrows knit together with concern.

"Yes, those are the ones. There's reason to believe that they might be related, and that whoever took them may have been trying to take Priscilla, too."

"And you know all of this, how exactly?" Lorene asked.

"It's a long story. I'd be breaking confidences if I told you everything, at least for now. But I can tell you that me, Cyndi, Tavia, and Nancy are pretty sure we know what might be going on and why. Priscilla has been confiding in my Natalie and now me. Unfortunately, she doesn't remember enough to help us much, so we can't rely on her for anything concrete yet, but we think Doc Halsted might be able to help her with her memory. But time is running out for us because camp will be over before too long."

"What do you think is going on?' Lorene asked, shifting her weight as she stretched and crossed her legs at the ankles. "Pretty much everyone thinks those missing ones left on their own, at least at first. Except Priscilla, of course."

"We believe that all of the missing ones were taken against their will and for very nefarious purposes. Possibly forced prostitution or servitude. Even the boy."

Lorene stared at her for what seemed like several seconds. She looked out of the attic window in the Castle at the green treetops against the sea of blue sky.

"How do you think they are being taken?"

"We think possibly through one of the lumber camps around here. Since you said your father had a lumber connection, do you know anything about the lumber camps or mills or businesses that operate near here?"

"I can tell you what I know of the history." Lorene responded.

"Used to be that the timber industry up North was quite productive. Before the Civil War, that is. When the Toxaway builders and wealthy industrialists began to both work and play in North Carolina, they recognized the huge supply and variety of virgin timber we have. Lots of soft and hard wood trees from which to choose." She stopped to tug at her bloomers and continued.

"At first, there wasn't much big commercial logging stuff going on and the transportation of lumber was limited to what oxen or horses could pull. A lot of small lumber companies have come and gone because they couldn't adequately transport the logs on the Tuck or without the spur lines."

"I think I've heard Hugh say something about a dam breaking on the river a good while back and that logs on the river presented danger to both the men and the land." Tricia said.

"Yes. But now, the Blackwood Lumber Company has bought up a sizable amount of land here in Jackson County and they are building a sawmill at East LaPorte. It's on the banks of the Tuckaseegee River, and there are many creeks and tributaries around to float the logs a short distance from the lumber camps to the main sawmill or a spur line. Blackwood will be the only real mill town here and it will be good for the area. My father says that employees will be paid well, and they will even have a church, a school, and a general store, and housing too. The biggest thing is that the company is smart enough to construct a small spur line railroad, runs maybe twelve miles or so, I guess, to move the logs in a way that other companies could not. They will allow transportation for people, too, and have picnics, play baseball, and stuff like that. The students from Cullowhee Normal and Industrial School will be able to come there, too."

"So, there are mostly just logging camps in the area for now? Just the ones that can transport logs by horse and oxen?"

"That's it. Mostly privately owned by either a local or one of those industrialists. My old man says he's not sure which is worse, the government's allowing lots of timber to be cut or the locals not knowing how much their land is really worth and selling it cheap. He thinks Blackwood coming here may be a good thing and he hopes to work for them as a timber cruiser."

"What's that?" Tricia asked.

"It's someone who can scout the land, the hills, and find the most promising areas and trees to cut. But aside from all that, you still haven't told me why you think a lumber camp is involved in the movement of the missing people."

"Well, we're not totally sure how, but we know that one of the locals runs a lumber encampment somewhere not too far from here, and is likely involved in the attacks, and that he and his friend – the dead man, Chester Graves – were involved in trying to take Priscilla. I'm not at liberty just yet to tell you how I know that. But I hope I can tell you more soon."

Lorene stood and moved to the window that overlooked a large part of Arden Woode. Leaning against the wooden wall, she rested her elbows on the windowsill and propped her chin on folded fingers, staring across the expanse of the camp.

"Okay, so I'm guessing this local fellow is the one that you think Cyndi is going to somehow trick into talking by pretending to be someone of substantial means?"

"I know it sounds crazy," Tricia mused, "but it's all we've got right now. We're hoping that she can trick him into believing that she needs some young girls and maybe boys for some kind of business endeavor. We need evidence or proof that he is involved so we can go to the sheriff with more than just a hunch."

"But you have more than a hunch, or you wouldn't be doing this, right?"

"Yes. We know for sure who, and we think we know why. We just can't connect the pieces as to how exactly. And the ones who have confided their secrets will not risk coming forward, with good reason."

"You have to be talking about Harvey Bryson." Lorene said, her voice devoid of emotion. "He's from my hometown and his father's family are descendants of the town's namesake.

"You know him, then?" Tricia asked. "Do you know where his lumber camp is?"

"I know where his main operation is. He's a pompous bag of hot air most of the time. I must say, you've come to the right person for help, though." She turned from the window to face Tricia.

"How's that?" Tricia asked.

"Because Harvey Bryson is my cousin."

Lorene saw the stunned expression on the face of her once enemy and added, "Not to worry, I've never liked him. His father, the judge, is my uncle. He's married to my father's sister. The ones we see at Christmas time, remember?"

"The ones that remind you of what you don't have?"

"The very ones. My uncle is a nice man. Wife's a bit pretentious, which irks the fire out of my old man, because he knows she's putting on airs she never had. They spoiled Harvey beyond rotten, though. He's out for himself only."

"You still want to help us, knowing it's your cousin?"

"If he's involved in something this evil, then yes. You know for a fact that it's him?"

"I'm so sorry, Lorene. I do know that much, for sure. When I can share the rest, I promise I will"

"Then that's all I need to know. Cyndi's tall and shapely, and she's pretty. Harvey will definitely like her. Let's see what we can find in the costumes. Maybe we can just add items to something she already has, like a black skirt, maybe?"

"Yes, I have an idea about what she has, even a little bit of jewelry. None of us brought really nice or dressy things here to camp, so we are at a bit of a loss."

"You're going to need some information about him. We will need a solid plan. And a whole lot of good fortune, too." Lorene smiled and brushed the light brown hair from her face. "Maybe the Wampus Cat will kiss us all when this is over."

CHAPTER TWENTY-ONE

The week had been routine thus far for all at Arden Woode, with campers and staff alike enjoying the remainder of their idyllic summer and the activities that had come to define the fun-filled and challenging days of camp. Tricia stretched her legs the length of her cot and flexed the cramped fingers in her right hand. These would be the final letters home to the parents of each of her campers, and she wanted to be sure they reflected all of the growth and accomplishments of each of her Du Kum Inn girls, who were also busy writing their own letters home.

Doc Halsted's visit would be in lieu of an evening program toward the end of the week, to accommodate his schedule, and Otha was preparing a sumptuous camp dinner especially for the event. Ewan had also spoken with the good doctor, as had Hugh, about the possible use of the hypnosis process, which would be explained in detail to Tricia and administrative staff before the evening meal. He had made a point to come by the camp as often as time and tasks would allow and had paddled across the lake at night to spend even an hour with Tricia out on the dock after all were asleep.

An unexpected soft rap on the cabin door interrupted her musings. She looked up to see Lorene outside with Cyndi and Nancy. Tavia was missing, probably had line duty. All motioned for her to come outside.

"Don't worry, Tricia, we will be quiet," Gaylen smiled. "May we play cards or just talk after we're done with our letters?"

"Yes, thank you girls. I'm right outside the cabin by the boats, if you need me."

She tied her hair in a scarf before exiting the cabin, then found Lorene and Cyndi whispering, deep in conversation about the upcoming Friday night at Hannah's Barn.

"Now that we have my outfit and the details almost together, we thought we'd better tie up the loose ends," Cyndi explained. "We've worked it out so that you, me, Lorene, Tavia, and Nancy have that night off, too."

"We can go across the lake to the Laurel Valley Inn in the canoes." Lorene said. "That's the simplest way without having to saddle up horses or try to get the camp carriage. Cyndi can have her hair and cosmetics done mostly before we get in the boats. We should only need two canoes. Once there, you and Nancy can walk across the road to Hannah's and check things out. See if Harvey is there. Tavia and I can help Cyndi before we come over, and she will wait a few minutes before making her entrance. Of course, we will not acknowledge her in any way, but can see if Harvey takes the bait. If he doesn't, she and I will make it a point to run into each other while there and she will use my name to make contact with him, if we have to force the issue. Then, we let it all play out, hopefully as planned."

"Once I have what I need, I will make sure one of you sees me when I leave to go back to the Inn. I'll change clothes and meet you at the canoes. You wait a little bit before you leave Hannah's, too, so it doesn't look suspicious." Cyndi said.

"Ewan says he will be there, also, playing his fiddle and such, if anything goes awry, he can help, as could his musician friends, if needed." Tricia said. "Let's pray that doesn't happen," she added. "Once we get what we need, we go to Dammie, Mary, and Hugh, who will, I'm sure, help us find the sheriff around here."

"Playing devil's advocate here," Cyndi raised a hand. "What happens if I don't get anything we can use from Harvey? Then, what?"

All were quiet until Tricia spoke up.

"I've thought about that," she said. "Then we have to play the hand we've got and lean on him some."

"What do you mean, Grimball?" Nancy spoke up, the concern mounting in her voice. "Lean on him, like how? That sounds like a mob boss in Chicago or something."

"I say we let Cyndi tell him she thinks he's involved in Priscilla's attack and the others, too, and that there was a witness. She can make the witness go away if he agrees to help her find the workers she's going to pretend to need."

"What? Tricia, you can't be serious!" That's way too dangerous for Cyndi!" Nancy was adamant. "All kinds of things could go wrong."

"Okay, wait, hold up." Cyndi interjected. "Harvey doesn't know who I am, and I will be using a deliberately fake name and background, so he won't find me at the Laurel Valley Inn or anywhere else, even if he looks. Ewan and other men will be there in case Harvey decides to behave in any ungentlemanly manner."

"Oh, he's no gentleman, for sure," Lorene piped up, "but I think Cyndi's got a point. If we walk away with nothing, then nothing is what we will have. At least, this way, we force his hand a little. I can tell you that he's all about easy money. And pretty women who he thinks might have money or access to money."

"So, if we get lucky, and Harvey bites on all this, and agrees to help Cyndi, then what?" Nancy asked, her eyes wide. "What will we do then?"

"I tell him to meet me the next night or two at the Inn for a drink and to collect half the money for what I want, and that we can discuss all the terms there." Cyndi said. "And of course, the sheriff and anyone else that needs to be waiting, will be. What other choice do we have, if we want to force anything to happen? Even if he doesn't cooperate, it would force him to make a move of some sort to cover his tracks and the sheriff can choose to investigate him or no."

"Remember," Tricia said, "we don't yet have permission to share the name of the witness, nor anyone else that was there the night of Priscilla's attack. So, we still keep everyone safe, but try to push Harvey enough to have him act. He still will think that Priscilla knows nothing, and we will all be going home, so we won't be around here after that. Except for Ewan, with whom I will remain in contact. If that happens, we will just have to let it all go or I will figure something out with Ewan's help maybe."

"I don't know," Nancy said. "I mean, it sounds good in theory, but holy geez, so much could go wrong. Harvey Bryson is a bad man – sorry, Lorene – and he isn't one to be trifled with, even as much of a cad as he is. He's the kind that will do away with his mistakes if he can."

"Nan, I think I can handle it," Cyndi laughed. "I mean, I'd like to try. I don't think he's as smart as he is greedy. He's probably just a stooge for somebody bigger anyway. If we can help find the missing, it's worth the risk, isn't it? We'll be careful and safe. I say we go for it. I don't have to play that card unless there's no other choice."

"One thing we have to do, as soon as we have anything we can use, is to tell Dammie, Mary, and Hugh. We've managed to keep it all under wraps for a good while, but I know we can't much longer. Hugh already suspects we are up to something, but he hasn't pushed me on it. At least not yet. Baudette, here, has pushed me on it," Tricia smiled at Nancy, giving her shoulder a gentle shove. "And she's right. We have to tell them and soon."

"If we all live that long, Grimball." Nancy shot back. "They may yet find our bodies somewhere down the Chattooga."

"No," Lorene said, shaking her head. "I'm afraid if we ever get caught, whoever Harvey is dealing with up the food chain from him will see to it that we are never found."

For a moment, no one spoke. Tricia put one hand on Nancy's shoulder and another on Cyndi's, next to her, and tried to smile.

"Then we have to be sure. We just can't fail. Let's go get ready for Doc Halsted. We can catch up again tonight after Taps, those of us that can."

Dr. Halsted and his wife, Caroline, appeared relaxed and jovial in their exchanges with the Arden Woode campers and staff throughout their tour of the new camp for girls. Mrs. Halsted in particular expressed admiration for the skills the young girls were learning, the love of the land and mountain culture that was evident in every aspect of camp living and daily routines.

"I should like to speak with the nurse here, if there is time," she asked of Dammie. "You know, I was a nurse. It was how I met Dr. Halsted."

Hugh smiled at Tricia, nodding his head. That was her cue to bring Priscilla Parker to escort the doctor's wife to the infirmary. While there, Mrs. Halsted, who was a fair assessor of amenability to prescribed treatment, would spend several minutes chatting with Priscilla about her camp experiences and willingness to participate fully in the procedure of hypnosis.

In the meanwhile, Arden Woode administration, along with Ewan and Tricia, would move to the dining hall to discuss the nuances of such treatment, as it pertained to appropriateness for Priscilla's case. Once seated at a table in the rustic building that overlooked Emerald Lake, Dr. Halsted sipped on a cup of hot tea and gestured to the small gathering.

"I should give you a bit of history with this most intriguing process, and my own experiences with it," the doctor began. Ewan smiled and leaned against Tricia's shoulder, his clean, warm scent was intoxicating, as he whispered in her ear.

"He can be a bit verbose, especially when talking about medicine, but we will try to keep him on topic and apprised of the time before dinner."

Tricia returned his smile with affection, as Dr. Halsted expounded on his knowledge of the subject at hand.

"In current medical circles, the process is referred to as 'fixed focus hypnosis induction,' as any object can be used as a facilitating object of focus. As early as the mid 1700s to about 1815, Franz Mesmer believed that iron would manipulate magnetic fluids in the body – animal magnetism, if you will – and this became the basis for what was known as 'Mesmerism'. Mesmer was also quite the showman, garbed in purple robes and silver slippers, with an iron rod, or wand, as the article of fixed focus. He even sat participants in baguets made of iron, that held iron rods in the water. Using this method, he conducted mass sessions, or seances, as the French referred to them. Even before the fascinating Mr. Mesmer, Fr. Maximilian Hell – interestingly enough that was his real name, attempted to exorcise demons using an iron cross. Spiritualism and such, was all the rage of course."

"The procedure used by Mr. Mesmer – is that the one used still?" Tricia asked.

"Oh, dear, no," Dr. Halsted adjusted his spectacles. "James Esdaile and James Simpson, both Scottish physicians and contemporaries, did a great deal of work and experimentation with anesthesia and such for pain relief, with ether and chloroform, even experimenting on themselves. They eventually, in the early to mid 1800s, performed surgeries using the process of hypnosis as the only means of anesthesia. Why, up to that point, pain relief was done frequently by only consuming alcohol and biting on a leather strap. It took one more Scottish physician, James Braid, who believed that the process had nothing to do with the charisma, gaze, or magnetism of an element or the person conducting the hypnosis. He believed that all it needed to be effective was the fixity of vision on an object of concentration. A true and accurate psycho-physiological phenomenon. He even was successful in auto, or self- hypnosis."

"Doctor, what exactly was your involvement while in Europe?" Ewan pressed with a gentle nudging for specifics.

"Ah, yes," the esteemed physician smiled. "I had the good fortune to spend time in Europe from 1878 to 1880, and again in 1885. During that time, Ambroise-August Liebeault and John Milne Bramwell, who were greatly influenced by Dr. Braid, spent time at the renowned Nancy School of Hypnosis in France. I was able to learn from the masters."

"If I might clarify for us non-medical folks," Hugh asked, "you believe that by having Priscilla engage in this procedure where she concentrates on an object, that you can assist her in accessing accurate memory of the night in question?"

"Precisely," Dr. Halsted smiled. "It is not magic at all, but access into the emotional part of the brain where experiences are internalized and more accurately recorded."

"And you can do this without putting words in her mouth?" Hugh asked. "Her recollections will truly be her real memory of the actual event?"

"Indeed, yes." Dr. Halsted smiled. "I believe it is not only possible, but likely, given that I proceed with the required professional due diligence. The next step will be obtaining the informed consent of both Priscilla and that of her family."

"I want to do it, Dr. Halsted. Please." Priscilla Parker stood in the entrance to the dining hall, holding the hand of Mrs. Halsted. "I don't want to be afraid of what I can't remember." She smiled at the small assembly. "Being here at Arden Woode has made me stronger in lots of ways. I'm not afraid anymore to face whatever happened to me that night."

Dammie rose from her chair to embrace the young camper.

"Then, it's settled. We will talk with all of the Parker family about this possibility. In the meanwhile, I think that for Priscilla's safety, and to keep camp life as normal as possible, this information should stay under wraps at least for the time being. If everyone agrees, I think it's time to get ready for dinner and for our exciting presentation from Dr. and Mrs. Halsted."

As the group stood to prepare for the evening meal, Dr. Halsted put a hand atop Ewan's shoulder and motioned for the attention from all.

"Before it slips my mind, I would like to announce that I have some very good news for this young man." He beamed at Ewan. "Johns Hopkins has agreed to accept Mr. Munslow into the medical program there, under my supervision."

Surprised and delighted congratulations were offered by all. Tricia felt the knot in her throat grow as she thought of being away from him, then fought back the immense disappointment in her initial reaction. Afterall, this was a most fortuitous opportunity, and Ewan deserved as much good in his life as he could find. Tricia reached to embrace him, trying to stir up an appropriate amount of excitement for the man that she had grown to love more than anyone. Sadness at the prospect of both leaving Arden Woode and being apart from Ewan was almost more than she could bear. The remainder of the evening proved difficult to endure.

"What's eating you, Grimball?" Nancy would ask, noting the quiet demeanor of her friend during the evening program presentation. "Somebody take the salt out of your grits?"

"Yes," she whispered back. "Dr. Halsted has made it possible for Ewan to continue his schooling way up north at Johns Hopkins."

"Wait, that's what you wanted, isn't it?" Nancy looked confused.

"Yes, it is. I mean it was. I'll be even further away from him now. I know I should be happy, and I am for him, because he is so deserving of the chance. But that was all before I fell in love with him. Now, the thought of possibly of a life without him is hard to imagine."

"Okay, hold up here. You know that, if this is meant to be, it will, right?"

Tricia smiled. This was what she loved about Nancy. Always the faithful optimist, the finder of the silver linings in life.

"Yeah, I know. Ewan asked me to meet him out on the dock later tonight, so I guess we will have to talk about it."

"Then tell him how you feel. If it's real between you two – and I think it is – it will all fall into place, and you will figure out how to navigate the distance."

"Thanks, Nan," she whispered, already counting the minutes until she was with him.

The moon hovered over Bald Rock Mountain like a sentinel, casting an ethereal light over Emerald Lake and the dock where Tricia sat waiting. The silhouette of Ewan gliding across the slick waters to spend time with her still brought a warm smile to her face. But the ache in her heart was growing with each hour that brought the end of camp closer and the distance between her and Ewan, further. So many evenings after her girls slept, she had spent with him, discussing everything from the political issues of the year to books, to their deepest beliefs and questions.

There were times when he had held her close, with no words spoken between them, and yet the moments were filled with the knowing that this was more than enough. His kisses awakened her heart, made her feel that she could never be too close to him. One of the many things she loved was the honesty they had cultivated with great care. Tonight, she would have to tell him how much she would miss him and the depth of her feelings for him.

"Good evening, *mo mhuirnín*," Ewan whispered, referencing the recently bestowed Irish endearment for *my sweetheart*.

Tricia tried to speak but was surprised at the unsettling emotion that threatened to erupt. Feeling the struggle intensify, she could no longer hide the tears that rose in her eyes.

"What is this?" Ewan placed sturdy hands on her shoulders, then gently lifted her chin with a finger. "Have I done something to displease you?"

"No," she stammered, looking into the frowning gray eyes. "No, of course not." She paused, her lower lip quivering. At least now he would know how much she cared for him. "It's just that, when Dr. Halsted announced the news about your going to Johns Hopkins, I was so happy for you." She stopped to gather composure. "But I found myself beyond sad that you would be so far away. It is selfish,

I know, to feel this way, when this is everything you've wanted and such a tremendous opportunity. I've come to care for you more than I thought possible. I got caught up in my own feelings of sadness at being away from you. I'm sorry. You know I am so happy that you have this chance to follow your passion."

Ewan pulled her close, wrapping her body in both arms, and tucking a strand of long brown hair behind an ear so that his lips and breath, warm and sensual, brushed across her earlobe as he whispered.

"I'm the one that's sorry. I wish I'd known that he was going to make that announcement. I wanted to be the first to tell you." He held her at arm's length, the steel colored eyes searching hers. "Did you know that the first time I heard your name, I thought it sounded like the wind, rustling through the treetops? Triciaaaaa," he whispered, waving a hand in the air. "It only enhanced your beauty and my attraction to you. I have been quite enamored with you from the moment I saw you that night at the home of Chester Graves, when you had no idea who I was."

Tricia smiled through the tears, feeling his hands slide the length of her arms until he held her hands in his.

"You've heard me talk about my faith, of creating a rule of life, so that my own life is lived more purposefully and joyfully. Part of that rule involves honest care in my relationships with others, and especially now with you." He squeezed her hands. "Tricia, next to being dedicated to trying to live my life as God would have me do, you have become the most important person to me. I've seen childbirth in all of its miraculous and messy glory and know that the process is a metaphor for much in this world, from intense agony to boundless joy along the way." He paused, his eyes searching hers, his gaze burning. "Humankind, even countries, go through such pains of birth, of growth. So do relationships." Ewan held her close once more.

"What I'm trying to say, is that I have come to care for you, to love and cherish you more than I ever thought possible. I know our lives could take many directions. But I know that I can also no longer imagine a life without you. I love you, and I want to love you in every way that a man can love a woman, and I want you to know it every single day. The thought of growing old with you, of sharing this life, is what I want more than anything else. When I draw my last breath, I can think of no greater sweetness to behold than to see your eyes looking into mine, and to know that I loved you well."

Ewan dropped to one knee, still holding her hands.

"I can only promise to love you beyond measure. I'm asking you to marry me, Tricia Grimball, to be my wife and partner in this one life we have here on this earth. Go with me to Baltimore and follow your dream to write, or teach, or anything else. And if we are blessed with children, they will have parents that will raise them together."

Tricia knelt beside him, grasping his hands to steady her descent. Never had she been more certain of anything than she was of this monumental decision.

"In all of my imagination, I could never love a man more than I love you, Ewan Munslow. Yes. Yes, I will marry you and spend the rest of my life loving you."

"Yes? You will marry me?" Ewan's smile was grand enough to compete with the glistening moonshine. Reaching into his pocket, he retrieved the most uniquely beautiful silver ring that Tricia had ever seen.

"My father had this made in Ireland for my mother. It is yours to wear as you like. If you would prefer to choose another, we can do that also when we have access to such."

Tricia held her hand out for him to place the ring on her finger.

"This ring is perfect," she breathed, running a finger over the mine, or cushion cut diamond in the Celtic setting. "That it was your mother's only makes it more precious to me."

"We have many decisions to make and much to do to prepare. I want to do right by you and your family and ask for your father's blessing. I know this is not what they expected for you."

"Well," Tricia smiled at him. "Someone once told me that I could not spend my life always trying to please others, or I would never know my own path. You are my heart. There is no other."

"The Irish have a word for that. *Anamkara. Soul mate.* And you are mine."

"What a lovely sounding word, *anamkara.* I would love to see your Ireland, your heritage, and perhaps even where your Uncle Richard is buried in England."

"Then we will go. There is one more thing. I have to decide about the ultimate fate of the Sin Eater, and how to proceed with all that is involved there."

"I know you do," Tricia held his hand. We will figure it all out very soon, I hope. If all goes well, Doc Halsted will help Priscilla to recover her memory, we will find those missing souls, and let the Sin Eater belong to the ages, with the dignity that he deserves for loving others."

Under the cover of the chilly mountain dark, the eyes of The Wolf narrowed as he once again watched the couple now embracing on the dock in the shadow of moonlight. This changed everything. Getting rid of Ewan Munslow would take some coordination but should be easy enough. He was sure the girl would fetch more than a sizeable amount of money.

CHAPTER TWENTY-TWO

Friday night had finally arrived amid the preparations for the final week of camp. This would be the last night off that Tricia and her friends would have together, and it was planned and discussed with great attention to detail, within the confines of the Ark. At rest hour, Tricia had read to her girls from Aesop's Fables, a tradition they had started at either the noonday quiet time or just before lights out. She gave them hugs and reminded them that she would return in time for breakfast the following morning.

As planned, the counselors met at the canoes as the rest of Arden Woode had moved toward the Castle for an evening program of skits that had been prepared by the camp administration. All agreed that Cyndi looked the part of a somewhat older, sophisticated lady, with her dark, thick hair piled intricately atop her head and secured with a stylish hairpin. Her lips were a darker shade of pink, and her nails had been buffed with an emery board and painted pink with the new nail paint they had procured from Caroline Halsted.

Her black skirt, fitted at the waist and paired with a white silk blouse with pink embroidery at the wide, round neckline, was accentuated by a short-waisted black wrap jacket with ties that were secured by a silver mother-of-pearl brooch and petite pearl earrings. Her gray top shoes were carried, so as not to be sullied in the dirt or mud. Only the hiking shoes were out of place, for now, but Cyndi would leave them in the boat when they arrived on the shoreline of the Laurel Valley Inn.

Tricia and Nancy, garbed in their camp uniform attire, went ahead of the others, thankful for the calm, glassy waters on this particular evening that rendered the trip across the lake not only faster, but also more smoothly and quiet, as well. When they rounded the bend in the curve of the lake, Tavia, Lorene, and Cyndi would begin the ride over, so that the parties would not be seen together.

"I don't mind saying, I sent up a few extra prayers for tonight, just in case," Nancy said. "I'm really nervous about this, even though Lorene and Cyndi are convinced that it's all going to work out."

"I'm trying not to think any more about what could go wrong," Tricia responded. "This has to work. It just has to. It's all we have."

"At least we can certainly say we found our adventure, right?" Nancy tried to smile.

"Definitely right about that, for sure. I know Hugh knows we are up to something. He commented earlier about how great it was that we had worked our last night off so that Lorene could join us. But he sounded a little suspicious. No turning back now."

Upon arrival at the Laurel Valley Inn, they docked the canoe and climbed ashore. A handful of resort guests were playing croquet, while a sprinkling of men and women in their fashionable garb sipped cool summer beverages on the great stone verandah. Ripples of laughter wafted down to the grounds below as the girls made their way across the grounds of the Inn and found the path that would take them to Hannah's Barn, just across the dirt road. They could hear the sound of merriment and the strumming of banjos and fiddles in the soft twilight that deepened to shades of purple behind the western tree-tops. No rain was in sight; the evening temperatures, near perfect. A few carriages and horse drawn wagons dotted the outside area of the white barn-like board and batten building. Overall-clad men and gingham-frocked women made their way inside while two or three couples who had wandered over from the inn crossed the lantern-lit walkway to the entrance of the weathered building. Children meandered among the adults, laughing and playing with one another. Tricia was reminded of the occasional festive church covered-dish gatherings back home. She wondered what it would be like to see her folks dancing, relaxed among such an odd but delightful pairing of mountain folk and genteel guests from the inn.

Inside Hannah's Barn, wooden benches and a scattering of chairs dotted the perimeter, with large solid tables at one end, while the worn wooden floor provided an expansive dance area. A simple raised stage opposite the tables held the musicians, consisting of fiddlers, banjo players, a piano, an old drum set, an upright bass, and guitars. Tricia recalled that Ewan had told her all of the musicians were either self-taught or had learned their craft from generations of mountain dwellers. At the thought of Ewan, Tricia looked around the room for him.

"He must not be here yet," she said to Nancy. "Must've gotten tied up at the Inn or the farm."

"But look who is here, over there already, galivanting about with some unsuspecting gal." Nancy nodded her head toward a corner of the room where Harvey Bryson was engaged in exaggerated gesture as he positioned himself close to a rather innocent looking girl. "No doubt there's lots of tall tales being told. Poor girl."

Tricia could tell by the way his gaze darted about the room and the preening way in which he positioned himself, that Harvey Bryson was far from attached to any one female in the place. Like a seasoned hunter, he was always on the prowl for the most available and best game.

"Over there," Nancy whispered, motioning with her eyes toward the door. "Lorene and Tavia are here."

The girls waved as they made their way over to Tricia and Nancy. Tavia glanced around the room, immediately spotting Harvey.

"I see that he's here, at least. Who is that with him?"

"He's been flirting with her since we've been here," Tricia said, "but I'm pretty sure she's not with him. That man that just walked up to him, I have no idea who he is. Looks kind of shady with that black hat and hair. His eyes just look mean."

"I know who he is," Lorene offered. "That's Dan Wolf. He's one of the remaining native Cherokee in the area and works for Harvey. His full name is Danuwoa. It means, 'warrior'. He's got a reputation for being as slick as Harvey, too. There aren't many of the Indians left in this area, but the ones that are still here are salt-of-the-earth people that would help anybody. Don't judge them by this one."

Tricia watched as Dan Wolf whispered something to Harvey. Both men smiled and laughed, clapping each other on the back. Harvey grabbed the girl by the hand, guiding her to the floor for a square dance. The Arden Woode girls watched in amusement as adults and children alike swirled and stomped to the directions of the caller and the rhythmic music. Even those on the sidelines clapped and tapped their feet. When the dance was over, the musicians stopped for a needed break. One of them stopped Tricia to say that Ewan had indeed sent word that he was held up on the farm but would get there as soon as he could.

Given a gentle nudge from Nancy, Tricia looked up in time to see Cyndi Turner make her entrance. Tall and stately, she appeared elegant and fashionable, easily passing for a guest at the Laurel Valley Inn and drawing the attention of many a male patron. Tricia grinned at her faux detached demeanor, watching as she intentionally made her way across the room via a path that directly crossed Harvey Bryson. His eyes followed her all the way to an empty table she chose that was close to a corner of the building. As if to add an exclamation point to the *femme fatale* persona she had manufactured, her careful and deliberate motion in crossing those long legs at the knee only added to her allure.

"She's perfect for this," Tavia whispered. "Rat's ass, Cyndi!"

Laughter from their table also drew the attention of Harvey, who recognized Lorene and made his way toward them.

"If it isn't the camp counselors from Arden Woode." He gave them a lazy smile. "You off duty tonight, Cousin?"

"Yes, we are," Lorene said, not smiling. "Just enjoying being out and about for an evening away from camp."

"This must be quite the experience for you. How does it feel to be making a little money and getting away from home? I guess the family will be glad to get some monetary help from you."

No one said a word. The expression on Lorene's face soured to a blend of embarrassment and anger. Before Tricia could take up for her, Tavia jumped into the fray with verbal guns blazing. The group of girls smiled at each other. Tavia was going to take him down and would cut him to ribbons if he made another wrong move.

"Why, Harvey, what an odd thing to say to a lady. Where are those gentlemanly ways you were bragging on, not too far back?" Tavia's eyebrows rose as she confronted him.

"My pardon, ladies, no harm intended. Lorene, here, is my kin. I'm sure she appreciates my deep concern for her welfare, always. You all have a good evening. Perhaps a dance or two later."

They watched as Harvey moved away, once again eyeing Cyndi as she sat in casual observance of all in Hannah's Barn.

"What an absolute and pompous jackass!" Tavia shook her head. "Lorene, no wonder you don't care for him. I'd love to be able to stomp his behind!"

Lorene watched as Harvey procured two glasses of sweet iced tea and moved toward Cyndi. A slow grin spread across her face.

"If he bites on this, it will be better than anything I could do to him. It's showtime, I do believe."

Harvey set a glass of tea in front of Cyndi, who regarded him with aloof curiosity.

"What's a pretty lady like yourself doing here without the finest of gentlemen to escort you?"

She crossed her arms, giving him a thorough perusal.

"My husband is otherwise engaged in a business transaction at The Laurel Valley Inn. I was bored and decided to look for some amusement. He's older and amusement is not a big part of his repertoire." She paused, flashing an inviting smile at him. "Are you in the amusement business?"

Harvey seated himself across from her, not waiting for a formal invitation.

"I could be. My business is lumber, but I do love amusement."

"Lumber business. I hear it is good around here. With transportation improvements and such." Cyndi sipped on the tea, tilting her head toward the dance floor. "Many young, pretty girls in these parts?"

"Some," Harvey responded, resting his elbows on the table and leaning toward her. "Most of them are dirt poor, anxious to marry, I suppose. A very curious question. Why do you ask?"

"I don't believe I caught your name." She gave him a beguiling smile.

"Harvey. Harvey Bryson. And you?"

"Dorothea," Cyndi said, rubbing the wedding band that had been created in the camp jewelry making "Bang Shop".

"No last name?" Harvey countered. "You're definitely a southern belle, by the charming accent, Dorothea."

"In due time, with the last name. Southern, yes. Mississippi, originally. But currently residing in Texas."

"Long way from home. And your husband, what does he do?"

"Banking. Lots and lots of banking. He dabbles in several entrepreneurial endeavors as well."

"I'm an entrepreneurial man, myself."

Cyndi took a breath and gathered herself for the next move.

"Are you, now? You seem familiar with quite a few of the females in here. Tell me more about the young women and girls in this area. Are any of them anxious to leave?"

"What is it you want to know exactly? Why so interested in the girls around here?"

Cyndi smiled, hesitating just enough to make him more curious and herself less anxious to move the discussion along.

"There are some solid business prospects for young, especially attractive, women in particular areas of Texas on into Mexico. An obscene amount of money to be made with good, old-fashioned hard work. We, of course, are looking to be on the managerial end of such a venture."

Harvey smelled opportunity and money, as Lorene said he would. Cyndi could sense his growing interest and curiosity. He was already taking the bait, leaning across the table and lowering his voice.

"What kind of business?"

"Sporting, of course. High-class, with first rate service and clientele. The total entertainment package, with billiards, gambling, drinks. We know where the ideal setting would be. Discreet procurement is a priority, of course."

"Tell me more."

"Ever heard of the Chicken Ranch in La Grange, Texas? It's only two blocks from the Houston to Austin road. They do actually have chickens there, and sell the eggs, although that's not the main offering." Cyndi paused. "Two years ago, two sisters who worked there began an ingenious plan of advertising to the local fellows fighting in the war. Sent them packages and letters. As automobile ownership began to increase, so did the traffic flow to the business." She smiled, taking another sip of tea. "You might be amused to know that the sheriff there visits each night to hear the gossip and see if any of the patrons had boasted of involvement in criminal activity. Seems like a mutually beneficial arrangement to me, don't you think?"

"Indeed, it does," Harvey beamed. "So, what do you have in mind?"

"The sporting industry has been successful in certain areas; others, not so much. Now that prohibition is almost here, with gambling and such already being discouraged in many places, there are a couple of areas down there that are becoming even more of tourist destinations, with plenty of disdain for these cumbersome ordinances." Cyndi leaned forward, her lips only inches from his. "We simply aim to start a competitive business venture and expand needed goods and services where they are desired and would be most welcome."

"This business opportunity you have, is there room for partnership?"

Cyndi pushed a wave of dark hair back from her eyes, raised her glass of tea, and smiled, never thinking that any of the home-grown stories and rumors could prepare her for conversation such as this. She had him where she wanted him, at least thus far.

"That depends heavily on how reliable and helpful the partner is willing to be. The possibilities are many, as law enforcement in such areas are quite cooperative, if one knows where to look." She smiled, recalling the information gleaned from relatives that lived close to the areas in question in Texas, thankful for the knowledge she thought she would never need.

"Well – Dorothea – it seems that we might have a great deal in common and I might be able to help you."

"How do think you could possibly help me, Mr. Bryson?" Cyndi asked.

"Please, just Harvey."

"Do tell, then, Harvey. I'm all ears."

Cyndi smiled, making a quick glance at her friends. Tricia and Lorene were watching the exchange, while Nancy and Tavia were dancing. From their nearby table, Lorene and Tricia gasped, as Cyndi became more friendly to the odious Harvey.

"She's good. Real good. I'm impressed." Lorene giggled.

"I think she's far smarter than Harvey Bryson on any given day, and twice on Sunday." Tricia added, laughing. "So far, it looks like things are going pretty well. I wish we could hear what they are saying. But at least we can watch." She smiled as the business discussion between Cyndi and Harvey continued.

"I'm in the procurement business, as well," Harvey bragged. "I have many important contacts, most in the northeast or Florida for whom I have provided similar goods and arranged transportation to wherever necessary. Added train lines in these parts have helped with that. Expansion to Texas could be a real possibility."

"The question is," Cyndi continued, not taking her eyes off of Harvey, "can you help find or provide such merchandise? Discretion is, of course, of utmost importance."

"I'm able to do that," Harvey said. "I've provided such already. There are numerous small towns around, with enough distance between to make rotating the hunting grounds a little easier. Some are willing to leave without my – how shall I say it? – assistance, which is only necessary if certain traits are desired and enticing the potential subject is not an option. On occasion, an opportunity simply presents itself and my associates and I must act on the fortuitous chance."

Cyndi surmised that Harvey Bryson grew more self-confident the more he heard himself talk. He appeared quite impressed with his own over-inflated ego. She relaxed for a moment, letting him talk on.

"My lumber business is located not far from here, but quite secluded. I can obtain any type of good needed. A variety of ages and types. As I mentioned, towns are spread out here, and a lot of transportation is still done by wagon and horses on these back roads, with the railroads being available in a couple of cities, along with a few spur lines." He gave her a lascivious smile. "I've already provided some of what you have mentioned. It might surprise you to know that both male and female have been requested, for a variety of purposes. It matters not to me what for. I can do whatever is needed."

"How do you make that happen, this necessary assistance?" Cyndi ventured. "I need specifics, to ensure that the goods are not compromised in any way."

Harvey made a thorough perusal of the area around them to be sure he was not overheard.

"Ether," he whispered. "The anesthesia stuff used for surgical procedures. We make it to our own specifications. It can also be obtained at most apothecaries, but making it is safer. Less risky than chloroform, but more flammable. Once one becomes adept at administering, it's almost foolproof. Sometimes takes several minutes to work, but renders the subject quite cooperative, otherwise. On occasion, it has to be readministered, depending on traveling distance and the subject, too. With proper research, timing and practice, and knowing how to make selections, it's fairly easy to use. I'm a professional, darlin'."

Cyndi fought back the urge to backhand the insidious smile off his face as hard as she could. She caught another glimpse of Tricia and the others. They were faithfully watching all while trying to be inconspicuous.

"So, if one were to make a very specific request, you could accommodate and make a discreet delivery?"

"If the price is right, I can do just about anything."

Cyndi shifted away from Harvey, tilting her head as if deep in thought, and crossed her arms. He never took his eyes off of her, an ingratiating smile still plastered on the soulless countenance. She leaned forward once more, as close to him as she could bear.

"Well, this has been a rather productive, as well as amusing, evening, I must say." Cyndi smiled. She had everything she needed. "I should be heading back to the Inn. My husband will need to be a part of any further discussion, as well as other details, before we finalize any possible working relationship. He will want to meet you, of course. Would it be possible for you to join us for dinner tomorrow evening perhaps? Drinks before?"

"Nothing would give me more pleasure." His voice oozed sensuality. "Well, perhaps a few things might." Harvey rose and offered his hand. "I'll escort you out."

Cyndi flinched only a moment before regaining her composure. There had been no preparation for this possibility. The evening had moved along even beyond her expectations. Now she just needed to get back to the boats at the Inn as soon as possible. She had to make a quick decision and hope the others would adjust. Taking his hand, she rose with as much dignity as she could muster.

"Oh, good lord!" Nancy exclaimed. "She's going to dance with him. Think that's a good sign?"

Harvey followed behind, as Cyndi made her way past their table. She looked sideways at Tricia, making the most clandestine of winks as the pair headed to the door.

"Whoa, wait," Tavia said, "What's she up to? This isn't good."

"Stay here," Tricia motioned, as she rose from her seat. "I'll go keep an eye out on her. Hopefully, she gets away from him as soon as possible. If I don't come back in in a few minutes, get help."

Harvey gestured toward the area to the side of Hannah's Barn that was left open for parking both carriages and automobiles. Tricia made a frantic check of the area from the top of the steps and saw the direction in which they were headed. She made her way down the side of the building to avoid being seen by Harvey. Hiding behind a bush next to another wagon, she could hear Harvey's voice as they moved near her hiding place.

"Before you leave, let me show you a little more about how the whole thing is done," he said. "Of course, there is a holding area, too, while specific transportation and accompaniment details are finalized."

When they reached Harvey's buckboard carriage, he motioned Cyndi to the side where a small barrel had been placed in the back, just behind the front seat, and chained to the side of the wagon. A stack of folded blankets and a large tarpaulin sat next to the barrel. Harvey put an arm around her shoulder, his efforts to impress becoming more evident.

"There's a hidden compartment carved into the barrel that holds the ether and rags.

That way, it is kept insulated and safe away from other elements and harm."

"Impressive. You've clearly gone to great lengths to carry out your work. This is the way you move the merchandise?"

"Most of the time, yes. Then the transport is made to my holding place until the final arrangements are made. We've been quite successful."

"How do you determine the best selection," Cyndi asked.

"Depending on what the client wants, we go from there. Of course, we know in general the availability of the draw in Laurel Valley but make it a point to scout other close areas, allow for time between orders, of course. There is a train station in Dillsboro where we obtained two, simply by listening to their conversation, then convincing them that we were there to retrieve them. Worked out, as one was a young colored male, and the client was willing to pay for such, along with the sister."

Tricia felt her heart jump to the back of her throat. Harvey Bryson had just confirmed his undeniable involvement in one of the known cases of missing youth. She tried to steady her nerves, wondering how Cyndi was handling this news, and leaned as far as she could toward them.

"Well, Harvey," Cyndi took a long, slow breath, "this has been the most fortuitous – and dare I say, amusing – evening I've had in quite some time. My husband will be anxious to meet you tomorrow after he hears of this."

Harvey moved in close enough to kiss her, as Cyndi prepared herself for whatever his next move might be.

"Then, my lovely Dorothea, we will have to toast to more amusing evenings, perhaps."

"Perhaps. Until then, Harvey. I look forward to seeing you again."

She turned to move away from him, turning only once to give him a coquettish wave before making her way to the path toward the Laurel Valley Inn, as he once again headed back to Hannah's Barn.

Tricia crept to Harvey's wagon and hoisted herself into the back, looking around to be sure no one saw her. Feeling along the barrel, she slid her hand back and forth across the rough wood until she was sure she had found the secret compartment. She pushed gently, then harder, along the edge until the piece of wood popped out. Just as she felt her fingers grasping something hard inside, she felt the wagon shake as a dark figure jumped aboard, seizing her arm and shoving her to the floor. A strong, sweet smell permeated the air around her.

"No!"

She tried to scream, but the massive man with the long dark hair and menacing black hat was upon her, covering her mouth and nose completely with a thick rag. Terrified, she struggled as hard as she could against him for what seemed an eternity, but to no avail. He pressed harder, squeezing her mouth and body. A feeling of giddy weakness overtook her senses and she could no longer fight him.

Dan Wolf stuffed another small rag into her mouth and bound her wrists with rope and secured the bondages to the side of the wagon so she could not escape. Once more, he covered her nose and mouth with the anesthesia. This time, Tricia felt her world collapsing to darkness. Was that Ewan calling for her or had she only imagined him trying to save her?

CHAPTER TWENTY-THREE

Tricia felt the rough-hewn floor of the wagon against her face and the deepening chill of the mountain night air, even from underneath the heavy blanket and tarpaulin that had been thrust over her. Her head was throbbing. No telling how long she had been unconscious. She struggled to rub her forehead, and to remove the rag in her mouth, but the restraints that held her wrists in place would not allow the range of movement. Shaking right and left and pushing with her shoulders, she was able to wriggle the covers from off her face. The sky boasted of myriads of stars, and there were thick treetops visible on either side of the starry display. They were still on a road somewhere. She strained to hear the sounds around her. The rolling of the wheels slightly uphill over dirt road, the rickety sounds of board rubbing against board, an occasional night creature stirring. But no talking at all. She was alone. And now, she was another of the missing. Dan Wolf was likely the driver of the wagon and they were headed up a small grade, before finally leveling out. *Think, think! Have to get out of here!*

Without warning the wagon stopped, lurching Tricia forward into the side of the barrel. She felt the man in the carriage jump down, as the wagon shifted with the distribution of weight. Footsteps. Without warning, her wrists were loosened, and her ankles were grabbed and pulled with such force that she feared falling. Her body was covered, lifted up without any semblance of gentle care, and she was slung like a potato sack over the shoulder of the man she assumed was Dan Wolf. He carried her up a small set of stairs, then banged several times on a door. A faint light emanated from wherever she was being carried to and a lady's voice, soft and shaken, was barely audible.

"Who's there?"

"Dan Wolf. We need your house, just for tonight."

A door opened, and the woman's voice sounded more agitated, afraid.

"I told Harvey I don't want no involvement in this, none. I done all I could. Don't involve me in this."

Where had she heard that voice before? It was sadly familiar.

"Which room?" The Wolf's deep menacing voice demanded.

"Please, I don't want no part of this at all. I done what Harvey asked. And I told the truth. You got the Sin Eater, ain't that enough? Don't drag me into this. And don't bring no dead body in here."

Tricia felt a nauseating wretch in her gut, as if someone had actually pummeled her senseless. It all fell into place. Ewan was in danger now. The woman was Chester Grave's widow, and she had no idea that a live girl had been brought to her home, the exact place where Tricia had first laid eyes on Ewan Munslow. Her mind swirled in confusion. Why were they at Chester Grave's house?

"Which room?" He insisted once more, a hint of thunder rising in his voice.

"Down the hall on the right." The widow cowered underneath Dan's mounting irritation.

Tricia felt herself thrown unceremoniously onto a soft bed. She closed her eyes, pretending to be unaware, as the covers were removed from her and she was secured to the iron bed.

"Where's Harvey?" The woman asked, wringing her hands. "Who is she? She dead?"

"Harvey will be here soon. Had to carry a message to someone at the Inn. She ain't dead. We have to hide her until tomorrow."

"Why here? I helped you all I could, don't do this to me."

Tricia heard the front door burst open. Harvey's voice was angry as he strode into the bedroom.

"We now have two pieces of prime merchandise. Seems Miss Dorothea, here, is an imposter. I took Dan's horse to catch up to her, once this one stuck her nose where she shouldn't have." He glared at Tricia, who had opened her eyes to see him carrying Cyndi, who was also bound and covered. The room was the same in which she had observed the sin-eating ritual for Chester Graves.

"I was going to inform my future business associate that we might need to rearrange our dinner plans. When I caught up to her at the Inn, she's sneaking across the grounds, headed to the boating area. Put on quite an entertaining show trying to change back into her uniform." Harvey smiled at Cyndi. "Soon as I realized the whole thing was a set up by you foolish damned Arden Woode hussies, I had no choice but to take her, too."

Tricia winced as he slung Cyndi off of his shoulder and shoved her hard onto the bed, where Dan Wolf proceeded to secure her also. Cyndi squirmed in fury, attempting to free herself from her bonds and making angry growls underneath the rag stuffed in her mouth. Harvey yanked the cloth from her, grinning with satisfaction, and stooped to get close to her face once more.

"What's that you're saying, Dear? Speak up. Nobody can hear you out here."

Cyndi spit as hard as she could manage into Harvey's face.

"You're nothing but low-class cheap white trash," she hissed at him.

Harvey wiped his mouth with the back of his hand, a wicked smile on his face.

"Some of our clients like 'em spirited. Not to worry – they'll break you fast. Ironic, isn't it? You and I were gonna be big partners. And now, you're nothing but a business transaction. I'll get a pretty penny for you, though. And enjoy doing it."

Cyndi glared at him and motioned to Tricia.

"Gonna let her breathe, or keep her uncomfortable like that?"

Harvey removed the rag from Tricia's mouth and stood, crossing his arms and gloating even more about their capture.

"Where is Ewan?" Tricia demanded. "What have you done with him?"

"Ah, you mean the now infamous Ewan Munslow, the Sin-Eater? Yeah, we know about that and more. Dan, here, is very skilled at hiding and scouting for information. Why, Munslow is likely being arrested, as we speak, for the murder of Chester Graves, and attempted kidnapping of Priscilla Parker. Before long, he'll also be charged with the disappearances of you two and a few others. Won't be long before an angry crowd demands that they hang him. Folks don't like being deceived by one they trust, you know." Harvey smiled again.

"Ewan's a better man than you could ever hope to be," Tricia lashed out at him. "Lorene knows everything, so does Ewan, and some of the others, so you'll never get away with this."

"What do they know?" Harvey challenged, an edge of anger in his voice. "They don't have proof of anything. As for dear cousin Lorene – she might send the law on a wild goose chase to the lumber site either tonight or in the morning – where they will find not a damn thing, of course. While they're done digging around my place, they will also find me at home, minding my business. No proof of anything." He smiled again. "As for Munslow, it's my word against his." Harvey gestured to the widow Graves. "Of course, Chester's grieving wife, here, has already told the law that she heard the Sin Eater apologize to poor Chester the night he came to take on his sins. He pretty much admitted his guilt. He can take on mine, as well."

"You know that's not the whole truth. Please don't do this!" Tricia pleaded with the widow, then turned to Harvey. "What about me and Cyndi? How are you going to explain our being missing? Everyone at Arden Woode knows he would never do such."

"Do they, now?" Harvey teased. "They know nothing. I walked a lady outside at Hannah's. And came back inside like the gentleman I am. You went outside after her. Ewan Munslow, of course, must've decided to take the both of you for his own profit, much as he has done with the others. From here on out, it's his word against mine. Doesn't matter what any of you fools at Arden Woode believe."

"They will believe Ewan!" Tricia was defiant. "People love him."

"Don't be so naïve," Harvey snapped. "They may love him. They don't love the Sin Eater. It never takes much for people to turn on someone they think may have been trying to trick them. People are more than willing to condemn another to make themselves seem more pious. All we had to do was plant that seed. Priscilla Parker doesn't remember enough to convict me. In fact, rumor has it that she can only remember 'the dark, scary man'." Harvey raised his hands in mock fear. "How fortunate that Chester's wife will attest to the sins of the Sin Eater. Not one bit of evidence will they find that I was involved. All else is hearsay. Legally and otherwise. My father's a judge, you know. As soon as we make the arrangements, you two fine ladies will go to your new homes, somewhere far away. I'll be richer, and Ewan Munslow will be out of my way for good. Perfect."

"You can't keep us here," Cyndi said with firm resolution.

"You'll remain here tonight," Harvey smiled. "Tied to this bed and the door bolted from the outside. No window for you either." Harvey gestured to Dan. The pair of men struggled to slide the massive wardrobe in the room in front of the window. Harvey placed a hand on the widow Graves' shoulder.

"She's also quite good with a shotgun. So, rest up, my lovelies, you're going to need it. The accommodations won't be as warm as this, tomorrow." He motioned for the others to follow him out of the room, then turned to his captives once more.

"Good evening, ladies. Sleep well."

"I swear," Cyndi took a deep breath. "I will see him locked up, if it's the last thing I ever do."

"It may be," Tricia said, "Unless we can get ourselves out of here. We're in deep trouble, Cyndi. No one knows where we are. We have to get out, somehow. Ewan's life, as well as others, may depend solely on us. The good news is, we know where we are and how to get back to the Inn and the camp."

She studied every inch of the room. There had to be a way. If even one of them could break free, they could do it.

"Okay," Cyndi gathered her wits and began to analyze their situation the way Tricia had seen her do so many times before. "Our options, as I see it: One, harass the stew out of old Chester's wife and get her on our side. Two, bust the hell out of here and get help from the Inn, since it's closer than the camp is."

"I think that pretty well covers it," Tricia tried to smile. "If we can get out, the Inn is our best bet. Harvey's sidekick may be prowling about Arden Woode, as he has apparently been doing all along. Everyone at Arden Woode knows we are missing by now. But Harvey is right about one thing. No one will look for us here, I don't think."

"So, it's just us and the widow now," Cyndi said. "What do you say, we try to play on her sympathy some?" Cyndi didn't wait for a response from Tricia but began shouting through the bolted door.

"Mrs. Graves! I know you can hear us. You're in this, too, and you will be charged when the truth comes out. Help us! It's your only chance, and you know it!"

No response.

"Think about it, Mrs. Graves! You know Harvey Bryson will own you forever, if you let him do this. Please, help us! Help yourself!"

Three rapid and hard banging sounds against the bedroom door let the girls know that Chester Graves' wife had heard them.

"Shut up! Shut up, you know nothing! I've lost everything. No income, because Ewan Munslow killed my husband!"

"Mrs. Graves, listen," Tricia pleaded. "What you say is only half the truth, and you know it. I was here that night. I was here, right under this window, and I heard everything."

Silence. Tricia tried again.

"Please, Mrs. Graves. You know what I'm saying is true!"

"You're lying! You're trying to trick me! You was never here."

"I was!" Tricia shouted. "You want proof? After Ewan performed the ritual in this very room, you asked him if he killed your husband! You thanked him for it. You know he did it to save that girl, you know it in your heart, don't you?"

More silence. Then, soft sobs.

"Ewan came here for you, Mrs. Graves. For you, not Chester! He wanted you to have peace. He left the money, too. For you! Not because he felt guilty, but because he knew you needed it. Please, you know it's true! Help us! Let us help you!"

"You can't do nothing for me. Nobody can," the woman sobbed, "I have nothing now."

"You have us, Mrs. Graves," Cyndi interjected, glancing at Tricia. "We can help you out of this, but you have to let us."

"Harvey promised me money. Gave me money that I need," the widow sobbed. "You can't help me. I have nothing. You can't understand where I am!"

"You're in a hard place, Mrs. Graves, I know you are," Tricia tried again, keeping her voice as calm as she could. "I understand that much. Stop and think. You'll never have any peace if you do this. And Harvey will use you for all kinds of evil, you can bet on that. Let us go, and you come with us!"

Cyndi shot her a surprised look. *Come with us?* She mouthed back at Tricia.

"Yes, come with us." Tricia answered them both. "Come with us and everyone will know what you've been through. People will help, I know they will. Arden Woode will help. Please, Mrs. Graves, please. It's the only way for all of us. Ewan cared about you, and so do I! Help us! Help yourself!"

Silence still.

"Now what?" Cyndi whispered. "I think she's gone."

Tricia yanked instinctively at the ropes that bound her and looked around the room. A small bedside table stood next to the bed on her side, containing a bible, a plate of some sort, with a rosary atop it, a folded handkerchief, and a glass figurine of an angel.

"If I can reach that plate or angel thing, and break one of them, maybe we can use the pieces to cut this rope."

"See if you can grab one of them and get it to the bed. We can slam it against the iron posts and break it. It's worth a try." Cyndi said. "Can you reach one of them?"

Tricia pulled the tied rope across the bed with as much force as possible. It would not stretch much.

"I think I can grab the plate, maybe. Think we can inch the bed a little closer somehow?

"Try bouncing up and down, and kind of rocking that way," Cyndi suggested. "Both of us. Lean that way."

The bed was heavy but began to move, making loud scraping noises in the process. The glass angel teetered a moment, then fell to the floor, shattering into an innumerable number of pieces.

"One down. Literally." Cyndi quipped. "We have to get to the plate."

"I'm almost there!" Tricia breathed, straining with all her might against the ropes.

Without warning, the bolt on the bedroom door unlocked and swung open. A frail and swollen-eyed Mrs. Graves stood in the doorway, clad in an oversized work-shirt, and trousers secured at the waist with a large belt, a pair of old work boots, with a shot gun at her side, and a large knife in the other hand.

"You didn't have to break it," she whispered. "We should take this rifle here, in case of a bear or bobcat. Or coyote."

Chester Graves' wife laid the shotgun next to the door and began trying to cut Tricia's bindings. Tricia and Cyndi stared in grateful disbelief, both smiling at her.

"We will help you, Ma'am. You have my word on that." Tricia reached for her hand.

"I know a short cut through them woods to the Laurel Valley Inn. Ain't nothing but a small path, but it's a lot faster than taking the road. Blankets, in that closet there. Wrap up in one. You'll stay warmer and less scratched up. We have to go through the woods.

"Then we'd better hurry," Cyndi said. "All of us are in enough danger."

"And Ewan, too. If they want to kill him, we have to stop it."

"We can't take no lantern. Too easy to spot us. Just let your eyes adjust to the night."

Chester Graves' widow extinguished the lantern light in the house and the three women crept out into the cover of darkness.

Chapter Twenty-Four

As soon as she saw them, Tricia swore that the electric lights at the Laurel Valley Inn were the most glorious sight she had ever seen. Both exhausted and exhilarated, they pressed on around the far side of Emerald Lake to the grounds of the great stone inn and scurried up the steps of the wide verandah.

"I wonder what time it is?" Cyndi asked.

"I reckon it's maybe an hour after midnight," Mrs. Graves noted, looking up at the sky. "Or more like thirty minutes."

Tricia banged on a window until a gentleman in a dark suit and cigar appeared on the other side. He frowned at the bedraggled group."

"Help us, please!" Tricia begged. "We are from the camp. Someone tried to kidnap us! We need to contact the sheriff."

"The man called out for assistance and opened the heavy door. Once inside, the women smelled the scent of a blazing wood fire, cigars, and the remnants of a hardy evening meal that lingered about and wrapped the chilled travelers in welcome security.

"We have to find the sheriff," Tricia repeated to the managing innkeeper and a handful of inquisitive staff. "And we need to contact the administrative staff at Camp Arden Woode, so they know that we are safe. Can you help us?"

Attentive assistants hustled the women into a private room where they were provided warm towels to freshen up, then given cups of steaming tea with fresh lemon and honey. Someone had volunteered to go to the camp and the innkeeper himself used the only telephone other than the one at the jailhouse to contact the sheriff.

"Sheriff Strother, he's been called to an emergency. There's a deputized man at the jail keeping watch, with a few others. Ewan Munslow is there." The innkeeper smiled at Tricia. "We gave him the message that you are alright, as well."

Tricia set her second cup of tea on the stone hearth. She felt the emotion welling up in her eyes, her body shaking. Unable to speak, she nodded her thanks to him. Cyndi rushed to embrace her, as Hugh Carson appeared, visibly relieved. He ran to the girls, hugging them both, and placing a hand on the widow Graves' shoulder.

"Thank God, you're here! Is everyone okay?" His eyebrows knit together in deep concern.

"We're fine," Cyndi offered. "Thanks to Mrs. Graves. She helped us."

"Mighty obliged to you," Hugh shook her hand.

The widow gave a weak smile and nodded her head.

"Nancy, Tavia, and Lorene, are they alright?" Tricia asked, "and our campers?"

"All fine," Hugh motioned for the three to sit, as he found a seat on the side of the hearth. "People from Hannah's helped our ladies get back to camp. Mary and Dammie are going to each cabin to tell them that you two are safe now." Hugh finally smiled. "I'm sure everyone is awake. Of course, someone from Hannah's also went to fetch the sheriff and I'm sure he was already dealing with the accusations against Ewan. Probably has a deputized group still at Harvey's lumber mill looking for any evidence they can find."

Tricia glanced at the widow Graves, who wrung her hands and bit her lower lip, as Tricia and Cyndi filled Hugh in with the many details that had brought them to this moment.

"I'm so sorry," Tricia shook her head. "We should have probably come to you all sooner, but we wanted to be sure we had the right information. I'm the one that kept pushing for more. And truly, if it weren't for Mrs. Graves' courageous and wise decision to help us, instead of Harvey, it could have been much worse."

"We're all thankful that it did not end that way," Hugh said. "Let me tell you all what's been happening otherwise. When your friends got back to camp, Mary and Dammie and I were awakened immediately, and told everything that had happened of which they were aware. All they knew then was that you both were gone, but they told us all that had happened before." He looked at Tricia. "They have also told us about the promise you made to keep a certain beloved lady safe, too, as she could very much help Ewan now."

Tricia looked at Cyndi, then back to Hugh.

"I feel terrible. I promised her. I promised she could trust me to keep her family safe. And now I've failed." Tricia brushed more tears away from tired eyes.

"No, no you haven't." Hugh was insistent. "She was awakened with the others. When she heard what had happened, that you two were missing and Ewan was arrested, she came to us. The sheriff himself will hear her and her son tomorrow. Tonight, she's sleeping in your cabin with your girls. Cyndi, Mary is with yours. And a few deputized men are standing guard."

Tricia raised her eyes to the massive ceiling, fighting back the tears as hard as she could, but they flowed freely. The thought of Otha spending time with her girls, watching over them for her, was more than she could bear.

"I'm sure that Ewan will be cleared after tonight, and Harvey and Dan Wolf will be charged on multiple counts. We will know more by lunchtime tomorrow. Dr. Halsted has met with Priscilla's family and she is cleared for the hypnosis procedure with him. Although I think this will all be resolved so that the case is not dependent on her memory recall, I think she very much wants the closure about what happened. Judge Bryson will be notified, when Harvey is arrested, and will likely come to Laurel Valley. As sad as it is, the judge is of high character and I expect he will encourage Harvey to cooperate."

Hugh stood, stretching his arms above his head and yawning.

"And of course, the sheriff will want statements from all three of you in the morning, as well. If you'd like, we can try to get word to your families now or wait til morning."

"My family is asleep, why wake them now?" Tricia smiled.

"I agree," Cyndi added.

"How about you, Mrs. Graves? Who can we contact for you?"

"Nobody. Ain't no family for me," she whispered, looking down at her hands.

"Then, we'd be pleased if you came to the camp in the morning for devotional with these girls. The Inn has graciously offered for you all to stay here tonight, also for safety, and eat a hearty breakfast in the morning once you're awake." Hugh winked at Tricia, smiling. "I understand that there are two camp canoes here anyway. Perhaps a morning boat ride would be therapeutic for you all."

"Oh, my gosh, yes," Cyndi said with great enthusiasm. "And please, Mrs. Graves, come with us."

"Call me Martha" the widow whispered with a half-smile. "Yes, that sounds quite lovely. There is one thing that I need to do."

She looked at Cyndi, then Tricia.

"I have to apologize to Ewan Munslow. I've done terribly wrong by him."

"He will understand, I'm sure of it," Tricia said. "So, Martha, you will come with us to Arden Woode? I know you will love it as much as we do."

"I'd like to get some sleep now, if that's even possible, then."

"I think that's a good idea," Hugh agreed. "We should all do that. It will be another full day tomorrow and we all will need the rest. One of the staff here is going to drive me over to the camp in one of the vehicles here at the inn."

"Let me walk you to the door, Hugh." Tricia offered. "I'll see you ladies upstairs," she said to Cyndi and Martha.

As they made their way through the red carpeted lobby and down the wide staircase, Tricia took the opportunity to share more with Hugh.

"You know that my folks know nothing of Ewan, right? I'm struggling with how to tell them that I'm marrying someone not of their choosing and moving up north to finish my schooling and do something they didn't want me to do. Writing, that is. All of those things are going to be almost impossible for my mother to handle," Tricia shared.

Hugh cocked his head to one side, regarding her with care, and pulled out his favorite pipe.

"This calls for a smoke," he grinned. "You want my opinion? I think anyone who has done what you just have, will have great success and joy in this life. Tell them with love, Tricia. That's all that really matters. The rest will take care of itself."

Before she could reply further, the innkeeper rushed out to stop them with news they had just received.

"You should know," he said, "that Harvey Bryson and Danuwoa Wolf, along with another man, have been arrested for the kidnappings and the disappearances of five other people thus far. Three from around these parts and two from across the Georgia line. That may not be all, but we know those for sure. Bryson has been helping some high rollers with a trafficking ring that spans from here to north and south, and out west. Even a few connections in some of the barrier islands in North and South Carolina, Georgia, Florida, and possibly on into Mexico and the Caribbean. This is going to be a huge story, young lady."

"How did they find the evidence they needed?" Hugh asked.

"Apparently they found it in two places. Seems there was an underground stash of written records that Harvey had in one of the outlying buildings on the lumber site. He thought they would only look for live bodies, and of course those were not there, but the sheriff was pretty hot that all this was going on in his jurisdiction, so the search was quite thorough. You know Sheriff Strother," the man smiled. "Yep, Sheriff has always thought Harvey a bit of a braggart, anyway, never trusted him. Also found some records hidden in his home. Found an anesthetic type of substance in a barrel in the back of his wagon, too. Ether, I think they said. He's going away for a long time. And in a day or two, this place will have reporters crawling all over the place. So, at least you can prepare for all that."

The innkeeper turned to go back inside when Tricia grabbed his arm.

"Ewan Munslow, has he been released yet?"

"No, ma'am, not yet, at least not officially. Sheriff thought he'd be safer for now staying put til daylight. Give people time to adjust to hearing the news about who he really is, you know? Lots of big news around here, for sure. Well, goodnight. Rest well. I'm sure we will all have plenty of excitement to come in our little Laurel Valley."

"Happy?" Hugh smiled at her. "I think it will soon be over. But you know what this means now, don't you?"

Tricia gave him a quizzical look and shook her head.

"A major ring of crime has been interrupted by young women. The story will be heard near and far, you know. It means that you girls and our camp will be very well-known for what you all have done. As will Ewan. If we ever wondered about the integrity and mission of Arden Woode, you all have given the world the chance to see it."

Tricia stared up at the sky. The stars lit up the night like a million fireflies as a chilly mountain breeze blew through the treetops.

"I don't care about being famous. Ewan once told me that, when he first heard my name, that it reminded him of wind in the trees. '*Triciiiiaaa*,'" she exaggerated, waving her hand and smiling. Her voice trailed off as emotion caught up with her once more. "But what I do care about is that I would be sorely deprived if I could never hear him call my name again. If I had never met the likes of Otha Moses, or the people here who have so enriched my world. Ewan also told me about a rule of life, about living with great purpose and joy. Being the person God intended him to be and living to be of service. Coming to Arden Woode, to these mountains, has been the best experience of my life. I'm finally alive in every possible way. Living the way Ewan has chosen, and living my life with him, through the good and the challenging, is what I want, too."

Hugh smiled, hugged her once more before heading down the massive steps. At the bottom, he stopped, puffing once more on his cherished pipe, and turning to face her.

"What a wonderful thing, to be so alive in this splendid, divine creation of a place. I can't think of anything more magnificent than being a living beacon for who we are and whose we are. See you in the morning. And Tricia?"

"Yes?"

"I'm so proud of you."

She smiled, watching him saunter away.

"There goes a really honorable man," she whispered into the night.

CHAPTER TWENTY-FIVE

By morning, word had spread through the Laurel Valley Inn about the sensational events that had occurred overnight. Well wishes and donations for the camp, as well as for the wife of Chester Graves, were given to the innkeeper for the three overnight guests. Patrons pressed their hands, cheered, and wished them the best of luck as they readied the canoes for the return trip across the lake.

"I ain't never been treated so kind," Martha Graves gushed. "These people wouldn't even see me, most of the time." She rolled up the sleeves of the casual yellow summer dress that had been given to her and stepped into the boat with Cyndi. Tricia noted how relaxed and happy she seemed to be, even making direct eye contact with others. Her soft brown hair, brushed and braided around her head, accentuated her brown eyes that had lost their empty emotionless stare, and now radiated warmth and friendliness. There was only a remnant of the scared waif of the woman they had seen last night. The thought of the welcome she would receive at camp made Tricia smile.

"People get distracted and caught up in their own lives," Cyndi laughed. "But if you give folks half the chance, they want to do the right thing, more often than not. My daddy always tells me to hold my head high and smile at everyone, even if they don't smile back."

"You won't have to worry about that at Arden Woode," Tricia grinned. "These little girls will be all over you, and they will ask you a million questions, too."

"I have not seen the camp yet. But I'm glad it's there." Martha looked out over the lake as they glided through the calm waters. "I always wanted a little girl. Chester, he didn't want no kids, at least no girl. He was happy when I miscarried. Me, I wanted a little baby so bad."

Tricia felt a pang of sympathy for this woman that had kowtowed to the likes of Chester Graves for so long.

"Martha, you know you are not responsible for what Chester chose to do. The minute you made a decision for yourself, you broke free. Now you can choose. And who knows? You're not too old to have a child. Lord knows, you're going to have more girls than you can imagine in just a few minutes." Tricia nodded her head forward, as the full expanse of Arden Woode came into view. Bald Rock, the overseer of all below, stood in majestic beauty, the solid rock face reflecting the morning sunlight that sparkled the pristine waters and warmed the docks and footpath along the front line of cabins. The lush green of the outdoor chapel and the sound of the nearby waterfall rendered the most picturesque of views. Martha Graves fell silent, a hand rising to her lips.

"It's heaven," she whispered.

"Yes, it is," Tricia agreed. "It is definitely that."

"And all of it is for girls?"

"That's right," Cyndi smiled, pointing toward the area around the Ark, "But I do see one thing that is especially for Tricia."

Ewan Munslow, carrying a large bouquet of field flowers, was flanked by the sheriff and Dr. Halsted. When he saw Tricia, he called out to her and ran to the dock to meet them.

"Ewan!" She embraced him, refusing to let go. "I was so afraid I was going to lose you."

"And I, you, *mo muirhnin*. You are alright? I was beside myself, not knowing if you were safe."

Ewan reached for the hand of Martha Graves to assist her out of the canoe. For a moment, the pained expression returned to the widow's face. She could barely look at him.

"I am grateful to you, Mrs. Graves, for helping these ladies. Thank you."

"I should be thanking you, Mr. Munslow," she murmured, embarrassed as she grasped his hand in return. "I don't deserve your kindness. You've done that for me twice now. I thank God that you did."

"That's enough for me, then." He continued to hold her hand. "Your choosing to do right by this woman is the greatest gift to me." He turned to Cyndi, smiling. "I hear you put on quite a convincing performance last night. I hate I had to miss that."

Cyndi laughed, glancing in the direction of the dining hall, where campers and staff were just beginning to exit before the morning devotional in the Castle.

"I actually enjoyed myself, up to that part. Relieved that it's all over. I hope the missing can all be located and returned."

"I can address that," Sheriff Strother took a step toward them. "It will take some time, but all of the records Harvey kept are being coordinated with information from the other towns of the missing ones. The tracking will be tedious, but with help from the Feds, we hope to find them and bring them home to their families, as well as find all of those responsible for their disappearance."

"I hope that Harvey Bryson and Dan Wolf will one day admit their wrongdoing," Tricia said.

Sheriff Strother removed the large ten-gallon hat from his head and rubbed his tired face. No doubt his night had been the longest of all.

"Good news, there, at least. When Judge Bryson received the news about his son, he came immediately to the jailhouse in Laurel Valley. Insisted on seeing Harvey. Convinced him that a guilty plea, and a promise to help locate the missing would go a long way in alleviating the need for a trial that would ultimately find him guilty, regardless, and would work in his favor in terms of sentencing. Harvey has agreed to those terms and admitted his involvement in all if it, including the attack on Priscilla Parker."

"That's wonderful," Tricia beamed. "That means Ewan is cleared of all charges, then?"

"Indeed, it does, Miss." The Sheriff continued, "I will need a statement from you three for the record before I leave, though."

Tricia reached for Ewan's hand.

"One more thing. What happens to the Sin Eater?" Tricia ventured. "Are people angry about that part of all this? What about his work at the Inn?"

"I believe I can answer that one, even in my non-affiliation with the Church," Dr. Halsted responded. "Ewan is a much-respected young man. The Laurel Valley Inn still values his reputation there. Certainly, no one suspected that the Sin Eater was he, but I believe that the resulting positive publicity from this entire affair will negate any negative perception that the Sin Eater is to be shunned. He acted to save a young girl. Most are quite grateful for what he did. I understand – correct me, if I'm wrong, Ewan, – that you have been invited to speak at the summer chapel of Good Shepherd about the Sin Eater, but not about any details of this case?"

"Yes, Dr. Halsted, that's right." He smiled at the doctor. "I hope to see you there regardless of your standing with the Church. Visitors always welcome, you know. They also will eventually be very interested in the hypnosis procedure for Priscilla Parker, and I'm sure will want you to speak, too, once the case can be discussed more openly."

"Priscilla still wants to do the procedure?" Tricia was surprised.

Before the doctor could answer, campers and staff alike rushed to greet them, Tricia's and Cyndi's girls, along with Nancy, Tavia, and Lorene heading the charge, followed close behind by Dammie and Mary. The counselors all embraced, with the young campers jumping up and down and rejoicing around them, then hugging Tricia and Cyndi.

Martha Graves watched in silence until the campers took note of her presence.

"Are you the lady that saved Tricia and Cyndi?" Gaylen inquired.

Martha looked nervous, wringing her hands once more and looking at Tricia.

"Yes," Tricia's reply was firm. "Yes, she is. This is Mrs. Martha Graves. And these," she gestured to the campers, "are our amazing Arden Woode girls."

Martha smiled, at a loss for words, and overwhelmed by the number of people that were present.

"Mrs. Graves, would you like to sit with us at our devotional?" Priscilla Parker stood before the reluctant woman, taking her hand. "Please sit with us."

"It's okay," Tricia smiled at Martha. "Thank you, Priscilla. You show her how we do things."

Dammie and Mary motioned for Tricia and the other counselors that had been to Hannah's Barn to remain behind.

"First of all, we are so thankful that you all are safe. And very grateful for what you did. That took incredible courage. Arden Woode will reap the benefits." She smiled at them. "I would be remiss if I didn't tell you that you should have said something to us about all of this earlier."

Tricia opened her mouth to accept responsibility, but Dammie held up a hand.

"But then, things might have not turned out this way. Each of you are heroes and the very essence of what a woman of integrity and honor should be. We could not be more proud of you. Go on to the Castle with your girls. Stay there afterward so that the sheriff can take your statements."

"Tricia, a moment, please?" Dammie said.

Nancy mouthed the words *see you soon* and gave her a thumbs up signal.

"Your parents were finally reached this morning. Your mother is extremely upset. Angry, I think. Your father was much calmer, but of course rightfully concerned. I thought you should know."

"Angry with me?" Tricia asked.

"My guess is angry with all of us that you were in danger. I understand. Whatever you decide to do, we will honor."

"Wait, I don't understand. What do you mean?"

"They are coming to Arden Woode for you."

CHAPTER TWENTY-SIX

Hugh Carson walked with Tricia on her way to see Otha Moses down in the dining hall. Stopping a moment to rub the head of Hala, who lapped up attention, ever loyal in following him with relentless dedication, he was careful in his response to Tricia.

"Yes, Dammie shared with me also that your folks were coming up from South Carolina to get you, and that you had made the decision to stay."

"The end of camp is only a few days away now, and I would never leave my duties. I couldn't do that to my girls or to you all. I just can't. My mother won't take it well, I'm certain of it. As it is, she will be upset when I tell her I'm going to marry Ewan."

"That's a tough one. We will back whatever decision you make. Cyndi is staying also."

"But her parents aren't raising a ruckus by insisting that she come home now."

"True," Hugh smiled, "but they were deeply concerned, which is quite understandable, given all that has happened."

"I'm pretty sure it's my mother driving this and not my father. She can be unbelievably stubborn and tenacious."

"So that's where you get it from."

"Okay, yes, point taken. I'm reasonable, though. She never gives me credit for anything."

"Oh, I think she does. You're her child, and she loves you. Her vantage point is different from yours."

"Ewan is glad they are coming. He wants to meet them and ask for my hand the proper way. Not for us, but for them."

"This will work out, Tricia, one way or the other. Let it. You can't fix it all."

"I know, but I want to. I don't want to hurt them."

"Look there."

Hugh pointed in the direction of the waterfall and the morning fire that was still burning in the cooking area. Otha stood, arms akimbo, with Samuel on one side and a young girl that she was sure must be her niece on the other. As soon as Otha spotted Tricia, she started down the small path to meet her, arms spread wide.

"Lawd, have mercy, here's my girl, back safe and sound. Child, I was worried sick about you!"

Tricia ran to meet the beloved cook, tears falling once more, as she wrapped her arms around Otha's neck.

"Thank you, Otha. And Samuel, thank you, too, for what you did for Ewan, and for all of the missing ones. I will never forget."

"I couldn't let my baby and Mr. Ewan be in harm's way like that, no. All these bad things going on, no, not no more. Lawd, it's a happy day around here today!"

"I have a request for you, Otha. An important one." Tricia held Otha's hand. "When Ewan and I marry, we want to do it right here at Arden Woode. Would you let us hire you to prepare the food for the reception? We want it all right here, with you there with us. No one cooks as magnificently as you."

"Oh, this is a great day, indeed! Ain't nobody else but 'ole Otha could take care of your wedding day like I will. Yes, lawd, we will have ourselves a fine feast."

"Otha," Hugh interjected, "we have a surprise for you, as well. Actually, Tricia does not even know this, yet. We want to make it so that your family can stay much closer to the camp, so that you don't have to be away so much. Next summer, Arden Woode campers and staff are going to fix up the old Hollingwood place over there next to the widow Graves' house for you all. It will be more room for you and close enough to camp that you could even take a decent walk here, if you wanted to do that."

Otha's eyes glistened with tears and she hugged Hugh, then Tricia.

"I don't know what to say. You so good to me 'round here."

"There's one more thing," Hugh smiled at Otha's niece. "We'd like to extend an invitation for Miss Celia, here, to be an Arden Woode camper. We have received donation money, and more will be coming in. Priscila Parker will also be here, and we are making plans to open our gates here even more, once we work out those details. Samuel, we want you to continue your schooling, but anytime you can help Otha around here, we'd be obliged and can pay you some, too."

"Yes, Sir, I'd like that very much," Samuel said, his usually quiet demeanor gave way to a happy smile.

"Can I come, Auntie, please?" Celia begged. "Can I learn to ride a horse?"

"Yes, indeed," Hugh grinned. "You can learn whatever you want here. So, it's settled, then. Arden Woode will be a visionary place in many ways."

Otha studied Tricia for a long moment before speaking.

"I hear tell your folks is coming up here to take you home."

"Yes, I've heard that, too," she shook her head, "but, I'm not leaving until camp is over."

"I didn't think you would." Otha replied. "You got to honor your folks, though. They family."

"What do you mean?" Tricia asked.

"You got to love them. Got to look past they anger. You their child and they just want to do right by you. You can stand up for yo'self, but you still got to show them the love. They gonna come around. If not today, then another day."

"I love you, Otha Moses. You are, without a doubt, the wisest and most genuine person I've ever met.

"Aw, now, I don't know about that at all. But, if I don't get busy 'round here, ain't nobody gonna have food to eat, come supper time. So, it's time for ya'll to let 'ole Otha git to work."

Tricia smiled, watching the beloved cook move about the outdoor area, issuing instructions and enjoying her reign as the dining hall monarch. Otha Moses was quite a lady.

As she and Hugh made their way back up the path to the trip

craft hut to begin the task of readying the last of the summer hikes, Tricia stopped to look out at the view of Emerald Lake over the tops of the cabins along the front line.

"I'm so glad I came here. It's been a life-changing summer for me in every way possible. Honestly, I've learned as much here, perhaps more, than in my formal schooling, which I thought was the best thing I could ever do to improve myself."

"Different kind of learning." Hugh commented. "It takes all kinds of learning and experiences, to grow. Learning should never stop. I'd like to think that formal education and common sense both grow together, but sometimes, that's not true. What ultimately matters, is what is inside one's heart."

"Dammie said reporters from many places were scheduled to start arriving here as early as tomorrow. Is that true?"

"Well, yes and no. That was the plan. But we met and decided to let the next couple of days be as normal as possible for everyone, so the decision has now been made to not have them here until the campers leave. That way, their presence here won't be so disruptive."

"So, we won't have to speak with them until that time?"

"Correct. We will have them all in one place, either in the Castle, or the Laurel Valley Inn has offered to provide a meeting place. Of course, you counselors that went to Hannah's Barn will have the opportunity to speak. Sheriff Strother and Dr. Halsted will be there, as well as Ewan Munslow, whom I'm sure they will be most interested in interviewing. Priscilla Parker is undergoing the hypnosis process this afternoon, I understand, and may or may not choose to participate."

"It all sounds a bit overwhelming and intimidating." Tricia responded.

"That's why we felt strongly about limiting the involvement. If you don't mind, I have a suggestion for you to think about."

"What's that?

"They will want to hear your words. You want to write; perhaps, even begin a career in the journalism field. I think you should consider telling them that you will write an article for the papers or a magazine, like *Life,* or *The Saturday Evening Post,* but that you want it to be your story, written by you alone. Then, you craft the most well-written piece you can. This is a singular opportunity for you while the nation and beyond is focused on this story. That way, the story not only gets told with accuracy, but you have the opportunity to show the world what you can do."

Tricia was quiet for several moments, thinking hard about what Hugh had said.

"You really think so? That I have a chance?"

"More than a chance, young lady. But you have to act with prudent care, if it is what you want.

"Alright, I will start giving it some serious thought, then."

"Very good. Let's go get on with the business of camp life while we can."

"I have a feeling this place will always be a part of my life. Always."

CHAPTER TWENTY-SEVEN

" Tricia, I remember it all now!" Priscilla Parker was ecstatic as she ran to catch up with Tricia and the Du Kum Inn girls before rest hour. "I know what happened to me. And you know what else? I'm not afraid anymore. Dr. Halsted helped me so much. I don't know how to explain it. He said it wasn't magic, but it sure feels like it to me! And guess what else? I'm coming back to camp next summer!"

Tricia's girls were giddy with excitement at the prospect of having Otha's niece join them and for Priscilla to return. They had exchanged mailing addresses and planned to communicate until time to come back to Arden Woode. Even Martha Graves had found semblance of redemption, having cultivated a friendship with Otha in the dining hall and offering to share her home with her family while the house next door was being prepared for them.

"Only you won't be here, Tricia. We can't have camp without you." Natalie was despondent.

"She's getting married, silly. To Ewan. They are going to live in Baltimore until he can become a doctor."

"I can see her some there," Christa said, with added enthusiasm, "because I live in Baltimore."

"Girls, I will always come visit when I can, and you can visit me, too! Doc Halsted has invited us to come to High Hampton, as well. But you know, Arden Woode will always be about about making new friends any time you come here. You will have wonderful counselors. Just think – one day, you might even be a counselor here."

"Yeah, I wanna be the boss," Gaylen laughed. "And see the Wampus Cat."

"No! Chuck shouted "You know you can't see him, nobody can! But we will always know when he's been around."

The girls laughed at the thought of all the orange-colored noses. They babbled on about the hikes they wanted to do and the skills they wanted to perfect. Tricia was thankful that they all were planning to return next summer.

"Who's that walking with Hugh?" Christa pointed down the front line near the docks to where a man and a woman were engaged in conversation, dressed much like those in afternoon garb seen at the Laurel Valley Inn.

"Stay here. I will be back shortly," Tricia said, leaving the cabin before too many questions were launched in her direction. She would recognize the aloof way her mother carried herself from any distance, especially when disapproval was part of the picture.

"Mama, Daddy!" She called to them, trying to sound genuinely glad to see them but dreading the upcoming conflict that was sure to come.

"Tricia, thank God you are alright!" Her father held out his arms to her while her mother kissed her cheek. At least his first words had nothing to do with her getting into trouble or needing to come home. But that would be short-lived. Abigail Grimball squeezed her shoulder, then began the campaign that Tricia expected.

"We got here as quickly as we could, sweetheart. You've been through so much, and we didn't want you to be away a minute longer."

"Hugh, could I have a moment with my parents?"

"Of course. I'll go check on your girls. So good to meet you, Mr. and Mrs. Grimball. Your daughter has been an outstanding counselor."

Tricia waited until there was no one close by.

"I am so happy to see you both. I appreciate your being here very much. But I cannot leave Arden Woode until my job is done. I don't want to leave. I love it here."

"Tricia! You must come home now. You were violently attacked!" Her mother was adamant. Tell her, John. This is the proper thing to do."

John Grimball studied his daughter. She had always been obedient and respectful to them as parents. A well-mannered young woman. But he could sense the new-found assertiveness, an inner strength of character and determination.

"Why do you feel compelled to stay here? The camp will release you from your obligations."

"Yes, I'm aware of that. But I'm not hurt. It was a terribly frightening ordeal, yes, but I am alright. Camp is almost over and I want to be here until the end. It has been the most incredible summer of my life. Two more days."

"Are you sure about this?"

"Yes, Sir. Very sure."

"John, you can't be serious? She needs to come home with us!"

Otha's words kept repeating in Tricia's head. *Show them the love.* She reached for both of her mother's hands.

"Instead of leaving immediately, please consider staying at the Laurel Valley Inn until camp is over. I can finish my responsibilities here and we can spend some wonderful time together before all going home." She took the deepest of breaths. "There is someone very special I want you to meet. He means everything to me."

"Abigail, I think it is a reasonable and honorable request." John Grimball insisted.

"Honorable?" She stared at Tricia; the disdain evident in her voice. "What about Daniel Middleton?"

"Mama, I don't love Daniel. I love someone else. I've made it quite clear to you and him, and that was the honorable thing to do." She let her words sit for a moment, giving her parents time to assimilate them. "I would like for you to meet him one night for dinner. You've come all this way and he is anxious to meet you as well. Please say you will stay."

"I don't know," her mother replied. "I'm disappointed that neither you nor your father can be reasonable about any of this. Your place is back home." Abigail Grimball was insistent, turning on her heels and walking back toward the carriage that had brought them over from the Inn.

"Give your mother some time, Tricia. She was very distraught about your being in grave danger, and you know she has had her heart set on a big wedding for a while now. We are staying at the Inn tonight, of course, and I expect we can stay a couple more nights. Let this settle in for her. I understand your wanting to meet your obligations and I'm proud of you for that. Plan on our being here for you when camp is done for the summer." Her father whispered in her ear. "We will meet your young man soon, I hope. Hugh Carson has already shared with us how special he is, and that the renowned Dr. William Halsted has full confidence that he will make an excellent physician and surgeon. It wasn't totally lost on your mother. Don't tell her I told you, but she did say that you had more courage and strength than she ever could. She loves you so. And she's set in her ways and plenty stubborn, you know."

"I guess that's where I get it from, then," Tricia smiled.

The remaining days at Arden Woode were blissful; full of the camaraderie, spirit, and challenge that she had searched for, embraced, and come to love, as she did the campers and staff. Saying goodbye to Otha Moses, her girls, and Nancy, Cyndi, and Tavia would be difficult. Harder still to leave Ewan, though she took solace in knowing that it would only be temporary. She knew she had made lifelong friends with people who had enriched her soul in every possible way. More important, she had made the choice to face this transitory life with singular faith, purpose, and service. Of a certainty, there was exceeding joy in that decision to move forward with thanksgiving and new self-confidence.

The last night of camp was both solemn and sacred. The oldest Arden Woode girls, dressed as the knights of King Arthur, told the tale of the search for the Holy Grail. When the final song had been sung and the last of the floating candles placed on Emerald Lake to symbolize their light and love going out into the world, the gathering grew silent; embracing, weeping, smiling as they reflected on their time in this place of rarest beauty.

After the last Taps sounded, Tricia kissed each of her Du Kum Inn charges goodnight and waited for the familiar sound of rhythmic breathing, the restful culmination of time well spent. Retrieving paper and fountain pen, she had intended to either began the epic story of all that had happened or to begin work on discerning and creating her own rule of life, having gleaned all the knowledge she could from the writings and books that Ewan Munslow had shared. She wanted her own rule of life process to be as rich and as life-giving as the time at Arden Woode had been, in hopes that it would help to carry her through this world of inherent good and evil, triumph and tragedy, life and death. She listened to the familiar night sounds that called to her from the mountain woods, from this place that had changed her life.

Laying aside the writing implements, Tricia wrapped herself in a warm woolen blanket and crept outside to sit at the top of the cabin steps. Leaning back against the wooden door and looking across the glistening waters of Emerald Lake and the towering girth of Bald Rock Mountain, she took in the serenity of this last Arden Woode night. Perhaps – if she were still and listened closely – she could hear the wind whisper her name one more time.

AUTHOR'S NOTE

Like most works of historical fiction, *A Rule of Life* is a blend of factual and fictional places and characters. For me, the story was a labor of love, as it was partly derived from the personalities of real places and people, either with whom I had the pleasure of working and getting to know personally, or with those beloved souls who were integral in the formation of the real Camp Merrie Woode in Sapphire, North Carolina, in 1919. Dammie Day, one of the founders who named Merrie Woode, often referred to the camp as "a place of rarest beauty" and to this day, it remains magical and cherished, with its Adirondack-hewn buildings and majestic Old Bald Mountain rising above the pristine waters of Lake Fairfield.

The historic Fairfield Inn is no longer there, sadly, nor is Helen's Barn in Highlands, nor Burrell's Place on SC 107 – but all have a re-configured and special place in this story. High Hampton, however, is still in existence, a remodeled and beautiful resort, once the summer home of the prominent Hampton family from South Carolina, where the young Wade Hampton III learned to ride before he became a Confederate commander during the American Civil War. When the property was inherited by Wade Hampton II's three daughters in 1880, they subsequently sold it (1890) to their niece Caroline Hampton, who had just married Dr. William Halsted, the famous surgeon who was one of the "Big Four" founding professors at Johns Hopkins Hospital. He was later called the Father of Modern Surgery. High Hampton was their summer home for many years. Dr. Halsted plays an important part in this story.

In 1906, the last known sin eater in Europe died. However, the strange and macabre custom was brought to the mountains of western North Carolina, where there are documented accounts, even into the 1950's, of local sin eaters conducting their bizarre ritual. In this story, the mysterious Sin Eater figures prominently in the plot and presents a dichotomy of sorts regarding past and contemporary faith, caring and sacrificing for others, forgiveness, and love.

Finally, all of the camaraderie, tradition, challenges, personal growth, and crazy fun that are evident in the fictional Arden Woode are only a small part of the real Camp Merrie Woode. One truly does have to "be there" to fully appreciate this exceptional place that is the embodiment of young women discovering and developing their best selves. While I only spent the summer of my junior year in college there as a counselor, it was a life-altering experience for me in so many ways. From learning new skills, traveling through the stunningly beautiful western part of the state as a part of the tripcraft staff, to developing lasting friendships, building self-confidence, and honing the important values in life, it was a magical summer. How fortunate I was to meet both campers and staff from all across the United States and beyond! Some of my campers, my special group of counselor friends (three of them) and myself *(now there's a makeover!)*, were utilized in the creation of fictional personalities and characters. There is one individual staff member, integral to Merrie Woode history, with whom I had the privilege of working closely. Hugh Caldwell, Philosophy professor at Sewanee, beloved director of the tripcraft program, expert outdoorsman, and the eventual first executive director of the Merrie Woode Foundation, was a metaphorical giant of a man. There was nothing common about this life-loving, pipe-smoking, felt-hat-wearing, singing, laughing, caring, canoeing, hiking, kaya-king, and spirited man. Hugh loved Merrie Woode and all of her charges passionately and unconditionally. It was my honor and good fortune to know him, learn from him, and to embrace life in all of its pageantry, as Merrie Woode allowed us to experience it.

Thank you, Merrie Woode, for the wonderful memories! Ah, the memories...